DANIELA HOFFMAN IS NOT STUPID

angela j. phillip

|C

Lame Crow Press

First published in 2020 by Lame Crow Press.

Book design by Paul Way-Rider based on photo by Christian Stahl on unsplash.com

ISBN 978-1-913669-04-1 (paperback)
ISBN 978-1-913669-05-8 (ebook)

For
Paul Way-Rider

1

Disaster! We had another test and Mandy didn't turn up. It was a bugger. I couldn't write fast enough and Alison marked mine. Gave me 1 out of 10. When I swap tests with Mandy, I make a note at the bottom to say what score I want. Alison won't mark like that because she says it's not ethical.

After Mrs Richards has written everybody's scores down in her book, she comes and stands next to my desk and breathes on me. Smells of stale onions. This is the second time today that she's having a go. It was bad enough this morning over the homework. She tells the class that I'm lazy. Won't do any work. Tells me to stand up, and I do, not knowing where to look and banging my knee on the desk. I hate her.

'Look at Daniela,' Mrs Richards tells them. 'Have a good look. Now, what do you see?' No answer from the class. 'Look at her hair,' she goes on and I wonder what's wrong with it. It's blonde almost white in the summer and I've got bunches so it stays tidy. I realise that I've lost the ribbon off one side. There's just the elastic band left, but so what. 'Untidy hair,' Mrs Richards pronounces, 'shows a girl who doesn't care about her appearance. Slovenly.' She pauses. 'Do you know what 'slovenly' means, Daniela?'

I nod, but she wants a pound of flesh (yes, we're doing *The Merchant of Venice* but Shylock's got nothing on Mrs Richards!).

'Answer me,' she says.

'Yes,' I mutter.

'Slovenly and lazy. The two go together,' she continues as she picks up my exercise book and waves it at the class. 'Look at this. Look how messy it is. Full of blotches. No proper writing.' Long pause. 'And no date.' She moves away slightly, then looks at me hard and orders me to go and write the date on the blackboard. Help. I can't remember what the date is. My mind goes blank and I stare at the two pinkish roll-down maps that hang each side of the central blackboard space. The world to the right and the British Isles to the left. No inspiration there.

'Here you are,' she says, handing me a long white piece of chalk. Unused. 'Write the date.' I heave a sigh as I remember what it is, but then the problem is getting it up there. Hard enough writing in my book. Impossible on the board. I start with 'Monday' and feel relieved that it isn't Wednesday - much too long - and almost giggle at my own thoughts. I'm still there at the front of the class, chalk poised. 'M' I attempt. Not too bad, so I rush on with o – n – d – a – y, but by the time I get to 'y' I've almost filled the board and it's sloped right down to the right. No space left for the rest of it.

'Stop,' she barks. 'Give the chalk to Alison.' I feel a wave of relief and look for Alison. Hand the chalk over and go to sit down, but no, Mrs Richards isn't having that. 'Who said you could sit down?' she says. 'Stand up straight and watch Alison write the date.' I watch as Alison makes it look easy. *- Monday 10th July 1978 -* It doesn't even slope. Why can't I do that?

I go once more to sit down, but Mrs Richards still hasn't finished with me.

'No, you can't sit down. Turn around and face the class.' I do as she orders. Then she speaks again, slowly with an emphasis on each word. 'This is a girl whose mother is a teacher. A girl who can do it but won't. A girl who is a disappointment to her family and who will definitely not succeed in life. At best she'll end up at Robertson's.' Pause. 'Packing biscuits.' Longer pause. 'If they'll have her.' Before she can say anything else, there's a voice from the back starting a whisper chant.

'No, she won't. No, she won't. No, she won't.' It's a boy's voice. Think it's Jaffa. Feel immense gratitude. Thanks, Jaffa, you've got Mrs R off my back at last. She's left me and is walking down to the back looking to see who's whispering. Then somebody at the other side picks it up and then somebody at the front. Suddenly, the bell rings and I'm saved. For today anyway. That's the end of Mrs R. for today. Hope she has a heart attack on the way home. I wish her either sudden death or a bad illness before tomorrow. Either would do, but it never happens. She's never away. Never ill. Don't think she's human. I need to forget about her, but it's not easy. I try to shake my anger off. I'm going to Mandy's to see why she wasn't at school today. She was all right on Saturday and it's only Monday.

I should go home first because Steve will be expecting me. It wouldn't take long to whip round to Mandy's, but I change my mind. Better drop in to tell him where I'm going. It's warm today. Sun still shining on the row of red back-to-back houses all the way down the left-hand side of the street. That's our side. Right-hand side is in shadow. Terraces on the right, back-to-backs on the left. Our house is about two-thirds of the way down. We're the only house with a hedge behind the wall. I like our hedge. We've all got low walls, but the others haven't got a hedge. All they've got are little fences.

Shouldn't take long to drop in and tell Steve I'm home. He's my dad, not my real dad, but as good as, and he won't mind me going to Mandy's. Through the little gate hanging off a bit on one side, up the stone steps (which people used to scrub in the old days), key in the front door and straight into the living room. Over to the stairs door at the back of the room. Yank it open. Takes seconds.

'Hello,' I shout from the bottom of the stairs. 'Steve, it's me. I'm home.' He always does his research upstairs, right at the top, that's where his office is.

'Dani?' I hear him call back. 'I'll be down in a couple of minutes. Will you put the kettle on?'

'No, I'm not stopping,' I shout to him. 'Got to go round to Mandy's. She wasn't at school today. Back soon.'

'I'm coming down,' he shouts, and there's a clattering noise as he comes down the stairs. As he appears in the doorway, he asks, 'How was school? Did you get into trouble with Mrs Richards?'

'No,' I say, 'not really.' No point in telling him what she'd said. He might go up to the school and complain. I wouldn't want that. And he'd tell Mum.

'Wasn't she cross about your homework?'

'Not really,' I say again. 'Got to go, Steve. Back soon.'

'All right,' he says and grins at me. 'Make sure you're back by half-past five for your dinner.'

And I'm gone. Outside already and looking for a stone to kick while I'm walking along. Street's empty. No cars at all so it's an ideal moment for target practice. but there's nothing suitable, not even an old tin can so I have to do without. I hurry up instead. Wonder what's wrong with

Mandy. I get to her house and knock, but there's no reply. That's peculiar. If she didn't go to school, she wouldn't have gone out. I try again, and this time her mother comes to the door and tells me that Mandy's got a stomach bug. Should be all right by tomorrow. So that's that. I turn back wondering where to go next.

Don't want to go home yet. I've got until half five. Decide to go down to the waste ground to see if I can find any old bicycle bits. I'm building a bike from scrap so I'm always on the lookout. I do a thorough search but there's nothing suitable so I go back home.

Mum's back from work and in a good mood for a change. Good job she didn't hear what Mrs Richards had to say. Mum would be up at the school ruck zuck. She thinks I'm clever and so does Steve and he's lived with us for most of my life. But at school, I'm not clever. At school, I'm useless. Not long till the summer holidays now. Maybe this week won't be too bad. Especially if Mrs Richards drops dead.

2

Esme looks at her watch. Only another half an hour to go. She wants to get back to see how Daniela got on at school today. She'd gone with no homework yet again. Same as Monday. Esme knows that she must have got into trouble at the beginning of the week, but her daughter won't admit it. Esme feels her stomach clench with frustration.

The sounds in the exam room bring her back to the present. Pens scratch, chairs scrape, and someone coughs. People fidget disturbing the silence. Esme looks around. The catchment area is mainly the council house kids off the estate beyond the ring road. She looks at the three large West Indian lads sitting in a row down the left-hand side of the hall and thinks of John. Nice thought.

John will be going with them to the Palace tomorrow night. Esme thinks of how he moves. Remembers the feel of him on the dance floor. He's sexy. Quiet. Doesn't seem to like talking, but it doesn't matter. Dancing is enough. The music is too loud for talk in any case. It's been getting louder all through the seventies. A decade ago, you could go dancing and still be able to hear yourself speak. She smiles at the thought of Bob Marley, the heavy beat and half moves in her seat in front of the table.

Esme has asked John questions. What was it like in Jamaica? How did it feel arriving in England? He tells her that he looked out of the train window and thought it was strange to see smoke rising from the chimneys but suddenly goes quiet. Says it was a long time ago. Doesn't think about it now. Her friend Kate says that he's married to Barbara, but before that, he had another wife who left him. Esme doodles idly on the pad in front of her, watching the thick black biro whirls growing ever larger and more satisfying. Her thoughts turn again to her daughter. If only Dani would just do the assignments.

'Miss, Miss,' someone's arm is waving madly. Esme gets up and walks over to put more paper on the girl's desk. Checks her watch.

'You've got ten minutes left,' she announces. There are a few sighs. Some people have already finished, written as much as they can and are staring around, looking bored. The rest are scribbling furiously. She and Steve spent more than an hour with Daniela last night trying to make her do her homework, but the longer they made her sit at the table, the worse it got. Dani sat staring at the exercise book, wrote a word, dropped her pen, chewed the end, made a blotchy mark, decided to start again and so on never getting any further. After an hour, just two sentences had been achieved and she looked so distressed that they gave up. Steve said there wasn't any point in making her sit there any longer and Esme agreed. But that didn't solve the problem. Dani had to go with no homework yet again. Once more Esme glances at her watch.

'Time's up,' she says, her voice carrying easily around the hall. 'Put your pens down and sit quietly while your papers are collected. No talking and no moving from your desks until I say so.' Esme walks around the room collecting the papers, feeling as well as seeing the increasing impatience of everyone to be up and gone. It feels like a battle of wills that she might lose.

'You can go now,' she says, but the *now* is swallowed in the screeching of chairs and the hubbub of noise as the prisoners hurriedly escape. She gets up, picks up her bag and the exam papers and follows everybody out of the room. In the staffroom, she puts the thick wad of scripts into Jenny's pigeon hole, says goodbye to the two or three people still working at the table and heads for the car park.

Impatience quickens her steps as she crunches down the gravel pathway through the shrubbery. Going through the bushes is the quickest route from the back of the school to the car park although not good when it's raining because the leaves are never cut back far enough. You end up getting soaked, but it's dry now. She keeps trying to light her cigarette but it's windy. Better wait until she gets to the car.

At least Steve will be there when Dani gets home, so that's a relief, but she wants to find out for herself how Dani got on. It isn't easy to get a thirteen-year-old girl to talk. Or to find out how she feels. Mondays and Thursdays are the worst days. The homework days. She sighs. Ess has to admit that Dani is often difficult.

The car seems to know its own way home. First, the short stretch to the roundabout, then the pause before edging carefully into the flow (the traffic is always heavy here) and finally the swing on to the ring road as she heads west. Before they had the car, she rode a motorbike and sometimes wondered if it was her fate to die on the ring road. Obviously not, or at least not yet. She gives a shiver of satisfaction as she drives along.

She's still got the bike. A Honda 70. It's at home, parked on the short slabbed path leading to the house, making it difficult for people to get past but there's nowhere else to put it. It's always ready for lift off. Her friend Howard had taught her to ride. He's a bike fanatic and owns a Norton 500, but even Howard admits that the new Japanese bikes are nice to ride and economical. You must always look behind you before turning he says. Always. On any bike. Or you'll end up dead.

Esme has taken Dani on the back of the bike and driven down the M1 to Grandma's so many times. A horrible journey. She and Dani would get so stiff from sitting that they could hardly move when they got off, but it was cheap. On the other hand, this car that she shares with Steve is much more comfortable. They've had it nearly a year already which is hardly believable because it still seems new. It's a second-hand Fiat 600. Esme suddenly smiles. At last, it's nearly the weekend and only one more week to go until the holidays. She finishes her cigarette, throws it out of the window and starts to sing as she drives.

There is no-one there when she opens the door into their house in Potter Terrace. She chose the house because it was all she could afford and thought that she'd hate having neighbours on three sides, but it's all right. More than all right. She's grown to love the place.

'Steve,' she calls. 'Steve. Dani. Where are you? I'm home.'

'Esme? Is that you? I'm up here.'

There's the sound of footsteps coming down the stairs and Steve opens the door into the living room. 'Hello, Essi. How was it? Do you want a coffee?'

'Where's Dani?' she asks. 'Isn't she home yet?'

'Been and gone,' Steve replies. 'Gone to Mandy's.'

'Oh no, not again. Dani's always gone when I get back. Why didn't you make her stay? I wanted to talk to her.'

'She was fine, Ess. Don't go on.' Steve frowns and Esme tries to stop her irritation rising into a snappy reply. 'Said she didn't get into trouble,' he says. 'She'll be back later, so you can talk to her then.'

Esme takes off her jacket, dumps the bag full of exercise books on the floor and sits down in her usual place at the table. She reaches down into the bulging bag propped next to the table leg and extracts her tobacco tin. Rolls a thin cigarette and lights up while she relaxes in the remains of the afternoon sun still coming through the window. Steve goes into the kitchen and puts the kettle on. Water coming to the boil. What a comforting sound and what a lovely smell, she thinks as she picks up the mug of coffee and feels the heat from the steam hit her face. It's the smell that goes with relaxing and chatting. She takes a sip trying not to burn her tongue on the near-boiling liquid. That's the downside. Black coffee is always too hot.

'And there's something to go with it.' Steve goes back into the kitchen and returns with two large, moist-looking hot cross buns.

'It's July!'

'I know, but I found them in the new supermarket up near the post office and I know how much you like them.'

'They're probably months old by now, but I don't care.' She bites into one. Steve brings two more and they stop talking.

'Mmm,' Esme says, 'Have you left some for Dani?'

'Of course,' Steve replies. 'There's another packet of six and two left in this one.'

'What happened then?' she asks again. 'Wasn't there any trouble over her homework?'

'I don't know,' Steve flicks the hair off his face. 'She seemed all right, but it's difficult to tell. I don't suppose we'll find out until Sunday night when she starts thinking about the homework for Monday. She won't get round to it before then.' He pushes his plate away. 'I hope this coming Sunday won't be as bad as last night.'

The homework nights were all the same. Long sessions of trying to get Dani to do her assignments. Last night, her face had set in stony lines and she had played with her pen until ink marks stained her fingers. In the end, there were a couple of smudges on her blouse, but in her exercise book only a hole with a dark rim around it. Esme was cross over the blouse. You can't get ink marks off. Milk was supposed to work, but it didn't. Another school blouse ruined and they're expensive.

This morning Ess had watched Dani set off up the road, shoulders hunched as though she was going to a torture session. Then Esme was late again herself. Ought to have left earlier. She is sure that Dani gets into trouble regularly, but she won't admit it. Won't talk about it. Doesn't want her mother to go the school and interfere. Why can't Dani just do the assignments? Thank God the holidays are only a week away.

Steve goes back upstairs. The work on his research seems never-ending, especially the literature review which is what he's working on at present. Esme goes to get changed. She'll have a bath and relax. Dani won't be back for another hour or so. There's time for a soak before getting the dinner ready. The bathroom is warm from the sun that has been shining on the window all afternoon. It feels luxurious to be having a bath in the daytime instead of just before going to bed. The immersion has been on since she got in so there should be enough hot water.

Ess pushes the little bolt on the bathroom door and runs the bath. She doesn't need to lock Steve out, but she does it out of habit. It feels nice to be shut away, not available for anything. She can lie there and relax. When the bath is about two-thirds full, she squirts some bath oil into the water and watches a few little golden blobs float on the surface. Slowly she tries to insert a foot. Too hot. Then again. Gradually her skin acclimatizes and she lowers herself into the bath. The water with the oil in it feels like silk. She touches her legs. Smooth.

The ends of her hair float in the water, dark at the best of times, black when wet. Perfectly straight strands. No hint of wave or curl. Her fringe is getting long again. It always grows too fast. Maybe she ought to get it properly trimmed this time instead of cutting it herself. It's well past her shoulders with plenty of split ends. Dani's could probably do with a trim at the same time. She grins at the thought of her daughter's blonde locks. No chance of missing her in the dark.

Esme lies back in the water. Nearly the weekend. She's looking forward to going to the Palace with Kate on Saturday night. Ess loves dancing and it's good for you. It's what she needs, and she's been going every week for nearly two months. It's kind of Steve to stay and look after Dani. Not that Dani is a baby anymore. She's a teenager. Growing up fast, but too young to be left alone although Dani doesn't think so. Says that all her mates stay at home by themselves. Esme doubts this, especially with the Yorkshire Ripper still out there. She wouldn't leave Dani by herself in the house at night. And certainly wouldn't let her go roaming about the streets after dark. For herself, it's different. Can't let the Ripper, the police and all the local misogynists control women's lives. It's as though women are the ones at fault. If a woman gets killed, it's her own fault. That's what they imply when they report these murders and advise women to stay in after dark.

Steve doesn't mind staying in with Dani. He says it gives him a chance to get on with his work, but Esme knows it isn't true. Dani never goes to bed early and it's not easy to get on with anything while she's there because she tends to talk non-stop when she's with someone she likes. The truth is that Steve enjoys Dani's company and Dani enjoys Steve's. A little miracle, she supposes, considering that Steve isn't Dani's father. Once upon a time, she would have wanted to stay at home, too. To spend time in his company. Could never get enough of him but not now. Steve is kind and Esme knows that he loves her, but she's getting restless. Can't help it and it's getting worse.

Her daughter has not had a father since she was two. Andreas died in a road accident and at first, everyone had thought that Dani had died with him. He had taken her from Grandma's and he'd been drunk and angry. Told Grandma he was taking Dani to Leeds to teach Esme a lesson. But he had left the child behind. They had found the two-year-old shut in the bedroom of her father's house and nobody ever knew why. Dani was safe, thank God, but the child had been upset for a long time. Kept shaking and saying terrible things like *Daddy kill Dani* which alternated with *Daddy loves Dani*. It didn't make sense. The little girl had suffered from trembling fits for weeks.

It was a long time ago but Esme still doesn't like to think about what happened. She feels guilty. Andy had been angry because he had found her in bed with someone else. He'd gone mad. Fortunately, Dani was so young that she barely remembers him. Her daughter's memories of those early times are more the things she's been told than the things she remembers, although Dani claims otherwise. Dani nearly always claims otherwise. About everything.

Esme lies back further, and more hair floats as the water approaches her chin. Bang. She hears the downstairs door slam with a force it was never built to withstand. At the same time, she hears Dani call up the stairs.

'Anybody in? I'm back. Dead on time. Did you get any ice cream?'

'Coming down,' she hears Steve call back. 'Your mum's in the bath.'

Esme is about to call down but changes her mind. Let them get on with it without her. The impulse to wash her hair as fast as possible and race downstairs to talk to Dani is held in check. Just. She breathes out slowly and tries to settle back into her dreamy thoughts, but they've gone. Displaced by the knowledge that her daughter is downstairs and that she needs to talk to her. Esme gives in. It takes only five minutes to finish in the bathroom and get dressed, but by the time she arrives downstairs, Dani has gone.

'Where is she?'

'Gone to Mandy's. I said she could go back for another half an hour.' Esme feels her stomach knot in frustration. Dani is avoiding her. And when her daughter comes in for dinner, there'll be another excuse. Another way to avoid talking about what has happened at school.

3

I've dashed out to go back to Mandy's. Don't want to be around when Mum comes out of the bath. She'd start cooking and consider it the ideal opportunity to try and talk to me. Dani, I want to talk to you. Dani, sit down so we can have a chat. Come here, I want to talk to you. Never-ending. For sure she'll want to question me about Mrs Richards and what happened about my homework. Steve isn't usually naggy, but my mother just won't let me be. I reach into my bag to check that my stone is still there. I keep it in the zipped inner compartment that is meant to be used as a purse. Yes, it's there. Good. As I hurry up the road, I hear a boy's voice shout after me.

'Hey, Blondie. Where are you off to?'

It must be Jaffa, Jaffa Johns. I'm grateful to Jaffa. He sticks up for me, but I don't want to talk so I ignore him and carry on.

When I first moved to this school not that long ago, the boys were awful. The girls called me Dani, but the boys were merciless. It's because of my name. It's Hoffman. It's a German name. Hey, Heidi. Heidi girl. Will you come up the mountain with me? We know what you do up there. Will you do it with me? Will you? On and on and they laughed. Every day they taunted me until one boy stepped up close and chanted in my face.

'Hey, Heidi. Will you do it with me? Are you ready, Heidi? Are you ready for me?'

'Yes, I'm ready,' I said and quite calmly (couldn't believe myself), almost without thinking, I leaned towards him and punched hard. Right in the face. That wiped the smile off him and I watched his nose bleed. Loads of blood all down his jumper. 'Still ready,' I said, looking around at the gathering crowd. Mostly boys. Some girls. "I'm ready for anybody.' I wasn't, of course. Most of the lads would have annihilated me, but I've learned to act. Especially when scared, act tough and it usually works. No-one else stepped up and I've had no trouble since then. Afterwards, Mandy walked straight up to me and linked arms. She's my best friend now and the boys call me Blondie, not Heidi. I don't mind that.

Back to the writing problem. What I need is a plan but I haven't managed to think of one. Not a workable one anyway. I need a way out rather than a plan. Something more like a miracle. It's a problem I can't solve and it bothers me more and more. There's no-one I can talk to about it. I feel ashamed because writing is such a basic skill. If you're intelligent, then you can write. But I can't. Everybody thinks it's just a matter of willpower. But it's not. Wanting to do it, willing myself to do it seems to make it worse. I'll think about it later.

My bike project is going well. That needs more work and there are a couple of problems that need to be solved but I know what I'm doing with the bike. With a bit of luck, I might be able to earn some money and become independent. That would be good! And now I'm at Mandy's. No bell so I have to knock.

'Hello, Dani,' Mandy's mum, Marsha peers at me as she opens the door. Marsha is nice but always looks as though she can't see properly. Maybe it's her glasses. They look too big. 'You're back quickly. Do you want to come in and wait? Mandy's having her tea.'

Oh bugger, that's early.

'No thanks, Marsha. It's all right,' I say as I massage the toe of my sandal against the step and watch it crease and bend. If I pull my toes in, I can almost get the end part bent double. I'm proud of the way I can bend my toes and I can pick up pencils with them sometimes. Marsha's still standing there in the open doorway while I'm daydreaming about my feet.

'I thought her tea-time was later,' I say. 'I'd better get back. I'll come and call for her tomorrow.'

There'll be trouble at home if they find out that I've disturbed Mandy's family while they're having their tea. Mum says that it's rude to go into people's houses when they're eating. Stupid actually because Marsha wouldn't mind. I start to walk back the way I've come. Yes, I'll go and see Aunt Suzanna. Suzi isn't my real aunt, and I don't even call her aunt, but she's the same as a real aunt. Or better.

After banging on Suzi's front door as loudly as I can for what seems like about five minutes, I have the eventual satisfaction of seeing the door open and there she is. Her door has a heavy iron knocker with a lion on it. The sound is great. Fills the street and you can do rhythms. I like doing rhythms and have thought of becoming a drummer but it isn't as easy as you might think to get the beats even. I did ask for a drum kit, but Mum said it would be too loud for the neighbours. Suzi doesn't ask what I want, just grins and says, 'Come on in.'

'I hope you aren't eating as well,' I say as I walk through the door.

'As well as who?' Suzi asks. 'Who's eating?'

'Mandy. I went to call for her, but she's having her tea.'
Suzi looks at the clock on the wall and then back at me.

'No, Pete's not home yet. We're eating later. But what about you? Isn't it about dinner time at your house?'

'Will be soon. I'll go back in a few minutes.'

'So what's new?' Suzi asks as she fetches a glass and pours some orange juice diluted with honey and lemon water. It tastes good. Suzi always makes the kind of drinks that nobody else does.

'Nothing,' I reply as I take the drink and settle myself down in front of the tv which is showing something that seems to be a news programme. 'Isn't there anything else on?'

'Help yourself,' Suzi replies and goes back to the sink to carry on preparing vegetables. 'How's Esme?'

'Same as usual,' I say and pull a face. Suzi grins.

I stretch out on the sofa with my feet up. Shoes are at the door. No shoes allowed in Suzi's house. And I forget about going home for dinner until there's a knocking at the door and I remember what Steve said. Should have gone home a while ago. Yes, it's him. He's come to look for me. I pick up my jacket, pull on my sandals and go back home.

***

Later on, when I'm in bed with the light off, and my mother has said goodnight and finally left me alone, when I have my book ready next to the bedside lamp in case I feel like reading, which I don't, only then do I finally start thinking about the day. Mrs Richards was beside herself just like on Monday. I knew it would happen. It was the usual. I was told once again that I'm lazy. That I can do it but won't.

That I'm a disappointment. Mrs Richards didn't say I was stupid, but that's what she meant. Stupid and useless. I can hear her thoughts.

She is evil. One day, I vow, one day I'll teach her a lesson. Mrs Richards is a bully and I'm not the only one she enjoys tormenting. My fists clench and I feel the anger start to rise. I think of my stone and wish it was magic. When I was younger, I was convinced that it had special powers and that I could change people's thoughts by rubbing it and making a wish. Stupid to have believed that. It isn't Aladdin's lamp.

I reach for my bag which, as usual, is beside my bed and take out the stone. It is smooth, small and oval like an egg. Jet black apart from a light grey patch underneath. I've had it for years. Picked it up from the beach at Scarborough where Mum often took me when I was little. My mum always said that the sea air would get rid of my cough and it seemed to work. When I was small, I had one cold after another and it always went on to my chest. Mum's cure was the seaside because she believes in sea air. Whatever the weather, she would take me to walk along the beach to breathe in the good air. My mother believes in ozone and is sure it can cure coughs. Can cure anything.

Every time we went, I collected stones from the beach until I had a shelf full in my bedroom cupboard, but my mother complained, so eventually, I got rid of every stone except one. The one I'm holding at this very minute. The black egg stone that I love even though it isn't magic and will never save me from Mrs Richards. It lies in my hand. Just like a small egg. It's black and mostly shiny.

I think again about the vicious cow. She said that I could write if I wanted to, but it isn't true. I can only copy. When

I try to write down my thoughts my hand cramps and the effort of writing makes me forget what I'm trying to say. I don't know why. It's always been like this, but it's getting worse. Still, I'll stand up for myself against Mrs Richards.

Better not think about it. I look at the stone that lies in my hand. Remember again that I used to think that the stone could change minds. A changed mind means a changed person and then you can expect changed behaviour. But it doesn't work which is a shame. There must be some way of making people think differently, but I don't know how to do it. And sometimes I don't think that I should even try. Tempting though.

I can sometimes send thought messages but know it won't help. Not with Mrs Richards it won't. I can hear her thoughts but I can't get anything through to her. Most people don't seem able to receive my messages. Mum can and she knows they're coming from me, but she only gets them sometimes. Most people don't get them at all. Mind you, I believe that my thoughts *do* reach people's minds. It's just that mostly, people are not aware that my thoughts are not their own thoughts and I see my messages get twisted out of shape.

My telepathic abilities are not as strong as they used to be. Sometimes I want them back. Over the years, I stopped listening to people's thoughts because it regularly made me either sad or mad. Mostly mad. But if you have any skill at all, you need to practise it. Use it or lose it as they say. But I still don't think it would help with Mrs R. I frequently find myself switching off so I don't hear her thoughts. Can't bear them.

A much better thing to think about is the bike project. The plan is to collect as many old bike bits from the local tips as I can find, make them into proper bikes and then sell them. The first one is going well. It's in the cellar. I wish Mandy would join me in the bike project, but she says no. She's not interested in building bikes. Riding them, yes. Building them, no. Mandy likes ballet and used to have lessons, but the classes stopped. The only human being I totally trust is Grandma, then there's Steve and Grandpa but Mandy comes about fifth. I almost trust Mandy. Almost.

Wishing something doesn't make it so, but Grandma says that you can pray for something and if God thinks it's a good idea then He'll grant the wish. I don't believe that, but still, I find myself praying from time to time. Please God let Mrs Richards have an accident. Please God let Mrs Richards be ill and have to stay off school. Please God let Mrs Richards die!

4

On Saturday morning I wake up feeling surprisingly cheerful. All sorts of good things are in the air.

1. It's Saturday.
2. Only one more week of school.
3. Will see Mandy
4. The Bike Project
5. Going to see Grandma Frances next weekend.

I wonder how long I'll be able to stay at Grandma's. Part of me wants to stay for weeks and weeks, the whole summer perhaps. But another part of me would prefer to stay in Leeds to get on with the bike and hang around with Mandy. I don't have any friends in the village where my grandparents live. Perhaps I could get a bike project going down there, but I would need space. And tools. Grandpa has tools, but there's no space to work on the bike in Summer Lane. There are two sheds, but Grandpa uses both of them and they look full. *However*, I think and roll the word around on my tongue. *How. Ever.* Nice word. Steve uses it a lot. It's such an ordinary word. Two little words joined together to imply possibility despite difficulties. Probability even.

However, building a bike would be something that both Grandpa and Grandma would approve of. Unlike the many things that they don't approve of. Like the way I sometimes call my mother Esme, for instance (not polite). Like taking anything that doesn't belong to you no matter what the reason (morally wrong). Things are black and white in Grandma's book. Right and wrong are non-negotiable. What if somebody steals because they're starving, I ask? They'll be forgiven, says Grandma, but it's still stealing. Still wrong. Steve and Esme don't agree with Grandma and neither do I. From time to time I argue with her about these things and although neither of us changes our opinions, we have interesting discussions.

I like being at Grandma's. It's like going home. Whoops. Better not let Esme hear me say that. My mother is super-sensitive about my feelings for Grandma and where home is. But that's Esme's fault because she's left me with Grandma so many times that it does feel like home and yes, I am close to Grandma. My mother gets upset because she says my home is in Leeds, not South Derbyshire. And yes, it is. But I've spent loads of time at Grandma's, so in some ways, Summer Lane does feel more like home. Except there's nowhere to go and hang out so I do prefer Leeds now that I'm older. There is a cafe in Swadlincote that might be ok, but I've got no bike down there and everything is difficult with no wheels. And I don't know anybody. Derby might have some good places, but it's even harder to get to. And once again I've got nobody to go with.

Grandma has so much more time for me than my mother. Esme is always busy with something so she can't be disturbed. Like marking. Or lesson preparation. Grandma, on the other hand, will stop whatever she's doing and listen. Or sometimes she'll carry on doing whatever it is but still concentrate on what I'm saying. Grandma is interested in what I have to say. She doesn't try to catch me out. Doesn't start listening waiting to jump in and criticise me like my mother does. I tell Esme less and less these days.

It's Saturday so Mum will be going out dancing again. I wonder why Steve never goes with her. When I ask, they say that one of them needs to stay at home with me but it isn't true. I'm already thirteen, old enough to be left on my own. Or I could go round to Suzi's and spend the evening at hers so then they could both go. But Steve never goes out much at all unless it's to work on his driving jobs or to the university to see his supervisor. He just seems to prefer staying at home to get on with his work.

Steve has talked to me about his research project, and it seems interesting. It's all about what was happening in the run-up to the Russian Revolution and about why people started thinking differently. The title is long and complicated and never seems to quite make sense, but when Steve explains it, everything becomes clear. Later, when he isn't there, the whole thing goes back to being vague, but the most important thing is that he's finding out what makes people change. Apparently, in 1905 the people in St Petersburg became politically conscious and wanted to change things. Steve is trying to find out what made them wake up. Me, too, I'm interested in what makes people change. I remember my stone and give it a quick stroke.

Steve likes doing his research and when it's finished, he'll be able to apply for lecturing jobs. My mum, too, would probably prefer to be doing research. Most of the time she moans about teaching. Especially about all the marking. Nearly every night, she sits for hours doing marking. I can't understand why anyone would want to be a teacher, so at least I can sympathise with her about that, but then Esme changes her mind and starts to say how marvellous it is to be a teacher. She'll say how rewarding the teaching is. Always changing. You can never rely on her.

I wonder again why my mother doesn't want to go out with Steve. I push away the thought that she might not like dancing with him. It's true though that Steve says he doesn't want to go. Doesn't like reggae. He prefers Pink Floyd and Jimi Hendrix and when my mother's out of the house puts records on full blast. Fantastic! Esme prefers jazz and sometimes folk. She only likes reggae for dancing, never listens to it at home. Mostly, I like the same sort of music as Steve but also some Carly Simon numbers, Queen and stuff by The Clash. Mandy likes *Hopelessly Devoted* from *Grease* but I think it's soppy. Punk is better.

It's breakfast time and nobody's up yet, so I can eat as much as I want. I get the Weetabix out and see that there are only six left. I put the first two in a bowl and heap sugar on top. I always put the sugar on before adding the milk. Mum does it the opposite way round which seems peculiar. Should I make a cup of tea? No, there's no time. Had better get a move on and get myself round to Mandy's before I get called on for shopping duties.

There are already noises upstairs. That'll be Steve. He always gets up first. Just in time, I get my sandals on. Wonder whether to change into the Doc Martens but decide not to. It might be sunny and it's nice having bare feet. Can see the Vivi varnish sparkle and shine on my toenails. I love that varnish. It's dark purple, almost blue, but with the faintest hint of silver that sparkles when the lacquer catches the light. It's a bit chipped. Must do some repairs but no time now.

I grab my jacket and call up to say that I'm off to Mandy's. I've had a good wash, brushed my hair and tied it both sides into the usual bunches. Think I look all right. Blonde hair and dark purple nails. Not bad. I like the Vivi look. They do a range of lacquers all in violent colours. Makes me look tough. Unapproachable. I like that.

My plans don't work out. After all the speed and getting to her house before nine, I find out that Mandy has to go shopping. Will be out all morning. Even worse, she can't come out this afternoon because her aunt is coming from Manchester. And not tomorrow either because Marsha has recently taken an interest in Buddhism and thinks that Mandy ought to learn about it. Marsha says that Mandy doesn't have to become a Buddhist but in order to make up her mind, she has to go to the Sunday meetings. Marsha even asked if I wanted to go with them. Definitely not.

Neither my mum nor Steve is interested in religious things. They never go to church or chapel so I'm safe there, but Grandma and Grandpa are Baptists, and they are true believers. It's part of their everyday lives. I'm not forced to go when I'm in Summer Lane because they know that Esme doesn't encourage it. But Grandma would like me to go to Chapel. In the past, when I was little and stayed there every year during the long summer holidays, I always went to Sunday School, but that was a long time ago. I don't feel like it now, not even to please Grandma. I no longer believe in God or Jesus but don't like to tell them because they would be upset.

I look around for something to kick and feel in my bag for the stone. No, I can't use that. It's too precious. I notice a can in the gutter and push it carefully a bit further into the road, then kick. Good one. I can kick better than most boys but should have put my Docs on. I kick another one. Not so good that time. Ok, so there's no Mandy for the weekend. Better go back and get on with the bike. It's time to solve the problem of the gears. Might have to go to the library and look it up because Mum and Steve won't have a clue about how to do that.

Just as I get back and go down into the cellar, my mother finally catches up with me.

'Dani,' she shouts. 'Are you down there?' I don't reply. 'I know you're down there, so come up here. I need your help this morning.' Oh, bugger. Bugger and shit. That'll be shopping for sure. 'Dani!' my mother yells. 'Get yourself up here!' No help for it. Had better go. Slowly I climb back up the stairs and go through the kitchen into the living room.

'Oh, God! Look at your jumper! You've got grease on the sleeve. You know you're supposed to change into old clothes before you start messing about with that bike.'

I look at the sleeve. 'Can't see anything.'

'Twist your arm.' I turn my arm, but still can't see anything. 'No, the other one!' Well, yes, my mother's right as usual. 'Go and get changed. We're going shopping.' I sigh. Knew it was coming. Saturday ruined by shopping. And my mother's already ratty. No point in arguing. I set off up the stairs and have just reached my room when I hear a knock on the front door. Who can that be? Steve's gone off on one of his driving jobs and won't be back until sixish. In any case, he wouldn't knock unless he'd lost his key. I listen to see who it is.

'Hiya, Esme,' I hear a familiar voice float up the stairs. 'Any chance of a coffee? Is Dani in?'

'Howard!' I yell as I turn round and rush back down the stairs.

'Hi there, Dani,' he says, 'How are you getting on with the bike?'

'Go and change!' my mother shouts at me, but she grins at the same time. Howard always puts her in a good mood. 'He'll still be here when you get back.'

And he is. I take him down to the cellar to show him what I'm doing. Howard can build bikes and mend cars and knows everything there is to know about engines. Unlike my mum and Steve, who are both useless at that sort of thing. Howard has taught me all sorts of things about engines. Taught me, too, about the importance of oil. Oil is something that Howard believes in. It's almost sacred. Oil, he tells me is the most important ingredient for any machine. Oil should always be kept at the ready. It should never be allowed to run out.

Howard leaves just before lunchtime, so he doesn't save me entirely from the shopping trip, but he's arranged to come and collect me tomorrow to go to a motorbike rally. Steve and my mum can't understand why anyone would want to go to a rally, but they like Howard. My mum's grateful that he does bike type things with me because I love machines, love bikes and cars and racing. They say I must get it from my father who also loved engines. So the weekend is turning out to be pretty good except that tonight my mother is going out dancing again. I suppose it doesn't matter. What matters is the thought of tomorrow night and I suppress a shudder. I already know that tomorrow night will be bad but am keeping those thoughts out of my head. Tomorrow night is Sunday, the homework night. I bite my arm to keep the bad thoughts away.

5

Esme hates putting the shopping away. Funny really. It should be a source of satisfaction to view the newly acquired provisions ranged on the shelves and in the fridge, but it isn't. Like her daughter, she's impatient to be getting on with the next thing. Suzi says that tasks like cleaning the house and doing the ironing can be calming and enjoyable. Her mother, too, says that she likes doing housework, but Esme finds this hardly believable.

Surely it is more sensible to be doing something worthwhile. If you spend time cleaning, for instance, it will only have to be done again. On the radio recently, she heard that dust never reaches higher than one centimetre so that if you don't have time to clean, it will reach its limit fairly soon and won't get any worse. She smiles at the thought of what her mother would think of that. Esme exaggerates what she says in order to provoke her mother. Makes herself seem worse than she is but doesn't know why. She doesn't like to admit it, but Ess always keeps her house clean even if it is not tidy.

Dani has already disappeared down to the cellar, but she did help with the shopping. Amazing how strong she is although she looks fragile. Looks older than her age, becoming attractive in a punky sort of way. She's growing tall. Soon be taller than her mother. Carried two huge bags full of the heavy stuff back from the supermarket. Ess tries not to use the car for short distances, but it does mean that they have to carry heavy bags of groceries back home.

She had hoped to be able to talk to Dani while they were out, but her daughter was offhand as usual. After Esme's second attempt to bring up the subject of Mrs Richards, Dani asked her to stop. And now she's gone again. At least after being nagged at only briefly, she went to change into some old clothes. Ess is impressed with the bike. It is beginning to take shape, although the hardest part hasn't been fitted yet. The hardest part, Dani says, is the gears.

Her daughter's talent for building bicycles makes Ess feel proud. The only thing she worries about are the trips to the waste dumps. She doesn't like to keep bringing it up, but her awareness of the Yorkshire Ripper and the fact that he still hasn't been caught bothers her more than she admits. The last murder happened in Manchester, but most of the previous ones were in Leeds. Maybe she ought to make Dani stay closer to home, but that's not easy.

A cup of coffee would be a good idea, but as soon as Ess puts the kettle on, she switches it off again. Decides to go and see if Suzi is in. Esme hasn't seen her friend since the previous weekend. Suzi teaches primary school at the same place as Marsha. They're like Esme, permanently tired and looking forward to the holidays, but the primary schools don't break up until a week after the secondaries.

Suzi is an old friend. Ess has known her and her partner Pete since she arrived in Leeds with Dani years ago. They had flats in the same student lodging house, hers and Dani's at the front, Suzi and Pete's at the back. Pete was a bit of a philanderer, but Esme never said anything. Not much to tell in any case because she never knew anything for sure. She always liked Pete. Used to fancy him a bit, but it was Suzi who became her friend. It was Suzi who helped her when she came back for her second year after the death of Dani's father. Suzi was not only a friend, she was a second mother to Daniela.

In some ways Esme reflects, she looks up to Suzi even though they are both the same age. Suzi always seems to be wise and sensible. Esme realises that she wants Suzi's approval and this desire, almost longing, affects what she says, the parts of herself that she reveals. Many of Esme's private thoughts and actions would be anathema to Suzi so she keeps these hidden, but they, too, are real, an essential part of her being. And often Esme's hidden side, the part she can't explain is the most powerful. It's what drives her. It's like being two people: the sensible Esme who chats to Suzi and agrees with her about almost everything and the other Esme, the one who rushes to the dance halls to flirt with the men, the one who will drop everything to pursue something that interests her. The one who is restless and ready for adventure, the one of whom she disapproves, but who definitely exists.

Ess calls down to Dani, grabs her tobacco tin and goes over the road to knock on Suzi's door. She's in. And Pete isn't. The ideal situation. They settle down with some strange tea that tastes of nothing much but which is supposed to be made of nettles and be good for you. And they light up. Esme's mother sends regular newspaper clippings to persuade her to stop smoking. Steve nags gently but continually and just lately Dani has started as well. Stop smoking, they say. It will kill you. Yes, she will. She will give up soon. Esme watches Suzi inhale her extremely strong unfiltered cigarette that she makes look like an elegant accessory. Suzi makes everything look elegant. She could have stepped out of Vogue. The house is elegant, too.

Esme, on the other hand, could have stepped out of a jumble sale. She is probably influenced at some level by the image of Leonard Cohen's *Suzanne,* who, according to the song, is dressed in rags and feathers from salvation army counters. This appeals to her and Esme often has various brightly coloured materials trailing from her neck or shoulders, but not rags or feathers. Scarves usually. The bright colours contrast with the plain shirts and jeans she wears and combine into a style that is individual and often dramatic, especially when taken together with her large earrings. For teaching, she wears more formal clothes but will still add earrings or a contrasting scarf. She says that it's easy to make a new outfit. All you need is a new scarf or a different pair of earrings. Voila.

Esme's style is attractive even if it's never been quite to her father's taste. These days she looks like a thin, well-groomed gipsy. Dark hair down to her shoulders. Long fringe. The days of her father threatening to throw her jeans in the back of the fire, which of course he never did, are long gone, but he still wishes that she would dress like a young lady. Fortunately, he has mostly transferred his hopes to Dani, although he won't have much luck there. Dani likes wearing worn-out jeans and Doc Martens accessorised with lurid nail varnish.

'Where's Pete then?'

'Not sure. Said he had to go into town to get some stuff from his office.'

'Are things any better?' Suzi shrugs.

'What about you? Anything new this week?'

'There's Dani as usual. Things are getting worse at school. Did she say anything when she came round on Thursday?'

'No. She just watched tv while I chopped vegetables. How is it getting worse?' Esme doesn't reply immediately. Instead, she asks another question.

'If Dani had said something, would you tell me?'

'Not if I'd promised not to. But she didn't say much about anything. How are things getting worse?'

'She won't do her homework. Says she can't do it and doesn't know why.' Esme watches as Suzi goes to fetch the biscuit tin. Homemade biscuits. 'Dani hates Mrs Richards,' she continues. 'But she doesn't manage other teachers' homework assignments either. Dani can't seem to write. She can read. Could read when she was four, as you know. But she can't write.' Esme helps herself to a biscuit. 'These are nice.'

'Lemon and ginger.'

'It's always been a struggle,' Esme goes on, 'but it's getting worse. When she was younger, it was easier because they didn't have homework and in school, it was mostly copying. She can manage to copy if you give her enough time. Even a few months ago, it wasn't this bad.'

'How bad?'

'She can hardly write a sentence. Sits at the table, drops her pen, moves around on the chair, bends over the paper, creases it, looks as though she's being tortured.' Esme inhales and then blows the smoke out slowly. 'At school, they tell her that she's lazy and she gets into trouble all the time. She won't admit it but I'm sure she does.' Esme looks at Suzi. 'Mrs Richards says that her verbal skills are excellent and she reads a lot, so there's no excuse. No reason at all why she can't do her homework.'

'Why do you think it is?'

'I don't know. The more pressure you put on her, the less able she is to perform, but I don't know what else to do. I suppose I add to her stress by trying to force her to do it, but it's the only way I can think of. I want to make sure that she has the homework ready to take to school. But it doesn't work. I can't make her do it. What would you do?'

'Stop making her write. Go and see Mrs Richards and tell her how Dani is at home.'

'I suppose I could try. Problem is that Dani doesn't want me to interfere. She more or less made me promise not to go and talk to her teachers.'

'That does make things difficult.'

Problem unresolved. It's not the first time they've discussed Dani's writing, but it never makes sense. She can read, but apparently, she can't write, and nothing they can think of seems to help. Suzi is always sensible and seems able to see clearly what to do but putting the sensible thing into practice is another matter. They've both tried talking to Dani. To her mother, she says things like leave me alone and don't interfere. To Suzi, she denies there's a problem at all and gets cross because her mother has been talking about her again. They lapse into silence.

'I'm going down the Pally tonight,' Esme says changing the subject. 'Why don't you come with us?'

'I've told you before. I don't like reggae, and I don't like dance halls. I'm too old to go out dancing.'

'At just turned thirty?'

Suzi grins and then says, 'But you don't like reggae either. At least that's what you've always said.'

'Well, I wouldn't buy it to sit and listen to, but it's fab for dancing. It's the beat.'

'Or is it the men? What's wrong with Steve? Are you getting bored?'

'Of course not,' Esme replies but realises that Suzi is probably right. 'Anyhow,' she goes on, changing the subject, 'what's happening with Pete? Is he behaving himself?' Suzi tenses slightly and looks at her.

'I think so.'

Esme supposes that means that he isn't, but Suzi doesn't want to talk about it. 'And what are you going to do tonight? I bet you're just going to sit here and wait for him to come back.'

'No, I'm not. I've got a new Joni Mitchell LP. Shall I put it on?' Suzi gets up to go and fetch it, but Esme looks at her watch and says she has to go.

'I'd like to, but I need to get back and cook. Steve will be home soon, and I've still got to get ready to go out.' As she's leaving, Suzi looks at her.

'Be careful what you get up to at the Pally, Ess.' There's a note of concern in her voice, but Esme just laughs.

'Of course, I will. See you later. Thanks for the tea.'

***

Several hours later, Esme is sitting on a padded leatherette bench with John on one side and Kate on the other. Kate's husband, Murray, is with them. Esme can feel John's leg touching hers. He keeps moving it away, but then it creeps back, almost of its own accord. Esme decides to pretend that she hasn't noticed.

This is the early part of the evening before the music gets loud. Later on, the volume cranks up to the point where all you can do is drink or dance. By that time, it's too loud to be able to talk without shouting. But not yet. She turns towards Kate who is telling them all, yet again, about how nice John is and how grateful she is to him. Apparently, he's been an angel this week. Was on the early shift but still found time to pick up their youngest daughter from school. Murray nods in agreement, and John's face shows a mixture of gratification and embarrassment.

This story is for Esme's benefit. She knows that it's to reassure her that although John is married, he is a good man and therefore a safe person to dance with. He can be trusted. Esme turns to speak to him.

'How's Barbara?' she asks, 'Doesn't she want to come out dancing?'

'Not anymore,' he answers. 'She used to, but not now. In any case, she's got to stay in and look after her kids.' He smiles.

'Not your kids then?'

'No, we've just got her kids, Cissie and Lorraine. My son used to live with us, but he's gone back to his mother.' There seems to be no answer to this, so they lapse into silence while Esme thinks of Steve looking after Dani. Who is not his. As she is mentally comparing John unfavourably with Steve, John adds, 'They're good kids and I stay back to watch them on Sundays so Barbara can get out. We take it in turns over the weekend.' Esme was wrong then, she thinks, in her hasty judgement.

'We're going to dance,' Kate tells her. 'You stay here and look after the bags and keep our seats, then you and John can go next.'

'OK.'

During the evening, she and John dance a lot, mostly the not touching kind of dances, but there are a couple of slow ones when John holds her. Delicately, she has to admit. There is still the sexy beat, but she prefers the kind of dances where you dance separately. Then she can move by herself and look around to see who is dancing nearby. A bit of flirting. Enjoyable. From time to time she catches the eye of a man who is dancing with someone else. And they half-smile at each other. There's one guy in particular. He wears a cowboy hat and walks through the place as though he owns it. Every so often she notices him staring at her, and when she looks his way, he grins.

The evening is soon over. Time to go home. John says he'll walk her back and Kate and Murray say goodnight. Before leaving, Esme looks around to see if she can see the cowboy man anywhere, but he seems to have gone. Earlier on when she was sitting with John doing their stint of looking after the seats, the cowboy man had walked up to their table, lifted his hat and bowed to her. She smiled in return but could feel John getting annoyed. After the man had gone, John had told her that she should be careful. There were a lot of men who would take advantage of her. She shouldn't encourage them. Yes, she had replied.

6

It's Sunday, and I'm out at last, but I've already had a row with Esme. She says that I can't go out with Howard because I didn't do my homework last night! And then she had a row with Steve and told him it was his fault. He was supposed to make me do it while she was out dancing. Poor Steve. Mum's a bloody harridan. I hate the way she goes on at him, at both of us.

After Mum had finished having a go at Steve, she walked out and slammed the door. Just think what would happen if I slammed the door like that! I was down in the cellar standing at the bottom of the steps. Could hear every word. After the door banged, I waited. Wanted to make sure that she wasn't coming back. I checked two minutes on my watch to make sure that she'd gone before I went back up.

We both felt better with her gone. Steve made a cup of tea which I didn't want, but he was being nice, so I went along with it. We talked for a while and Steve suggested a plan. What he thinks is that if I promise (cross-my-heart and hope-to-die no kidding) that I'll do my homework tonight, then Esme might, just might, change her mind and let me go out with Howard. So that's the plan. When she comes back, Steve is going to tell her that I've promised to do my assignments. And then we'll see what she says. I hate having to beg but I do want to go to the rally. According to Steve, there's a good chance it might work and I think so, too.

There's just about enough time to get to the dump, have another look for bike parts and get back in time for lunch. Everybody else has Sunday dinner at midday but not us. We have ours in the evening. Getting back for lunch means getting back for a piece of bread and cheese. Sometimes a limp lettuce leaf to go with it. Not worth it but no choice. I wonder how Mandy's getting on with the Buddhist meeting. I must ask her about it.

I feel in my bag for the stone, take it out and give it a little rub. I always do that when I take it out. Keep it with me at all times. Hope it will bring me luck. I want something to kick and notice a large, irregular grey lump of something on the pavement. Looks like a piece of broken concrete. Carefully, I place it in the middle of the pavement. Take aim. Kick. It hurts my foot. Unpleasant. Need something better and I find a good stone near the hedge. Kick again. Yes. Good one. And again.

'Good kick, Blondie,' I hear from somewhere behind me.

'Thanks, Jaffa,' I call back without turning round as I bend to inspect my sandal which now has an indented black mark all the way down one side. I spit on my finger, bend down and rub at it, but it won't come off. Bugger. I half turn and see Jaffa pushing his bike at some distance behind me. 'Can't stop,' I shout. 'Got to get back.'

I'm not sure about Jaffa. He seems all right, but still, I'm not sure. He's gangly with big hair that he gets cut every month or so. Makes him look like a shorn black sheep but the short frizz accentuates the shape of his head. His smile seems enormous. Not good looking but he's tall and sexy with wicked eyes. There's something attractive about him and he's sure of himself. A bit up himself maybe.

Always does well in class. Clever. Slouches about as though he's boss of the neighbourhood.

Best of all, he's good to me. Sticks up for me but I don't know why. Last Monday wasn't the first time. Don't think he's old enough though. I sometimes wish that Vee Jay who lives next door would notice me. He's in the sixth form, not as tall as Jaffa but good looking. Must be at least seventeen. All I get from him is a polite smile every now and then. Doesn't seem to know I exist although I've seen him looking at my legs. Still, I don't care. Don't need boys.

Lunch has already started by the time I make it back home so I get into trouble again but not so much this time. They've got the wine bottle out I notice, and Mum is looking relaxed and starting to smile again.

'Steve tells me that you've made a promise,' Esme says. I nod. 'Well, what is it?'

'I'll do my homework tonight if I can go with Howard this afternoon.' Oh, God. As soon as I've spoken, I know I've got it wrong. Damn. Before I can say another word, my mother shoots back at me.

'Well then, you can't go. You're not bargaining with me about doing your homework. You'll do it anyway.' Mum's face creases back into ugly. I try again,

'That's not what I meant. I'll do it anyway. I've promised to do my homework tonight so I hoped you might let me go out with Howard. He's coming especially.'

'Not sure I believe you. You've promised before.'

Oh God, there's no pleasing her. If it weren't for Howard, I wouldn't bother saying another word, but I do want to go to the rally. It's worth one last try.

'Well, I do mean it. I do promise.'

There, that's as much as I can manage but I'm lucky. The wine seems to be working in my favour and Esme likes Howard. Mum doesn't want him to come for nothing and have the treat thrown back in his face.

'All right,' she says. 'But if you don't do the homework later on, there'll be trouble.' Ah, trouble. I know all about that.

Howard turns up soon afterwards, and we set off in his car. On the way, he asks me how I'm getting on with the bike, but I haven't done anything more to it so there isn't much to tell. I half wonder whether or not to say anything about my homework problem and the battle with Mrs Richards but decide against it. It's true that Howard is one of the few people that I could tell but I don't think there's any way he could help. He would be sympathetic but what I need is something drastic, a plan to sort out Mrs Richards.

Sorting out Mrs Richards means putting her out of action and that might be too much even for Howard's easy-going standards. It might be too much for mine but I've got to think of something. He would probably just grin and try to talk me out of anything I could think of. Better keep quiet. I'm getting desperate. Getting determined to find a way to stop my tormentor because things can't go on the way they are. I don't know yet how I'm going to sort things out but there will have to be a way.

Howard is the only person I know who has been to jail. It was years ago when I was small and I'm vague about the details. Esme told me about it at the time and I remember feeling upset. I've known Howard since I was a baby and it was distressing to discover that I lived in a world where somebody as kind and lovely as Howard could be locked away. It was something to do with dealing cannabis, but I don't know any more than that. If it happened now, I'm sure he'd just be given a warning. Don't think anybody gets locked up just for cannabis but I might be wrong. Mum is always reluctant to talk about it. She told me that when it happened, I tied up my toys, especially Brown Bear and I played at prisons. But I can't remember any of that. Howard won't talk about it either. I asked him once but haven't tried again.

Nowadays, I feel that his past gives Howard a certain mystery. It adds a certain glamour to his person that nobody else has. But I know that Grandma and Grandpa would never consider prison glamorous. I know that my mother hasn't told them about what happened to Howard so I don't mention it either. I know they wouldn't like to think of me being taken out by someone who had been to prison. And they wouldn't understand how nice Howard is. My life is full of hidden pieces. Suppose everybody's is. It's like the dream I have about my Dad. My first dad, I mean. It's a weird dream and I try to talk to Mum about it, but she won't listen. Just a dream she says, it's only a dream. Forget it. But it keeps coming back. The same dream. I've always had it. Not so much a dream, more a nightmare. I dream that he's trying to kill me.

I look out of the window, but there isn't much to see. Just a few fields on either side of the dual carriageway. Howard announces that we're nearly there and once we get to the rally ground, I forget about everything else, even the homework. The racing is brilliant and no-one is killed or injured so it's a fab afternoon. You might think that's a heartless comment, but it's a fact. Death and injuries can happen at rallies, so we're relieved when everything's fine. It's part of the thrill though. The danger.

We eat cheeseburgers and chips with masses of tomato sauce that by some miracle I manage to keep off my clothes. I like to look good. Holes in jeans are ok but not in blouses or jumpers. Tops have to be ripped or frayed along the seams and you have to do it quite carefully. Easy to ruin them. Holes in jeans or preferably slashes can look fab but dirty marks anywhere. No way. It can take ages to get the careless ripped look. I'm good at it. Esme has no idea that I've done it deliberately. She actually believes that I *am* careless.

Howard gets cokes for both of us. I don't get coke at home. Esme says it's too expensive. And not good for you. Just think. Most of my classmates get beer at home and I don't even get coke! Everybody's always talking about it. And wine. And they say they get drunk. I've asked for beer when Steve's had some, but he grins as though I'm making a joke. I'm treated like a child. At thirteen! Some of the Vietnamese refugees that Mum used to teach had been married at twelve. (Not that I want to get married!)

It's nearly seven by the time we get back. Dinner is ready and Howard has been invited to stay and eat. Howard and I have eaten tons already and are both full, but we still sit down at the table. Howard says he can't manage any food but wouldn't mind a drink. Mum says there's a beer in the fridge so I go to get it and while I'm there, start to help myself to some orange juice.

'Don't forget to dilute it,' Mum calls through to me as I stand in the kitchen hastily drinking half a glass of pure before going to the tap. My mother can see through walls. This orange juice isn't meant to be diluted, but Esme says it's expensive so we have to make it last. Mum and Steve drink it diluted, too. I sigh, pick up my glass and the can of beer and take them back into the living room. Steve and my mother have already started eating and Howard is chatting with them.

I sit and listen. It's rare for me to be this quiet, but my mind is busy warding off the prospect of the homework that I still have to face. Eventually, the pudding turns up and I'm allowed to have some even though I haven't eaten any of the first course. It's because Howard is here. If it weren't for him, I wouldn't have got any, but I don't give a damn about the pudding. I'm no longer a child and I'd need something more than apple crumble to distract me from the worry about my homework. My stomach starts to clench. If only the dinner would last until bedtime. But it won't. Be realistic. What can I do? Yes. If I could keep Howard here for the whole evening, preferably until at least midnight, then I might be all right. Howard would keep me safe. Surely Mum wouldn't stand over me like last week. Not if Howard were still here. I shudder and try to think of how I can get Howard to stay.

'I need your help, Howard,' I hear myself saying. They all turn to look at me. 'It's the bike. I'm stuck with the gears. Will you come and help me after you've finished eating?' But before Howard has a chance to reply, my mother jumps in.

'No way!' she says with that edge in her voice that makes me shiver. 'In a minute, you're going straight upstairs to do your homework. Aren't you.' It isn't a question.

'I've got to be getting back anyway,' Howard says as he stands up to go. 'I'll try and drop in next Saturday and give you a hand with the gears, Dani.'

'We won't be here next Saturday,' I say. 'We're going to Grandma's.'

'No, we're not,' my mother announces. 'We're going on Monday.'

'Monday? You said we were going on Saturday.'

'Yes, but I've had to change it. There are some things I've got to do before we go and there'll be no time before the weekend.' I notice that Steve is looking as surprised as I am. He didn't know about the change of plan either. He looks cross but doesn't say anything.

'And when will you be back?' Howard asks.

'Not sure,' my mother replies. 'If you're coming on Saturday, we can let you know then.'

'OK,' Howard says, 'and thanks for the pudding. You're great at puddings, Ess. Bye, Dani. See you next week. Bye Steve.'

That's a joke. Mum hardly ever makes puddings. Only when somebody comes to eat with us.

'Bye, Howard,' I say with a sinking feeling. 'Thanks for taking me to the rally.'

As soon as the door closes, I turn to my mother. 'I'll do the washing up,' I offer.

'Upstairs,' she commands, 'and get your books out. I'll be up in a minute.'

7

Unbelievable! How can Dani not manage to write a few paragraphs for her homework? It would make her life so much easier. (And Esme's.) But she won't do it. Can't do it? Whatever Ess tries, nothing works and her daughter just pushes her away. It's Monday morning again and her heart aches for Dani. Esme has spent so long getting her daughter out of the house that she is going to be late once more. She swore she wouldn't let it happen again but getting Dani out of bed is a nightmare. She called her at 6.30 and then every half hour after that until eight, but Dani stayed stubbornly in bed, pretending to be asleep.

Steve left before six because he had a long-distance driving job. It's a pity because he would have turfed Dani out and got her off to school with less stress than when she does it. Her daughter seems to delight in pushing her to the edge of patience and these days the edge is easy to reach. But Esme is sorry for her. She watches Dani set off to walk up the road. Shoulders hunched, body bent, head bowed. Dani shuffles along. Looks as though she is studying the pavement, searching for something. Escape? Salvation? Dani moves as though she is forcing her legs to keep walking. By some superhuman effort of will.

Ess grabs her bag and puts on the helmet. Steve needed the car to get to his pickup point, so she'll have to use the bike today. At least there's only one more week to go. Only four days left in fact. As she sets off, her mind turns to focus on 7G and the first lesson of the day. At least she can start at ten on some days, now that she no longer has form mistress duties. It's a relief to have taken on the after-school drama club responsibilities instead. Another source of satisfaction is that all her marking is up to date so these last few days should be fairly easy.

It doesn't take long to get to school and she's soon riding into the car park. Not many free spaces today so it's good to have the bike which never presents any parking problems. Teaching can be good at times. 7G has plenty of difficult pupils but she likes them. The difficult ones are the most satisfying to teach, especially if they become enthused and start to do well and it sometimes happens. She parks the bike, removes the large bag of books from the luggage rack and heaves it onto her shoulder. She could do with a smoke, but there isn't time.

Philip is one of the difficult pupils in 7G but has ended up surprising her. Esme doesn't know much about his background except that he's always being moved from one foster home to the next, He barely speaks. Most of the time he occupies himself drawing pictures of knives, swords and broken bodies with blood dripping out of them. In every lesson, Ess tried to speak to him, asked him some question or other in a vain effort to get him to respond. One day, after weeks of this, Philip handed her a picture. It had a gravestone in the middle and a leafless tree at one side with a bird in it. Esme has no idea what the picture is supposed to mean (if anything) but the fact that he offered anything felt like an honour. She was pleased and showed it to Dani, but her daughter looked bewildered and irritated.

'What's that for, then?' Dani had asked and Ess had shrugged. There was no answer. Dani didn't understand. Or wouldn't. Her daughter was constantly awkward.

It's been a mixed weekend. The Pally was good, and it was nice seeing Howard, but the row with Steve was upsetting. He was angry with her for postponing the trip to her parents without consulting him. And she was angry with him for not making Dani do any homework on Saturday night. He will never be properly strict with her which is annoying. It would have been so much better for Dani if she had got some of the homework done before Sunday. Esme sighs. It's not often they have a row and Steve is right to be angry about the trip. She should have discussed changing the arrangements with him, but the worry over Dani's homework is a worse problem. Now they can't even talk about that.

Hopefully, she will be able to straighten things out over the summer holidays. It's getting harder and harder to talk to her daughter. 'Leave me alone. Leave me alone, will you?' is all Dani says these days. And then if Esme won't leave her alone, things get worse. But how can she? The school problem has got to be solved somehow. Esme realises that it's no longer just a homework problem. Her daughter's school stress has become a misery that hangs over them all.

The days pass and Dani seems to get slightly better towards the end of the week, although it's probably just because there's a general countdown to the holidays. At home, the atmosphere is not so good because Steve's usual good cheer has been absent. All week he has been angry so the house has been full of misery. The plan had been for all three of them to go down to Summer Lane at the weekend, and then Steve would have come back by himself on Sunday night ready for his working week. Now that Esme has altered things, Steve won't be able to go with them. He'd cleared the weekend of driving jobs and had organised replacement ones during the week. It's too late to rearrange them and he doesn't want to lose his reputation for reliability.

Steve shouted at her that she only ever thought of herself and that she'd changed the arrangements so she could go dancing on Saturday night. It was nothing to do with any tasks she'd got to do. Ess had denied it, of course, and almost believed her own excuses, but Steve is right. That was exactly why she had changed the trip. She had not paid any attention to what either Steve or Dani might have wanted. Should she change it back? She still could. Esme sits in the staff room and decides that she probably will change it back. She'll make a final decision very soon.

8

The trip is not rearranged, and on Saturday night Esme is once again sitting on the padded leatherette bench between Kate and John. It's the same bench they sat on the week before. Funny how human beings get into habits so quickly. Wanting to sit in the same seats. Drive along the same routes. Repeat a hundred little action loops and thought circles to fill up their lives. She looks around the room to see if Jackson is around. The cowboy man is called Jackson. Kate told her this when Esme asked about him. Casually, of course. Kate knows nearly everyone and their stories, but she frowned when Esme asked about Jackson and told her to stay clear of the man. Jackson is bad news. He's been done for GBH.

'What's that?'

'Grievous Bodily Harm,' Kate replies grimly. Despite this news, Esme still scans the room for signs of him.

'Want to dance?' John asks.

It doesn't take long for the familiar pleasure to kick in. Feeling the beat, watching the way John moves, letting her body sway. They dance, sit and drink, dance again. Esme is drinking lager. She prefers it to beer. Or are they the same thing? She doesn't think so. Lager is the kind of beer they had in Germany where she lived many years ago. It's where Dani was born. She hardly drank then because she was pregnant, but she often shared a beer with Andreas after Dani was born. That kind is the only kind of beer she likes. The English non-fizzy variety tastes awful.

'We're going now,' Kate says.

'But it's only half-past nine.'

'I know, but I told you before that we had to go early tonight. We've got family coming from Bradford. If we don't get a move on, they'll get to the house before we do. You'll be all right with John.'

'Sure,' she replies. 'See you next week.'

'How are we going to dance now?' Esme turns to John. 'There'll be nobody to mind my bag or keep the seats.'

'Can't you dance with it on? It's a shoulder bag. Should be easy.'

'I can try,' she says, but it isn't easy dancing with the bag swinging from side to side. It's heavy. She passes it to John so he can feel the weight and he can hardly believe it.

'What have you got in there, girl?' he asks. 'Feels like bricks.' They try again, but Esme can't get balanced so they go to sit down. John fetches more drinks but won't let her pay towards them. Then he asks if she's had a good week at school.

'It was, actually,' she says. 'I had a discussion with my third years about how to work out whether objects in German are masculine, feminine or neuter.'

'Oh,' he says and smiles, then after a pause, 'How do you do that?'

Undeterred by his lack of knowledge of the German language and almost certain lack of interest in it, Esme continues.

'There is no way of knowing most of the time. You have to learn each one separately. But what's interesting,' she pauses and looks at him, 'is to consider why those words evolved as they did.' By this time, John is looking bored but Esme can't stop. Somehow it has become important

55

that he understands what she's trying to say. No, that's not it. What's important is that he becomes *interested* in what she's trying to say. 'For instance,' she goes on, '*chair* is masculine, but *ceiling* is feminine. I asked the kids to imagine why that might be so. And *room* is neuter.' She pauses and looks at him again. He's grinning at her.

'Makes no sense to me,' he says. 'What did your kids say?'

'They got interested,' Esme replies. 'We got carried away imagining female ceilings and masculine chairs. And we laughed a lot. But *girl* in German is neuter. It's because the word means *small maid*. Everything with the 'small' ending is neuter.'

'You've lost me now,' John tells her, 'but I know that you're small and you're very feminine, so you can't be German. You're definitely an English girl.' He looks pleased with himself as he says this but Esme's brows contract.

'I'm not a girl,' she tells him.

'Not a girl?' he asks, and half giggles. 'What are you then?'

'I'm a woman,' she says and looks hard at him, but he's clearly baffled so she decides to give up. 'Shall we go and have another dance?'

'I've got a better idea,' John says. 'Let's go and have a cup of coffee at my friend's house. I'm keeping an eye on it for him while he's on holiday. It's only a few steps.'

'All right,' Esme agrees.

It's an unexpected relief to step outside into the cool, evening air away from the insistent beat and the harsh bright lights of the dance club. They walk along the street for a few paces before she sees John hesitate slightly and then catch her hand in his and start swinging her arm in time to their steps. It makes her feel uncomfortable. Esme has never walked along the street holding hands with anyone, or at least not since Dani was a small girl. She disengages herself, but then reaches up and gives him a little kiss on the cheek to show that she's not putting him down. He looks both surprised and confused. They keep on walking. He said it was just a few steps but it seems like a long way. They're walking in the opposite direction from Kate and Murray's house so Esme is not quite sure where they are.

'Are we nearly there?'

'Yes,' he replies but keeps on walking, quickening his step a little as though in a hurry to reach their destination before she decides it's too far and changes her mind. Suddenly he turns left into a side road and then right into a ginnel that leads behind some houses.

'Here we are,' he announces. 'Be quiet, Boxer,' he raises his voice to a speak to a dog that is chained to a kennel. The dog is barking furiously.

'Poor dog,' says Esme, backing away nervously. 'How long has he been chained up like that?'

'He's a guard dog,' John tells her defensively. 'Does a good job. But look, he won't hurt you. I'll bring him inside with us.' John walks up to Boxer, who jumps up and licks his face, rump waving madly. No tail. John unfastens the dog who stops barking and follows them meekly into the house. It's clear that John is at home here. He goes into the kitchen and puts the kettle on. Then he goes over to the record player in the living room and takes a Bob Marley record from the stack lined up on the shelf. He waves it at her. It's *Exodus*.

John looks pleased with himself and puts it on. Even though it was only released the year before, and despite the fact that usually, it takes several years before Esme catches up with record releases, she knows all the tracks because they've been played so often at the Pally. *Jamming* soon fills the room. It's the one she always told him she liked and he's remembered. She smiles at him.

'This is side two,' he says. 'Maybe I should start at the beginning.' He goes to stop the record and turns it back to side one.' From the kitchen, he brings two cups of coffee and puts them onto the little table in front of them. The large sofa on which Esme is sitting bears a heavy resemblance to the seating at The Pally in that it's soft, padded and made of imitation leather. Esme stares at the cup of coffee which is so milky she thinks she might not be able to drink it but decides not to say anything. After bringing the coffee, he goes back into the kitchen and returns with a couple of packets of crisps.

'Cheese and onion,' he says.

'Thanks, John, but I'm not hungry.' He sinks down next to her on the big, soft sofa and they listen to the familiar tunes. John gets up and turns the record over once more. *Jamming* starts again.

'We could dance,' he offers. 'Come on, Esme. Come and dance.' He stands up and starts swaying gently in time to the music. He holds out his hand to her so she gets up and starts moving. No shoulder bag to hamper her now. It's on the floor next to the sofa. She smells his aftershave as he moves closer. Too sweet and too much of it. It doesn't quite mask the faint smell of sweat that's there underneath the artificial scent. She prefers the smell of his skin. John's hips move, and Esme watches. *Waiting in Vain* is starting to play once more.

'Am I, Esme?' he asks, almost whispers. 'Am I waiting in vain?' How can he be so corny? She doesn't answer. He's holding her now and speaking into her ear. 'I've been waiting for you all my life.' Esme pulls away and goes back to the sofa. Can't believe such a crass chat-up line. Almost starts drinking the coffee, she's so distracted but changes her mind.

'What about Barbara?' she manages to ask.

'I'm leaving her,' he replies seriously. 'We can't get on with each other. It's a long story. I'll tell you another time.' He picks up his cup, then turns to look at her. 'I'm free, Esme. I'm yours if you want me.'

'But I'm not free,' she says. 'I'm with Steve.'

'I'm sorry,' he says and hesitates. 'I do know that. I'm sorry, Esme. I just can't help it. If you want me anytime, then I'm yours. Even if it's only for half an hour.' Esme relaxes and grins at him.

'Half an hour?' she says. 'OK, I'm up for that. Let's go to bed for half an hour. Then I'll have to go.' She sees the shock on his face as she says this. He's trying to make sense of what she's said. It doesn't fit with what he knows of her. It doesn't match what he expects her to say. But he gets up and holds out his hand.

'Come on then,' he smiles uncertainly. 'Let's have the half-hour.' He leads the way up the stairs and the dog follows them. When they reach the bedroom, he ushers her in and shuts the dog outside. The bed is a bit like the sofa downstairs. Soft and yielding. It is piled up with cushions which she thinks is odd. The whole room is red. The curtains are dark red velvet and look dusty. The carpet is red, too, but threadbare and stained in places.

'Come on,' he says pulling her gently onto the bed and starting to stroke her. He's tall. The length of him presses against her and she feels the hardness of him. He tries to take off her clothes, unwinds the scarf from around her neck and reaches to touch her breast. Then she feels his hand sliding down looking for the zip on her jeans.

'I'm on the pill,' she says.

'I don't care,' he replies.

'You should,' she tells him. 'What about babies?'

'I don't care,' he replies and hesitates. 'Yes, I do care, Esme. I would love it if you had my baby. I would be proud. I would look after you. Both of you.'

'What about Dani?'

'Oh, yes, Dani, too.'

Esme doesn't believe him. It's just another chat-up line. He doesn't seem interested in looking after Barbara's children and he didn't even remember that Daniela existed. She doesn't think he's half the man that Steve is. But she's being unfair. He does mean it. At least he means it at this moment. She watches as he gets up and takes off all his clothes except for his socks which almost makes her laugh. They're green. Then he watches as she, too, starts to take off her clothes then stops. Just her jeans she decides. It's too cold to take off her jumper or anything else. She shivers and realises that she's feeling the opposite of passionate but his body gleams and she stands up and moves towards him. For a minute they stand quite still while he holds her gently like he does when they're dancing.

It's quickly over and now he's holding her tightly, much too tightly and saying he loves her. Oh, no, she thinks and pulls away, puts her finger over his lips to stop the words.

'It was just the half-hour,' she says. 'A bit of fun between friends. It won't happen again.'

'What do you mean?' his voice starts to rise. 'Come here, Esme. Come closer. Let's cuddle. Come here, darling...' But Esme gets off the bed, pulls her knickers back on and then her jeans, feeling wet and ashamed in a way she has never felt before.

'I've got to go. Steve will be wondering where I am.' She sees that John is hurt and she's sorry. She's used him. He is a good man and she's treated him badly. She had thought she could have sex without it mattering whether she wanted their relationship to continue.

'I thought you liked me.'

'I do like you. We can be friends, but I have to think of Steve.' It's an excuse but giving Steve as an explanation is what she thinks John will understand.

In silence, they walk back through the poorly lit streets until they reach the main road. It's still quite a way to where Esme lives, but she says she wants to walk, doesn't want to catch a bus. He insists on going with her although she would rather walk alone. Eventually, they reach her house and she turns to thank him for bringing her home.

'See you next week.'

'Of course,' Esme replies. 'See you next week.' But she knows that her dalliance with John is over. From now on, it will be dancing only. She's been stupid and selfish and she's sorry. *Please God, don't let him tell anybody.*

9

I survived Monday because I managed to write two sentences for the weekend homework. Steve helped me with them and they were short but better than nothing. Mrs Richards didn't shout as much as usual. The final homework assignment, the one that should have been given in on Thursday, didn't happen because things were getting relaxed. It was the end of term and Mum said that the teachers were giving up. Wish Mrs Richards would give up. If she saw how hard I worked at my writing when there was no-one there, she wouldn't call me lazy. None of them would.

Mum thinks I'm lazy. I'm sure of it. She tries not to nag at me but still keeps on. 'You've got to get your homework done, Dani.' Over and over. She's like a record that's got stuck. Why doesn't she understand that I'd do it if I could? She must think that I like to look a fool in class. But it's over now until next term. I'll have to find a way to do it by then. If everyone else can do it, there must be a way.

I'm looking forward to seeing Grandma. We should have gone on Saturday, but Mum changed it and Steve's cross. He'd changed his driving jobs so we could all go together at the weekend and we know why she changed it. It was so she could go down the Pally on Saturday night. I wish she hadn't gone. Anyhow, Mum rang Grandma to tell her we were coming on Monday instead.

I spoke to Grandma when Mum rang although we didn't talk for long. Grandma loves having the phone, but she doesn't exactly chat on it. Just uses it for short bits of information. Grandpa held out against it for ages. Said they didn't need one but he doesn't mind now. He's been happier since he retired. Even I can tell that. He used to sit in silence as though he didn't want to be with us, didn't want to be with anyone. Would hardly say a word and sometimes didn't answer when you spoke to him. Grandma said it was his long working hours and because he was in pain with his arthritis, or was it rheumatism, but now he's changed. His hands are sometimes almost closed with pain but he still gets up every morning and hums, goes out into the garden and spends all day there. Grandpa hates having to go anywhere that cuts down his time in the garden. He won't go on holiday, won't even go shopping. He never wants to waste a single minute of precious gardening time, so we always know that he'll be in. It doesn't matter when we arrive.

We haven't seen them since Easter and now it's July. Mum said we'd go more often once she and Steve got the car, but it hasn't happened. Mum used to drive me down on the back of the Honda. It took ages and we got stiff and cold but we still went more frequently than we do now. I know why. It's because of the dancing. Mum's become obsessed with going dancing but she tells Grandma it's because she's got too much school work. Tells her that the marking loads keep going up. Mum does do a lot of marking I have to admit. I'm never going to be a teacher. On second thoughts maybe I'm never going to amount to anything just like Mrs Richards says. If I can't write, I won't manage to do anything apart from factory jobs. Maybe she is right. Perhaps I am stupid, but I don't think so and I'm certainly not lazy. Thank God this is the last week for ages that I have to see that spiteful cow. There will be the whole summer to forget about her.

Nobody in our family is lazy. Mum works hard and so does Steve and now Grandpa has retired, he works harder than ever. I liked it when Grandpa was at work and I could have Grandma to myself, but it's nearly as good now because Grandpa is out in the garden all day long. Even when it rains, or when it's so cold that the earth is too hard to turn, he still finds something to do out there. In the shed if necessary. He prefers the shed to the house. He's up by six-thirty each day (instead of the quarter to six start when he went to work), and day after day he beams and says how good it is to have a lie-in every morning.

'Ah, Frankie,' he says, and yes, he's started calling my Grandma, Frankie. Grandma says he used to do that in their early years together and I can tell she likes it. 'I never thought I'd live this long,' Grandpa says. 'Never thought I'd live to see my retirement. They said I'd be gone before I was thirty.' This is a constant happy refrain. Grandpa never tires of repeating it and we've all got used to hearing it. He has come back to life. He's relaxed and cheerful and sometimes almost chatty. He jokes. And I know that I can do no wrong. I've always been his favourite. Esme says he spoils me and that she used to get told off for doing the things that Grandpa just smiles about when I do them. Like sledging down the lawn in winter. Or climbing on the roof of the coal shed. He doesn't like me wearing jeans, but he doesn't nag at me like he used to nag at Mum.

I bet Grandma is shopping and cooking ready for us coming. She always bakes loads of our favourite things: fruit cake, scones and shortbreads, cheese straws, lots of puddings. And the house always smells of furniture polish.

Lavender. Smells a bit like Mum actually. She always smells of lavender. But not polish. Mum doesn't do much cleaning.

It only takes about two hours to drive down from Leeds but we never set off early so it is late afternoon before we arrive in Summer Lane.

'Hello, Grandma,' I shout as I race up the path to the back door. She can't understand why I usually run rather than walk, but it's simple. Walking is too slow. Grandpa tells me that I'm a young lady now and should behave like one. He means I should walk sedately, but it's a joke. He smiles when he says it. I look at Grandma and fling my arms around her and hug her hard.

'You'll squash me to death,' she says, but it's not possible. Grandma is thin and unsquashable. She's got strong bones. You can feel them.

'Where's Grandpa?' I ask.

'Up the garden,' she says. 'Where else. You can go up in a minute and tell him it's time to come in for his tea.'

'It still seems strange without Snowy,' I say, talking about the dog that was there when I was little. I loved him. Gone now.

'Yes, we miss him, too.'

I see Mum finally make it into the house lugging two huge bags and knocking the geraniums in the porch as she comes through. A trail of red petals lands on the floor. It's taken her ages to get out of the car and come in.

'Are you moving in?' Grandma asks her.

'Just for a few days,' Esme grins.

'It's a pity Steve couldn't come with you. How is he?'

'He's fine. Sends his love. Already had jobs lined up that he couldn't cancel.'

'Yes. I bet he would have had things organised ready to come at the weekend and then you changed the plan.'

'You're right. And it was completely my fault. There were some things I wanted to get done before we came, but I probably shouldn't have changed the arrangements.'

'It's because she wanted to go dancing,' I say before I can stop myself. I see that Esme gives me a filthy look but she doesn't contradict me. I should have kept my mouth shut.

'I didn't know you went dancing, Ess,' Grandma says.

'I've been going for months. Well, weeks anyhow. Since just after Easter. It's good exercise, especially after being at school all week.'

No more is said about the dancing or our delayed arrival, and after tea, I set off 'to check things out'. 'Where are you going?' Esme asks.

'Out,' I say and am gone before she can question me further. I'm off to see what's going on. If there are any new places to hang out, to see if there's anyone around, but I pretend that I'm going fishing. Don't want them to worry. Esme keeps warning me about strange men especially since the Ripper hasn't been caught yet, but I think he targets prostitutes rather than young girls like me. I don't worry about him, but I do keep my eyes open.

Every day after breakfast, I go out to check the place out. I see that Grandpa expects me to come back with fish and Grandma expects me to talk more. I don't think I've changed since Easter, but they do. I definitely don't want to talk about school. No point in telling Grandma how awful Mrs Richards is or that I can't write. I'm ashamed and, in any case, there's nothing she can do to help.

I'm not sure when we're going back to Leeds because Mum hasn't said anything and I'm almost afraid to ask. Snappy when I try to talk to her and even if she does tell me what she's planned, it can change at a moment's notice. You can't rely on her. Today when I get back, she invites me to go for a walk with her over the fields. That means she wants to talk to me privately where Grandma can't hear. Don't like the sound of that. I say that I don't feel like it, but she insists so we set off.

When we get to the top stile and there's a good field distance between us and Grandma's, she tells me that she'd like me to stay here for the whole holidays. I like it here, but a wave of worry washes through me. I ask her why she wants me to stay here and she says it's because it's peaceful and because Grandma would enjoy having me. That's true and I do like seeing Grandma, but it's boring. I want to hang around with Mandy and my other friends. Most of all, I wonder why my mother doesn't want me around in Leeds but I'm too scared to ask. Instead, I explain about wanting to spend the holidays with Mandy and she suggests that we ask Grandma and Grandpa if Mandy could come down here with me. I think about it. If she came down with me, we could go and check out the place together. We could find the local hangouts. There must be a fun place somewhere in the neighbourhood, at least in Derby. Yes, ok, I tell her, so we go back to see what Grandma and Grandpa think about it.

'The wanderers return,' Grandpa says as we walk in. I suppose we must have been gone for quite a while. Grandpa and Grandma have already eaten. 'Thought you'd got lost,' he says.

'We've been talking,' Esme starts off as we sit down at the table and start making sandwiches. 'Dani's made a suggestion which would need your consent. It might not work, but at any rate, you'd have to agree first.'

'What's that?' Grandpa asks.

'Mum wants me to stay here for the summer,' I tell them. 'It's nice here, but I'd be bored. There's nobody to hang out with. So I wondered ....' I trail to a halt.

'What,' Grandpa prompts me, 'what did you wonder, my ducky?' I can see that Grandma knows what I'm going to say next.

'Could Mandy come and stay with me?' I ask. There's no immediate reply, so I carry on. 'She might not be allowed, of course, but it would be great if she could.'

'I don't see why not,' Grandpa says looking at Grandma. He knows that Grandma won't mind. She loves having me around.

'What's she like?' Grandma asks. 'This friend of yours. Is she a nice girl?'

'Mandy's a lovely girl,' Mum jumps in. 'She's polite, well behaved. You'd like her, but Dani's right. We don't know whether her parents would let her come. Or even whether she'd want to.'

'Mandy would definitely want to,' I say, so it's agreed that Mum will take me back with her on Friday. We'll find out if Mandy is allowed to come down and ring to let Grandma know.

On Friday morning, Grandma stands in the lane and watches us drive off. I do want Mandy to come down here but at the same time, I'm miserable because Mum doesn't want me with her in Leeds.

10

'And what about you, Mum? What do you think? Will you be pleased for Mandy to go to Summer Lane with me?' Dani is talking non-stop as Esme drives back to Leeds.

'Yes, of course,' Esme says, reaching for the volume knob to at least turn the music down.

'Won't you miss me?'

'Yes, of course, I will.'

'I could stay in Leeds instead,' Dani says, 'I could stay with you and Steve.' Esme hears the change of tone and wonders what to reply. Yes, she wants some time alone, but she does think it will do her daughter good to spend the summer with Grandma and Grandpa. And she can see that if Mandy is there, too, then Dani will be happy with the arrangement. If it doesn't work out, Esme won't get the chance to have the time alone that she almost craves. She lets out a sigh.

'Yes, you could,' Esme says. 'You could stay in Leeds if that's what you want.'

It's the right response. She sees her daughter start to relax again.

Esme wants to get her thoughts straight. Needs to think things out and work out why she's so restless, but it's difficult with Dani around. Impossible. Like now. No peace. When she's on her own, driving is a good time for thinking. Ess glances at her daughter and pushes another tape into the player. Al Green this time, but it makes no difference.

Dani talks over it, like an endless waterfall, energy bursting forth and overflowing. She's stopped talking about the probability of Marsha's agreeing to the Summer Lane project and has switched to talking about prime numbers. They defy prediction apparently. Dani's interest in numbers is not new, but it's something Esme doesn't understand. At least Dani sounds cheerful. Ess reminds herself that it's a pleasant change from the times when her daughter is sullen and withdrawn. Those times have been all too frequent lately.

It's mid-afternoon by the time they get back, and Steve's not home yet. So many bags to bring in from the car even though they've only been away for a couple of days. She calls Dani to help unload, but her daughter is already on the way to Mandy's.

'You ok with those, Mum? I'll come straight back.'

'All right,' Esme says wearily and carries on fetching the bags in by herself. She feels worn out. It's exhausting just to be near Dani some of the time.

Finally, the bags are dumped in a heap in the middle of the living room. Ess has collapsed on to a chair for a minute before starting to sort them out when Dani bursts through the door followed by Mandy. Marsha stands in the doorway.

'Hello, Marsha,' Esme goes to the door. 'Please do come in. It's a bit of a mess. We've only just got back.'

'Thanks,' Marsha says and follows Dani and Mandy into the house.

'She wants to talk to you, Mum,' Dani tells her.

Esme sends the two girls down to the cellar with instructions to stay down there and get on with something while she makes a pot of tea for Marsha and herself.

'Haven't seen you for a while,' Marsha says.

'No, we should get together sometime. You ought to come round for a coffee.'

'You, too. Don't know where the time goes.'

Having fulfilled the need for a few polite pleasantries, Esme starts to explain about the invitation for Mandy to go with Dani to Summer Lane.

'Dani wants to spend time with her grandparents but she doesn't know anybody down there. It would be great if Mandy could go with her.'

She looks up and notices that Marsha is looking hesitant but, instead of stopping to find out what the problem is, continues to pour out information hoping to persuade her to agree. Ess hardly draws breath as she rambles on about the woods and the fields, the fishing and the tree climbing. Gradually she falters and Marsha begins to laugh.

'That's very kind of you. I'm sure Mandy would love to go, but I don't think she's into tree climbing and she wouldn't have a clue about fishing.' Marsha leans forward and helps herself to another shortbread. 'These are nice. Did you make them?' Esme shakes her head. 'Is that what Dani likes to do? Climb trees and go fishing?'

'I don't suppose I've seen her climb trees for a while,' Esme admits,' but she loves going fishing.'

'Well, I'm not surprised,' Marsha says, putting her cup down. 'Dani's an interesting girl. Always been a bit of a tomboy, hasn't she?'

'I suppose so,' Esme says slowly, although she has never thought of Dani like that. She pauses to consider how her daughter might appear to other people. 'Her grandpa taught her to fish when she was small and Dani took to it,' she grins, 'like a fish to water.'

'Mandy's never done anything like that, but she likes the countryside. I'm sure they would have a good time down there.' Esme nods. 'It would keep them from getting into trouble,' Marsha adds and laughs. Once again, Esme feels faintly surprised. What does Marsha mean or is she just making polite conversation? It had never occurred to Esme that the girls might get into trouble during the holidays.

'But whatever happens,' Marsha continues, 'I couldn't let Mandy impose on your parents for such a long time.' Esme is about to interrupt, but Marsha shakes her head. 'You suggested them going for four weeks.' Marsha puts her cup down and this time Esme keeps quiet and lets her finish. 'It's very kind of you, but that would be too long. We'd like her here with us for at least part of the holidays.'

'Of course,' Esme says, her spirits sinking. 'Yes, I completely agree. Four weeks is far too long. It's Dani getting carried away.' She crosses her fingers as she says this, hoping that Dani doesn't rush upstairs to inform Marsha that it's actually Esme who suggested the four weeks. Ess is sure the two girls will be listening at the bottom of the cellar steps. The realisation hits that Dani wouldn't want to stay in Summer Lane for that long. 'Me, too,' Esme says, 'I want Dani here for at least part of the holidays.'

But it's not true. Esme wants the summer to herself. Dani is her beloved daughter but so long as she's safe and well cared for, Esme is happy for her to be somewhere else. Relieved in fact. She wants her daughter to be somewhere else because Ess almost desperately wants to spend time on her own. She's lost in thought for a moment until she realises that Marsha is speaking again.

'Three weeks might be possible. If you're sure that your parents wouldn't mind having her?'

'No trouble at all. My parents would be happy to have them. It would be no trouble at all.' With an effort, she stops herself from thanking Marsha and saying once again that it would be no trouble at all.

'All right then, I'll ask Richard when he comes home from work. Can we let you know tomorrow morning?'

'Of course, you can. There's no rush.'

'And could you call Mandy for me? I'd like her to come back with me now.'

Esme duly calls down the stairs and as soon as they've gone, Dani grins. She doesn't need to be told what Marsha has said. Esme is right. The two girls have been shamelessly eavesdropping.

'What do you think?' she asks her mother.

'It sounds good,' Esme says. 'Just hope you don't get up to anything while you're down there.'

'*Get up to anything?*' Dani echoes in withering tones. 'We're not children, Esme.'

'It was a joke,' Ess replies half-heartedly.

By the time Steve arrives back, Esme has finished cooking. It's the special chicken stew that she knows he likes. After their row and his missed trip to Summer Lane, she's hoping to make peace between them. She has made a huge panful. Thick and aromatic. Creamy. Enough for the next few days. Usually, it's curry that she makes in liberal quantities to save having to cook every day. This is almost the same and the flavour improves with each day's addition of different fresh ingredients.

It's ready and has been kept simmering. The smell is making her hungry and from time to time she has been tasting it. At last, she hears the car door and the sound of Steve coming up the steps. She goes to the door with a smile and holds out her arms to give him a hug but he pushes her away. Walks straight past, dumps his stuff and goes to sit down.

'Not now, Esme. I'm tired.'

Since when has Steve been too tired to give her a hug? Esme says nothing and goes to dish out the food. During the meal, Dani starts to tell him about how Mandy will be going down to Summer Lane with her, but it soon becomes clear that he's not listening. Esme reminds her that Mandy's Dad has not yet given his consent, but Dani no longer seems interested. She falls silent. Steve is quiet throughout the meal. Hardly seems to be listening to anything they have to say. As soon as he finishes eating, he says he's going upstairs to work.

'Oh Steve,' Dani says, 'surely you don't have to go and start work now. You've been working all day and we've only just come home.' She looks at him again, adding quietly. 'And I'll be gone soon.'

'Sorry, Dani, I'll have a bit more time tomorrow and we can talk then.'

'Ok,' Dani replies and Esme watches her daughter's shoulders slump.

'Or play chess. We could play chess,' he says as he disappears up the stairs.

Esme wonders what's wrong and realises they won't be able to talk until after Dani has gone to bed. When will that be? Dani sometimes goes upstairs around ten, to read or to listen to music, but mostly it's later than that. And even if she does go up early, how long will it be until she is asleep? Sound travels easily in this house. It's hard keeping anything private. Ess feels worried. It's unusual for Steve to be moody so she decides she can't wait until later.

They could go out to talk. To the pub or for a walk. It would be nice. Dani would be all right by herself for a couple of hours or Suzi might be free to come over. Most of the people she knows leave sons and daughters of Dani's age in the house by themselves for short periods. *We're not children, Esme* echoes in her head. Ess realises that she's stricter with her daughter than most other parents are with theirs. It's because she nearly lost her. That time when Dani was little. What did happen on that day when Dani's father rushed off and left her behind? Esme doesn't like to think about it, but the disturbing memories linger. She keeps trying to bury them.

Esme goes upstairs to talk to Steve.

'Are you busy?' she asks. Steve nods and turns back to the book on his desk. He looks as though he's making notes and writing information on to index cards. 'I thought we could go out to the pub for a couple of hours. We never get any time to ourselves. Couldn't you leave that for now?'

'No.'

After Dani has gone to bed, Steve finally stops and comes down for a drink. Esme tries again.

'What's the matter?' she asks. 'What's wrong with you tonight?'

'Nothing,' he says. 'I'm tired.' He switches on the tv and starts watching a comedy programme. It doesn't look familiar. What Steve likes best is Monty Python. Esme remembers that when they didn't have a tv, Steve would drag her round to his friend, Paul's to watch it and Dani had gone with them. That was in the days when they did stuff together.

'Come on, Stevie,' she says. 'Please tell me what's wrong.'

'There's nothing wrong,' he says but moves away when she goes to sit beside him.

Finally, Esme gives up and goes to bed. She'll have to wait. Maybe he's still angry about the change of arrangements for going down to Summer Lane. Or maybe he doesn't like the idea of Dani spending most of the holidays away from them. But she thinks it's something else. Steve was stiff and angry when he came in tonight. It must be something serious. The memory of John flashes through her mind, but she pushes it away. Surely, John wouldn't tell anyone what happened. It's too awful to contemplate. She doesn't think that men like to advertise their rejections. Nor women either come to that, but women confide more easily than men. Don't they?

And then there's Dani. Sounds happy some of the time but then changes completely. She suggests staying in Leeds like she's throwing down a gauntlet. Esme drifts off to sleep with her mind full of uneasy thoughts.

***

On Saturday morning things come to a head. The first thing that happens is that Mandy's Dad says she can't go to Summer Lane. They couldn't possibly put Esme's parents to so much trouble. Mandy would miss the Buddhist meetings that they wanted her to attend with them. Mandy arrives in person to bring the bad news and soon afterwards, Dani announces that she and Mandy are going out.

'Where to?' asks Esme.

'Just out!'

'No, you're not. Not like that. Come here and tell me politely where you're planning to go. Then I'll tell you whether or not I'll allow you to do so.'

'Gledhow Valley,' Dani mutters.

'All right, but make sure you're back here by one o'clock. For lunch.'

'Don't want any lunch.'

'That's up to you, but if you're not back here by one, you'll be in trouble.'

'OK.' Dani sighs and looks at her mother. 'Can I go now?'

'Yes. But be careful. And make sure you're back by one.' The door bangs and her daughter is gone. Ess looks out of the window and watches the girls, one blond head with bunches and one head of short brown curls bobbing up and down, deep in conversation as they walk down the street. You wouldn't think they were only thirteen. *We're not children, Esme* echoes once again.

Ess fetches a cup of coffee and stands at the table staring out of the window while she drinks. She's sorry for Dani and Mandy. And for herself, of course. She's sorry that Mandy won't be going to Summer Lane. She looks up. There's a noise from upstairs. Steve is coming down.

'What was all the banging and shouting about?'

'Mandy can't go to Summer Lane so they're upset. They've gone off to Gledhow Valley.'

'So Dani will be here for the holidays, will she?' Steve stares at her with a strange look on his face. 'Won't that seriously cramp your style?'

'What do you mean?'

'Well, it's hard to run around Chapeltown if you've got a young daughter to look after and I might not always be available for babysitting.'

'Steve!' Esme feels a twinge of apprehension. 'What do you mean?'

'Exactly what I say,' he says, looking at her with disgust. 'I suppose you're proud of your power to wreck lives. How marvellous that you're so attractive. And I used to admire you.'

'I don't know what you're talking about.'

'I'm quite sure that you do. Kate said that John had already told you, so I'm sure that you do know. What is clear is that you don't care.'

'Don't care about what?' Esme is shouting now.

'The fact that John has left Barbara and the kids,' Steve pauses and pushes the hair out of his eyes. 'Because he's in love with you! Says he had to leave even though you're not interested in him. Says he can't stay with his wife anymore and live a lie.' Steve picks up the glass ashtray next to his hand and looks as though he might throw it at her. 'You've wrecked a family, Esme. And you don't give a toss.'

'Oh my God,' she says and sits down. 'Oh, Christ.' She reaches for the tobacco tin and rolls a cigarette. Lights it. Sucks hard. 'John did tell me, but I thought he was joking. I never thought that he really would leave Barbara. When did you hear this?'

'Kate came round on Thursday. Actually, she came to see you. Didn't know you'd gone to Summer Lane. Wanted you to persuade John to go back.'

'Of course, I'll try to persuade him to go back. I'll do my very best.' Esme stubs out her cigarette and reaches for the tobacco tin. Begins to roll another one. 'He did tell me,' she speaks slowly. 'Last week when he walked me home after the dancing, he did say that he was leaving Barbara, but it didn't occur to me that he was serious.' She stops. Steve looks tense. He keeps reaching up to push the hair out of his eyes like he does when he's upset. 'And yes, John did tell me that he loved me. He told me he was free, but I said that I wasn't. I reminded him that I was with you.' She lights the cigarette. 'I thought he was just saying that he'd leave her to see if he had a chance with me. I never thought for a minute that he was serious. Thought it was just a chat-up line. I'm so sorry.'

Esme sees Steve soften slightly. He doesn't want to believe the worst of her. But she *is* to blame. She did flirt with John. She had sex with him and made it into a joke. Said it didn't mean a thing. She prays that Steve will never find out. Wonders what John has told Kate. Esme stands up and goes to get her jacket.

'Where are you going?'

'I'm going to see Kate. Will you stay here and make sure Dani gets back on time? I told her she had to be back here by one.'

Steve sighs, 'I suppose so.'

11

'Come and have a cup of tea,' Kate says as Esme follows her into the kitchen. She is offering tea but doesn't look welcoming. 'What's the matter?'

'It's Steve. He says that John has left Barbara and that it's my fault.'

'Well, that's more or less true. At least it's true that John has left Barbara. He said that he'd told you.'

'Well, he did,' Esme admits. 'He said last Saturday when he was walking me home that he was leaving Barbara. Said it was a long story and that he'd tell me about it another time.' She sits down at the table and waits while Kate puts the kettle on. Ess reaches into her bag for the tobacco tin and starts to roll a cigarette. 'But I didn't believe him. I thought he was joking.'

'Did John tell you he was leaving her because of you?'

'No, he didn't say that. How could he? He hardly knows me.'

Kate frowns, 'Oh come on, Ess. You can't tell me you haven't noticed how he looks at you.'

'Well, I knew he liked me. Of course, I did, but I didn't think it was more than that. We flirted a bit for sure, but it was never serious. I had no idea.' Esme lights her cigarette and offers the tin to Kate, who shakes her head. 'And you encouraged me. You always told me that John was completely safe. That he was someone that I didn't have to worry about.'

'Well, it's true. You can trust him to treat you with respcct, but you led him on. We thought you fancied him and wondered if you were thinking of leaving Steve. You never go out with Steve anymore. And I'm sure John noticed that. He must have thought he was in with a chance.'

Esme's heart sinks. Some of it is true. There had been a time when she would never have wanted to go out without Steve. John wasn't around then, but Kate remembers and must have noticed that Esme had changed. She has, and yes, she was briefly attracted to John. But never seriously. A fleeting sexual attraction, soon taken care of. On her side that is but she knows she has treated John badly. It would be how a man would behave she thinks.

The thought that a man would probably behave like that should help, but it doesn't. Ess wants to be strong and principled in her relationships and at the same time honest. But she is not managing it. In any case, only some men would behave like that. Not the good ones like Steve. Dear Steve, whom she once adored, but who has now started to irritate her. She doesn't like the way he is super tidy, how he folds towels, jumpers (hers as well as his), folds everything even socks and newspapers and puts everything away. It's stupid to be irritated by such things and there was a time when his tidiness pleased her, but she can't help it. When he eats, he makes a faint clicking noise and it drives her mad. Not loud, but she always hears it. She can hardly believe that she could feel like this. Such unimportant things. What is wrong with her? Esme draws on her cigarette.

'I thought John knew I was with Steve,' Ess repeats half-heartedly, realising that she had known for some time that John wanted a serious relationship with her, but she hadn't paid any attention. It had been pleasant to be wanted. Now she's sorry for not being more careful. Sorry for not behaving better. Desperately sorry that it's turned out like this and that John has left his wife.

She catches herself thinking that she'll have to be more careful the next time. Next time? She examines this thought and tries to stamp on it but instead finds herself drawn to the prospect. It might be better next time. She draws again on the cigarette. Not possible to explain either her feelings or her actions to Kate, but she can try to make things all right again for John. Can try to get him back with his family.

'I didn't realise you thought I was going to leave Steve. I came out with you because I like dancing. And a bit of flirting, I suppose.' Esme puts her cup down. 'How do you think I can get John to go back to Barbara? Where is he now?'

'He's staying with a friend somewhere in Chapeltown, not far from the Palace he said.'

A vision of the house with the dog and the big soft sofa rises in Esme's mind. And the bedroom with the red curtains and the stained, threadbare carpet.

'How can I make him go back to Barbara? Will she have him back?'

'Oh yes, she'll have him. But he won't go. He says it's over.'

'I'll find a way,' Esme says. She stubs out her cigarette. She stares at it. It's the ashtray she's used a thousand times, the one with a bird at each corner. 'I'll find a way to make him go back, but I need to go home now.'

'Are you still coming out tonight?' Kate asks.

'Do you think I should?'

'Of course,' Kate replies. 'It will be a chance to talk to John, to try and make him see sense. You can make it clear that he has no chance with you.'

'I did try before,' Esme says. 'When he said he was free because he was going to leave Barbara, I told him that I wasn't. I did make it clear that I was with Steve, but I'll have another go tonight.'

'OK. We'll see you later then.'

'All right. Bye.'

***

When Esme gets home, Dani is in the cellar working on the bike after having eaten her lunch in near silence, according to Steve.

'She seemed upset that you'd gone to see Kate, but I might have got it wrong. Perhaps she's miserable because Mandy can't go to Summer Lane.'

Ess goes into the kitchen to put the kettle on. Of course, Steve is getting it wrong. Dani is not upset because of her. Her daughter is upset because of what's happening with Mandy, but it's not a good time to start arguing with him.

'Do you want a coffee?'

'Yes, please, and then come and tell me what happened at Kate's.'

Esme is carrying the cups into the living room when there's a banging on the door. It's Mandy!

'I can go!' Mandy shouts, breathless. 'I can go,' she repeats before she's even inside the house. Esme hears her daughter pounding up the steps from the cellar.'

'What did you say?' Dani asks as she appears in the kitchen doorway. 'Come in, Mandy. Come in.'

'Dad's changed his mind. I can go.'

'Hallelujah! Great balls of fire.' Dani smiles.

'Are you sure?' Steve asks Mandy. 'Why did your dad change his mind?'

'It's because Mum talked to him. I knew she would. Told you,' Mandy said turning to Dani. 'But she couldn't do it in front of me, so this morning it was a no.'

'And now it's a yes,' Dani beams at her friend.

'And now it's a yes,' Mandy echoes. 'Do you want to come round to our house so we can plan the trip?'

'Is that all right, Mum?'

'Go on then,' Esme says, feeling a surge of relief at the latest Summer Lane news. 'Make sure you're back by seven.'

'Yeah, sure.' And the two girls are gone.

Esme sits down at the table and feels her mug. It is still hot.

'Have we got any biscuits?'

Steve fetches the tin which is usually empty and opens it to reveal two packets of chocolate digestives.

'I just got them,' he says taking out a packet and putting it on the table. 'So what's the news? You still haven't told me what happened at Kate's.' Esme tells Steve what Kate told her, but there's nothing much to add.

'Kate says I should go tonight and persuade John to go back to Barbara.'

'Not sure about that,' he says. 'I don't think that's a good idea.'

'Why not?'

'Let's talk to John together so he can see us as a couple. He could come here.'

'I'm not sure,' Ess replies slowly, trying frantically to think of what she can say to avert disaster. 'but I do think I should go tonight because Kate asked me specially.' She looks at Steve. 'Maybe you're right. Perhaps it would be a good idea to ask John to come here and talk to us both together.' Esme picks up her cup, but it's empty and glances at the packet of biscuits. It is nearly finished. She has eaten without noticing. 'I know what to do,' she says. 'I'll go tonight and ignore him. If I cut him dead, he'll start seeing sense. He'll think how horrible I am.'

'Don't be stupid. That would get him going more than ever.' Steve bangs his mug down on the table and pushes his plate away. 'Don't play games, Ess. There's nothing more attractive than an unattainable woman.'

'You mean you'd be attracted to a woman just because she didn't want you?'

'Of course,' Steve replies. 'She'd be a challenge.'

'That's ridiculous,' Ess says and notes the growing frustration in his face, 'but I'll keep on thinking about it.'

At seven, Dani returns punctually for the second time that day. At least the Summer Lane trip has worked out Ess thinks and gives Dani a hug. Asks her if she's looking forward to going to Grandma's on Monday but Dani just shrugs. As soon as they've eaten, Ess goes upstairs to get ready for the evening out. Usually, it's a pleasure, but not tonight.

***

There is no cheery welcome. The atmosphere is chilly and both Kate and Murray look disapproving. Esme attempts to make light-hearted conversation but her words fall into the wind as Kate and Murray walk along without speaking to her. If passers-by were to glance at them, they would never believe that the three of them were heading for a fun night out. As she walks along, Esme makes a decision. She won't talk to John tonight and she won't dance with him.

They are early and sit down in their usual place while Esme goes to get the drinks. John's not there yet and she's asked Kate and Murray if she can sit between them so she doesn't have to talk to John.

'I thought you were going to persuade him to go back to Barbara,' Murray says, looking at her in surprise.

'I'm going to ignore him,' Esme says. 'That will be the best way to show him I'm not interested.' Neither Kate nor Murray looks convinced, but neither of them makes any further comment. When John arrives, he goes to sit with them as usual, but the only available space is next to Kate. John looks distressed but doesn't comment and when he says hello, Esme is careful to look away.

Instead of the usual cheerful chat, the four of them sit in near silence. Kate asks John how the preparations for the West Indian Carnival are coming on and he says fine. After that, the silence between them resumes while all four of them concentrate on listening to the music. *Wait in Vain* starts to play, and Ess can feel John's eyes on her as she resolutely fiddles with her bag then stares at the dance floor. Eventually, Kate and Murray get up to dance, and she and John are left sitting at the table with a large space between them.

'What's wrong, Esme?' John asks as he moves closer and she sees that his face is full of misery.

'There's nothing wrong. I just don't want to talk to you. Go back to your wife and leave me alone.'

'Can we have a dance?'

'Didn't you hear me?'

'Please, Esme. Just a dance.'

She turns away and starts to roll a cigarette. John tries to move closer, but she slides further along the seat and won't look at him. Suddenly she is aware of Jackson standing in front of their table.

'Leave her alone, man,' Jackson says to John. 'You're not the one.' He laughs and turns to Esme, lifts his hat and bows. 'Come on, girl.' She doesn't reply but gets up and follows him onto the floor. The dance is quickly over and Jackson escorts her back to the table. John is staring at her.

'Esme,' he says urgently after Jackson has gone. 'That man is bad. You need to keep clear of him.'

'I'll do as I please,' she replies and turns away.

'Oh, Esme,' he says as he gets to his feet and prepares to leave. 'I used to think you were the sweetest thing.'

Kate and Murray return after a couple of dances and ask where John is. Ess tells them he's gone so they look hopeful and the atmosphere lightens a little. She looks around in search of Jackson and sees him dancing with someone else. For the rest of the evening, she sits by herself. Nobody asks her to dance and the evening drags on. If she had any sense, she'd go home. Instead, she keeps looking for Jackson, hoping he'll come back and ask for another dance, but he doesn't. After dancing with a couple of women Esme hasn't seen before, he seems to have disappeared.

It's nearly closing time and as Ess comes out of the Ladies, she sees Jackson standing with another man chatting and laughing. He beckons her over and she walks towards him.

'Would you like to come for a cup of tea with me on Thursday?'

'What time?' Esme hears herself ask.

'Three o'clock,' he says. '15 Thompson Street.' Esme feels herself blush as she turns away. 'Don't be late, girl!' he calls after her as she walks away. She half turns. He looks at her and laughs before resuming his conversation with the man who is standing next to him.

'You've been a long time,' Kate says when Esme finally makes it back to the table. 'Have you seen John again?'

'No,' she replies. 'I think he's gone.'

'Well, let's hope he's gone home to Barbara,' Murray says. 'Maybe you did the right thing, after all, refusing to dance with him. But did you see his face? I felt sorry for the poor bugger.' Esme says nothing and heaves a sigh. Why did she go and talk to Jackson? How can she have been so stupid? One bad decision after another. There's no way she is going to his house on Thursday. Or any other day. She shivers.

By the time she gets home, it's gone midnight. Dani's gone to bed, but Steve is still up. He looks at her as she walks in, and she knows immediately that something awful has happened. There's trouble.

12

What a day! First bad, then good, then awful. Don't know what I'm going to do. At the start of the day, things weren't good, but now they're much worse. On a different level, as Steve would say. And I'm supposed to be going to Summer Lane for three weeks on Monday. How can I get out of that? Only tomorrow to sort things out. Mum is driving us down on Monday and Mandy's looking forward to going with me. We've made plans about what we were going to do. Like planning to stir the place up a bit. What a mess.

It's the middle of the night and the sounds from Mum and Steve's bedroom have finally stopped. I decide to risk switching on the light. Can think better with the light on and I want to make a plan in my private exercise book. It takes a long time and my writing looks weird, but nobody will see it. It's my secret place to practise writing. Used to do some nearly every night but not anymore. I've given up because it doesn't help. Practising makes it worse.

Can't figure out why everybody else can write so much faster than I can. Maybe I am stupid. That's what Mrs Richards thinks. And probably everybody else, too. Maybe even Jaffa, who likes me so much that he follows me around. Maybe even he thinks I'm thick. But I don't think so. And I'm not. I am not.

For a minute, I'm almost grateful to Jaffa just for liking me. But then I remember that he's my age. Clever and sexy but only my age. If I wanted to bother with boys. Which I don't. I'd choose somebody older. A boy like Vee Jay next door perhaps. But that's stupid. Forget about them. Forget about everybody. I'm on my own and there's nobody who can help me. Not Mandy. Not Steve. Not Howard. Not anybody. I'll have to sort out this trouble by myself.

It's funny. I get real pains in my hand and wrist when I try to write. Nobody believes me because it doesn't happen to them, but it's true. I've tried everything. I found out that it's easier to write with a thick pencil than with the biro that I have to use for school, but even the pencil only helps slightly. I borrowed the 3B from Esme's drawing set months ago. She didn't notice because she doesn't draw much these days. Too busy dancing, I think, and I clamp my teeth together in frustration.

I stare at my exercise book. *Daniela Hoffman 8B* and underneath, *General Science*. I'm going to try and make a plan to look after my mother. Most of the book is empty because I can't write. Or at least I can't write fast. While everybody else writes a page, I manage a couple of words. Or one. It's so hard to control my hand that I forget what it is I'm trying to say. That's the biggest problem. My brain goes faster than my hand. When I have to stop thinking to concentrate on the actual writing I can't remember what I was going to say. My thoughts and my hand are not in sync. But everyone else manages. There must be something wrong with me. I need to write, especially now. I've got to write this plan. Concentrate. I must concentrate.

It's not very warm because I'm sitting up in bed but I try to get more comfortable ready to add a new section entitled *Mother,* but it's dwindled to *Mum.* It takes quite a long time to write the heading even though by now it's only one short word. Three letters. After that, I stop to think, rule three columns and manage to write *date, loc(ation)* and *com(ments)*. I need to keep track of my mother. I'm planning to follow her.

I'm getting tired and cold and wonder if there's any way I can get myself a tape recorder. That would be a lot easier than writing notes. Maybe I could ask for one for Christmas. But recorders are expensive and Christmas is a long way off. Everything keeps changing. First Mandy had permission to come to Summer Lane, then she didn't, then she did. Now there's the problem with Mum. It started earlier, but it's got worse. When I got home for lunch, Steve was bad-tempered because my mother had gone to Kate's. We ate without her and Steve looked miserable.

'What's she gone to Kate's for?' I asked

'Something to do with helping somebody they go dancing with.'

'Helping them with what?'

'Not sure. Some sort of problem.'

Steve had sounded cross and worried. He could have told me then what he knew, but he didn't. Why can't Mum stay at home with us? We knew she'd be out tonight and then she went out all afternoon as well. Mum's too old to go dancing and if she did want to go, she should have gone with Steve. I clench my teeth again, but it doesn't help.

My Saturday nights with Steve are usually a pleasure. Sometimes we watch tv, but for the last few weeks, we've played chess. He's taught me how to play and I'm getting steadily addicted. Steve says that I'm improving fast. Anyhow, tonight we had just finished the first game when there was a knock at the door. Steve opened it, and there standing on the doorstep was a large, black guy.

'Hello,' the man said to Steve. 'I'm John Hall. It's about your wife. Can I come in?'

It turns out that John is one of the people Mum goes dancing with. He seemed all right. Agitated but still polite. Steve invited him to come in and went to put the kettle on. Then he told me to say goodnight and go up to my room. See what I mean? They treat me like a child. No point in arguing so I went. They spend their lives getting rid of me and *protecting* me. Even Steve.

Of course, there was no way I was going to miss this. I'm an excellent listener and do it whenever possible. Always have. From somewhere in the back of my mind, I remember a time when I could listen easily without even hearing what was said. Just had to focus to pick up what somebody was thinking, but as I said before, I can't do it so well now. I have to listen with my ears.

'What's the matter?' I heard Steve ask and then, 'I'm sorry, but Esme isn't in.'

'I know she isn't,' John replied (He's got a deep voice with a West Indian accent. It might be Jamaican. I think Jaffa's family are originally from Jamaica, but Jaff was born here. Jaff sounds pure Leeds and that's what I'm working towards. At the moment, my accent has got traces of south Derbyshire in it according to Mandy, but I can't hear it.) 'Esme is down at the Palace. That's why I've come.' I strained my ears. 'Your woman's not behaving herself and there's trouble coming.' By this time, I could hardly hear. John's voice was getting quieter, hardly more than a whisper and I was forced to come down to the first-floor landing.

'What do you mean she's not behaving herself?' Steve asked, but I couldn't hear the reply. I didn't dare go any lower, but then I heard Steve say, 'We were both sorry to hear that you'd left your wife. Esme was hoping to persuade you to change your mind.'

'Esme wouldn't have anything to do with me tonight,' John said. 'She wouldn't speak to me at all, but that's not why I've come.'

'What is it then?'

'I told you. She's heading for trouble. Sure as I'm sitting here, but she won't listen so I had to come and warn you.' There was a long pause and I listened as hard as I could. 'She playing with fire, man.'

'What do you mean exactly?'

'She's messing about with a man called Jackson. He's bad. Treats women bad. Everybody knows about Jackson, but she won't listen.' There was a pause and somehow I managed not to cough. 'That's why I've come. So you can keep her safe.' John's voice rose as he delivered this message and then there was more, but the voices dropped low. I tried holding my breath because the sound of my breathing was too loud, but it didn't work. I was about to give up and go back to my room when I heard John speak again. This time he was speaking much louder. I could hear that he was leaving and almost shouting as he went.

'I don't like to tell you this, man, but your woman, she sleeps around.' There was a slight pause and I could imagine Steve's face. 'It's the truth, man,' John said, and his voice was loud and clear, 'but I'm sure you already know that.' It went quiet. I thought he'd finished, but he must still have been standing just outside the door. John's voice came again, rising higher.

'She needs to steer clear of Jackson. If she messes about with that man, she'll come to a bad end.' And then louder still. 'Keep her in, man. Keep her in the house.'

I could hardly breathe. My mother does *not* sleep around. How dare he say such a thing! I nearly rushed down to tell him. To shout as loud as he had. Louder. But I didn't. I wasn't properly dressed and it would have made things worse. He might have shouted back. I crept up to my room and tried to stop my heart from thumping. I knew it couldn't be true. Yes, my mother does like to go out dancing, but that's not sleeping around. I know she wouldn't. She's respectable.

There is a boy in our class whose mother does sleep around and the girls whisper about it. They say that his mother would do it with anybody and they roll about laughing. But after that, it gets more serious and they whisper that his mother is a working girl. That means a prostitute. I can hardly believe that John has said that *my mother* sleeps around. I shiver. John must know that Mum is as good as married. Steve is Mum's husband. The same as. Everybody knows that. We've been a family for years.

The only explanation I can think of is that John is jealous. Perhaps John wants to sleep with my mother. I get a funny feeling facing this thought. Can't imagine my mother with anybody, but I have to admit that John sounded as though he believed what he was saying. I don't understand how this can have happened, but it does seem as though Mum is in danger from this man called Jackson. I can believe that part because Mum never listens when people try to warn her about anything. Always thinks she knows best. And she never thinks anything is dangerous. She's not even scared of the Ripper. At least not for herself although she's afraid for me and warns me endlessly to be careful. Seems to think she's always safe and I'm not. Think she lives in some sort of magic bubble.

After John went, I expected Steve to call me down, but he didn't so after what felt like ages, I got up and went down.

'Thought you'd gone to sleep,' Steve said. 'What have you been doing?'

'Nothing much. Reading.'

'What are you reading now? Is it still *Anne Frank's Diary*?

I ignored that and asked, 'What did John want?'

'It was some private stuff. I'm afraid I can't tell you about it.'

'Will you tell Mum?'

'Oh, yes,' Steve said and I watched him clench and unclench his fist even while he was smiling at me.

'All right. I'll go to bed now.' I watched Steve's face for signs of surprise. If I'd said that on any other evening as early as this, he would have thought I was joking, but he said nothing. He was hardly aware I was there except that he wanted me gone.

'OK, Dani,' he said. 'Good night.'

I knew Steve wouldn't tell me anything so my next task had to be waiting until Mum came home and then listening again. At least I could get into bed properly and get warm again, but it took hours. Not to get warm, I mean but for her to come back. She didn't arrive until nearly midnight. My eyes kept on closing as I tried to stay awake reading.

I finished reading *Anne Frank's Diary* ages ago. (Steve obviously doesn't listen when I talk to him. I told him about it weeks ago.) It was a marvellous book, but I'm reading *Lord of the Flies* now. Our English teacher read bits of it aloud in class. I can't quite believe that kids would behave like that, but perhaps it's possible. I preferred Anne

Frank's Diary especially because it's set in the second world war when the Germans were the enemy. My father was a German and I'm half German, too. I used to ask my mother about Hitler, but she couldn't answer my questions. Sometimes I can't bear to be German.

After an age, I finally heard something. There was a noise downstairs. I sat up and listened. I thought it was the front door. Yes, it was Mum. Back at last. I got out of bed and crept down to the landing below. It is supposed to be summer but it felt cold. I should have put my dressing gown on. I shivered as I listened to the voices from downstairs. Was that Steve? I'd never heard him sound so angry.

'What's the matter?' That was my mother speaking.

'Sit down.'

'I'm tired, Steve. I'm going to bed.'

'No, you're going to sit down.' It was an order, but Steve never sounds like that. I shivered again.

'All right. Tell me what's happened.' I heard Mum say. 'You look awful.'

'But you don't!' he said. 'What's happened to you, Esme? You've wrecked a family, treated John with contempt, gone off with someone else...' There was a pause, 'and you look as though you haven't got a care in the world.' Steve was almost shouting.

'What do you mean I treated John with contempt?'

'He said you wouldn't talk to him tonight. He came round.'

'Came here?'

There was no sound for what seemed like ages, and I wondered what was happening. Suddenly the stairs door opened, and I had to turn as fast as I could to get back upstairs.

'Is that you, Dani?'

'Yes,' I shouted down. 'Just been to the toilet.'

'Night night, love.'

'Night night.' Phew, that was a close call. I got myself back upstairs and realised there was no sound of the loo flushing because I hadn't been to the bathroom. Nobody noticed. I heard them coming up the stairs and going into their bedroom. They were talking again but not loudly. Suddenly I heard my mother shouting at Steve.

'Oh, Christ! How could you think that! Don't you think I feel awful about John? And then you accuse me of dancing with a bad man. Dancing with somebody isn't the same as going off with them. And who says he's bad? It's John. Of course, that's what he says. John doesn't want me to dance with anybody else. But I wanted to show him that I didn't care about him. That I wasn't interested. I wanted to make him go back to Barbara.'

'He says you're a slut. That you sleep around.'

'John said that? And you believed him?'

'I don't know what to believe.'

Now it is quiet again. There are no more sounds from below. I have the light on with my exercise book in front of me. My heart is still pounding, but I am making a plan.

13

Mum won't change her mind. I've told her I'm not going to Summer Lane, but she won't listen. Says she already sent a letter to Grandma and posted it on Saturday. Posted two in fact. The first one said that Mandy couldn't come and the second one said she could.

'Grandma is expecting us,' she tells me. 'And Mandy is looking forward to it. Of course, we're going. What's wrong with you?'

'Why didn't you just ring?' I ask her. 'You could ring now and say that we're not coming. I don't want to go. I've decided to stay at home in Leeds.'

'The phone's not working. That's why I wrote the letters. Somebody's coming round to fix it, but even if it were, I wouldn't ring to tell Grandma that we're not coming on the very day that she's expecting us. She'll have got things ready. I don't know what's wrong with you, Dani.'

'Well, you'll have to go without me. I'm not going. I've got to stay here.'

'What have you got to stay here for?'

'Things to do.'

'What things?'

'Private stuff.'

Mum looks at me as though I've gone mad. Whatever I say, she doesn't believe me. She's determined that we're going.

'You want to get rid of me, don't you? I know you do.'

'Don't be ridiculous,' she says and goes into the kitchen to check that everything's switched off. 'Go and get your things from upstairs. Mandy will be here in a minute and you won't be ready.'

'It's the bike,' I tell her in a flash of inspiration. 'If I don't get on with it during the holidays, it won't be finished before Christmas.'

'You didn't mention it earlier,' she says. 'I don't believe you. Now go and get ready.'

I've got no choice. I'll have to find a way for us to come back with her when she returns to Leeds. Once I've had a chance to speak to Mandy, it will be all right. If it weren't for Mandy, I would just refuse to get into the car, but it was me who asked her to go down with us. What a disaster.

After all the revelations and shouting on Saturday night, I was surprised to get up yesterday and see Mum looking normal, or at least, normal for nowadays. She was distracted. She seems to be in a kind of a dream most of the time. Often doesn't hear me when I speak to her. I know she wants me to stay in Summer Lane so she can have time alone in Leeds. What is she going to do? Why doesn't she want me around? Every so often she says she loves me, but not wanting me around doesn't fit with loving me so I feel scared. She's left me with Grandma so many times before and I do love Grandma, but my place is in Leeds. Even Mum says that my home is in Leeds so what's going on? Steve doesn't want to get rid of me. Or at least most of the time he doesn't. It's only Mum.

I'm hastily packing a few things when I hear Mandy arrive. Mum sends her up to get me so we go down together, get in the car and set off. Mandy chatters on for a bit. She's the only one who's cheerful, but she gradually realises that there's something wrong and goes quiet. She keeps giving me questioning looks. We'll talk when we're on our own, but that won't be until we get to Summer Lane.

I wonder what Mum has said to Grandma about how long Mandy and I are staying. Does Grandma know that we're staying for three weeks? Knowing Esme, she probably hasn't sorted out any arrangements. She might even have said four weeks earlier on and not changed it. I hope Grandma won't be upset when she finds out that I *won't* be staying not even for three weeks. In fact, I'll be going back straight away and I won't be able to explain why.

When we arrive and get our stuff out of the car, I can hear the piano. Grandma's always playing. Mum listens and says it's Mendelssohn's *Songs without Words*, but the music stops almost immediately. Before we reach the back door, Grandma has come outside to greet us.

'Grandma,' I go to hug her and then turn to introduce my friend. 'This is Mandy.'

'Hello, Mrs Gardiner. Thanks for inviting me.'

'You're very welcome,' Grandma smiles at her, then turns to me. 'You are going to sleep in the front room. Do you want to take the bags in and get sorted out? Grandpa's set up a camp bed so one of you can sleep on that and the other one can sleep on the sofa bed. Esme will sleep upstairs as usual.'

We go into the front room and I start explaining to Mandy what's wrong. I tell her that I want to go back to Leeds. Mandy is usually supportive so that's what I expect, but this time she is annoyed. Reminds me that we've only just got here. The problem is that I can't explain. It's impossible to tell her without betraying my mother so things are not looking good.

Back in the living room, I wonder why Mum's brought so much stuff with her. She's got that enormous rucksack she takes when we go on holiday and a bin bag. Looks as though she's brought enough stuff so that I can stay for a year.

'Hello,' Mum says after dropping the bags on the floor and giving Grandma a hug. 'We've arrived.' She smiles at all of us and collapses on to the sofa. She looks tired and Grandma goes to get her a cup of tea.

'It's a long drive,' Grandma says and although Esme would usually disagree and say it's not far, this time she doesn't say anything. Just thanks Grandma for the tea and settles down to drink it, while I pick the bags up and take them upstairs.

'Thanks, Dani,' she says and sounds as though she means it.

It isn't until after tea that I get the chance to take Mandy off so we can talk about things again. This is not going to be easy. Grandma already seems worried about Esme. I can tell by the way she looks at her. Grandma is not going to understand me wanting to go straight back to Leeds, especially as I can't explain why. But it can't be helped. I've got to go.

Mum says she's planning to go back on Wednesday, so we've got just one day to spend with Grandma and get things sorted out. I tell Mandy again that I've got to go back, but I can't tell her why. She's not happy about it but says she'll support me. I heave a sigh of relief. By the time we get back to the house, we're hungry again so we eat a second tea and I see Grandpa looking pleased. He always looks happy when I eat. It's easy to please Grandpa. Just like when I was little.

Next morning, I get up before seven so that I can tell Grandma what I want to do.

'You're up early,' Grandma says. 'Is Mandy still asleep? And are you ready for some breakfast?'

'Yes, and yes,' I reply. I refuse the porridge that Grandma offers and remember that porridge was all I wanted to eat when I was here the last time. Instead, I help myself to cornflakes.

'You've changed,' Grandma says and smiles at me nodding towards the cornflakes.

'Yes,' I say and then, 'Grandma,' but don't quite know how to carry on.

'Yes?'

'Will you help me get back to Leeds?'

'You've only just got here,' Grandma says in surprise. 'And what about Mandy?'

'Well, she'll have to come with me, I suppose.'

'Why do you want to go back? I thought you were staying for a few weeks.'

'I know,' I say, 'and I'd like to stay, but there's something very important I've got to do in Leeds. And I can't tell Mum about it.'

'Then tell me,' Grandma encourages.

'No, Grandma, I'm sorry. I can't. You'll just have to believe me that it's important. I know it will spoil Mandy's holiday, but I can't help it. I haven't got a choice. I've got to go.'

'Well, I'll try and talk to your mum but if you can't tell me why, then I'm pretty sure that your mum won't agree.'

'That's what I thought,' I say. I can see that Grandma realises I'm worried even though she doesn't know why.

'But I've got to go, Grandma. Please help me.' At that moment Mandy appears in the doorway and I go quiet. It's then that Grandma realises that even Mandy doesn't know why I want to go back.

Grandma can't persuade my mother. Esme says that she won't take us back with her. Grandma says that she ought to because there isn't any point in keeping me here if I'm anxious to be gone. Mum disagrees and says that she isn't going to upset Mandy without good reason. Until I explain myself, I'm not going back to Leeds. Mum is beginning to sound angry. It's clear that she doesn't want me in Leeds and Grandma can see that, too.

All I want to do is to look after her but Esme doesn't want me around. I don't suppose she would thank me for trying to look after her. She'd think I was interfering but that can't be helped. I'm going to do it. I've got to because I'm worried about her. I go into the front room to try and think of what to do next and Mandy follows me. Poor Mandy. I tell her again that I'm desperate to get back and this time she offers to help me.

'How can you help?' I ask her. 'I just don't know what to do.'

'I'll say that I'm homesick and I want to go home.' I look at her in amazement. That would be brilliant.

'Are you sure?'

'Of course,' she says and puts her arm around my shoulder. I try not to cry and I manage it. I've been practising how to get tough lately, but sometimes it's hard. It's when people are kind that it's hardest.

We arrange how we're going to do it. It will be better if I stay in the front room while Mandy goes by herself to tell Grandma that she wants to go back to Leeds.

'I'm sorry, Mrs Gardiner,' I hear her say, 'I do like it here, but I'm feeling homesick and I'd like to go home.' Although Mandy is speaking to Grandma, it's my mother who replies.

'I don't believe you, Mandy. It's Dani who's made you come to say this. And it's not fair. You can go back and tell her that it hasn't worked. I'm not taking either of you back with me.'

Mandy comes back into the front room on the verge of tears. Then I hear Grandma telling Mum that she shouldn't speak sharply to Mandy and Esme starts talking again.

'Mandy's perfectly all right. I'm not going to be manipulated by two teenage girls.'

I go back into the living room to try and talk to Mum but she's upset now and says she's going upstairs to have a rest and read. It's a miserable day. By the time Grandpa comes in for his tea, the household has split up and disappeared into separate rooms. Nobody is coming out to eat. There's only Grandma and Grandpa at the table for tea and even they don't look happy. Grandma explains what has happened and I hear Grandpa trying to cheer her up.

'Dunna fret, Frankie. They'll sort themselves out. It'll blow over.'

I feel both miserable and guilty, but it's Esme's fault that nobody is happy.

14

Esme is still in bed. It's Wednesday already, the day she's due to drive back to Leeds. She knows that she has upset her mother, but it was necessary. Dani should not have forced her friend to say that she was homesick. Esme will not let herself be manipulated. They wanted to come so now they're here, they can stay. Admittedly, Dani did change her mind before they left and said that she didn't want to come. But it wouldn't have been fair to Mandy or Grandma. At the same time, Esme tries to ignore the voice in her head that whispers insistently that she's the one who wants her daughter to stay in Summer Lane.

Grandma is now in the unenviable position of having to look after two girls who don't want to be there. Esme hopes they'll settle down once she's gone but privately, she doubts it. Dani can be terribly stubborn. Usually, she loves coming down to stay with Grandma. It's baffling. As though there were not enough to worry about. John's behaviour is unbelievable. That he went to their house and told Steve that she was sleeping around. She shivers in the warm bed. Looks at her watch. She ought to get up but instead turns over and pulls the covers more tightly around her shoulders. It feels comforting lying in her childhood bed.

Steve thinks that John came round with the best of intentions. Trust Steve. He usually believes the best about people. Except about her, it seems. With her, he seems to believe the opposite these days. What she can't work out is whether or not Steve believes John's accusation that she has been sleeping around. During all their years together, this is the first time that she's been unfaithful so it feels unfair of him to trust her so little.

On the other hand, she did invite John to go to bed with her. Did it without hesitation. She's been feeling restless for a long time. Knew it would happen sooner or later with somebody. And she was prepared. She was on the pill anyway. Had no intention of risking pregnancy with Steve or with anyone else. She has always been careful not to get pregnant even though Steve would have liked her to have his child. A brother or sister for Dani, he suggested but didn't insist. Steve lived in hope that she'd change her mind but Esme always knew that she wouldn't.

In a moment of shame, she remembers that John, too, had said that he would like her to have a child. He had meant it, but it was a throwaway remark spoken in the bedroom. Esme has to protect herself. The men are not the ones who bear the children and carry the responsibility for a lifetime. They might disagree, but she knows better.

Esme is sorry for John and for all the trouble her actions have caused but still, she can't bring herself to feel properly guilty. He was willing and he had enjoyed it *and* she had told him the truth before they had sex. Just half an hour of fun with a friend. The problem was that he hadn't believed her. She, too, had thought she would enjoy it, but she hadn't. She had thought it would be fun, but it wasn't. The memory makes her feel ashamed. She didn't foresee the consequences, didn't even think about them. Home life has been awful since then. Steve is angry and that's just from the mere suspicion of her infidelity. She hardly dares to think about what would happen if he found out. What a relief it was to leave on Monday and drive down to Summer Lane, but now it's time to go back.

She ought to get up. The curtains are open like she always has them when she comes home. The place of childhood. Lying propped up on the pillows, she stares at the sky as she has done a thousand times before. It's cloudy. Her thoughts turn to Jackson. Is he dangerous? Kate thinks so. Says he's a bad man. Ess considers whether or not to go to his house. Keeps changing her mind. She knows it's stupid, but she wants to go and doesn't understand why.

There's something about Jackson that simultaneously draws and repels her. Nobody would call him handsome. He is short and squat, powerful like a boxer. His face is ugly and frequently creased into a mocking smile. Or he can look hard, ruthless. There is a power in the man. You can feel his presence. She is curious, but it's more than that. Danger is not something that excites her. She doesn't like to be anywhere near fights, doesn't like fast cars or roller coaster rides, but she moves towards him despite herself. When he beckons, she responds and at the same time despises herself for it.

Time to get up and spend a couple of hours with her mother before she sets off back up the motorway. Esme wonders if the girls are up and if so, what they are doing this morning. Hopefully, the frantic pleas from last night won't be repeated but when Esme finally appears downstairs, the girls are waiting for her.

"We want to go back with you,' Dani informs her.

'I'm sorry, Mrs Hoffman, but I'd like to go home,' Mandy echoes. Esme's spirits sink and she looks around for her mother.

'Where's Grandma?' she asks Dani.

'Don't know. Up the garden, I think.'

'I'm going to have a chat with Grandma,' she tells them. 'Back in a minute.'

'We won't let you go without us,' says Dani. 'We'll lie in front of the car.'

'Don't be silly,' Ess replies as she goes through the porch and opens the door to the back garden.

Her mother is weeding the rockery while her father is further up, cutting the hedge. It's a big job because it's mainly hawthorn and stretches the whole length of the property. There's a bit of privet near the bottom end and that's easy, but the hawthorn is heavy going. Good for the birds to nest in, but hard to cut.

'Aren't you helping Dad with the hedge?'

'He's not ready for me yet. I'd be in the way.' Her mother stands up and winces slightly as she straightens her back. 'How are the girls this morning?'

'That's what I want to talk to you about.' Ess pauses to light the cigarette that's lying in the tin ready-rolled (despite her mother's constant anti-smoking pleas). 'They're trying to make me take them back to Leeds. Do you think they'll calm down once I've gone?' Ess looks at her mother who puts the trowel down.

'I don't know. I don't think so. You know how obstinate Dani can be when she's set her mind on something.'

'What we need to find out is why she wants to go back to Leeds. Have you any idea what's behind it?'

'No, she wouldn't tell me. What about asking her again? You could say that if she tells you why she wants to go back, then you'll consider it, but otherwise, you won't.'

'I suppose I could do. But what about Mandy? She's the most difficult one even if it isn't true that she's homesick. I can hardly tell her mother that she wanted to come home, but I insisted that she stay here.' Frances nods and waits for her daughter to continue. Esme bends down and grasps the bright yellow head of a dandelion, but it slips between her fingers and the top comes off leaving the root and most of the leaves stuck between the rockery stones. 'I think I'll try your suggestion,' she says as she drops the squashed flower head and sets off back to the house.

Half an hour later, she is back. Success, or at least partial success. Under duress, Dani had agreed to say why she wanted to go back, but the explanation turned out to be that she wanted to build her bike. Esme doesn't believe that for a minute but had to pretend that she did. Dani was offered a solution. If Grandpa would agree to make one of his sheds available, Ess would drive to Leeds and bring the bike back so Dani could work on it in Summer Lane. Mandy thought this was a brilliant solution, so Dani had been left with no choice but to agree.

Grandpa does agree, so Esme says she'll go and fetch the bike and bring it back on Friday. But she still won't let them go back to Leeds with her. Stalemate. Esme hasn't won, but Dani can no longer complain. The only good thing is that Mandy seems happy with the arrangement, so Ess no longer has to worry about what to say to Marsha if she sees her. Proof, she realises, that Mandy did pretend homesickness. And secondly, evidence that Mandy, like the rest of them, has no idea of the reason for Dani's desperation to get back.

In this way, Esme succeeds in leaving without the girls, but she knows that Dani is not happy and it bothers her all the way up the motorway. Her daughter's unhappiness will spread. It will affect Mandy as well as Grandma and Grandpa. Ess knows that the bike is not the problem but doesn't know what is. Anyhow, there's nothing further to be done until she comes back on Friday when she'll be able to talk to her daughter again. Ess wonders if Steve knows what the problem is. Since John's visit, he has been silent and withdrawn so it won't be easy to talk to him.

Finally, she allows her thoughts to return to Jackson. It would be stupid to go to his house. Esme knows exactly how a man like that would interpret her visit if she did go. But despite the constant repeating to herself of all the reasons to stay clear, she knows that good sense might not prevail.

15

On Thursday afternoon, Esme sets off to walk into Chapeltown. The address Jackson has given her is quite a way from where she lives. Nearly two miles according to the map, but the walk will do her good. A relief to be able to escape the heavy atmosphere in the house. Steve is barely speaking to her. He went out last night soon after she got back, saying that he was going to see someone.

'Who's that?' she'd asked.

'None of your business.'

Steve hardly ever goes out, so she wondered where he was going. Hopefully not to meet John. All evening, she was restless, drank too much coffee, ate biscuits, paced around the house. No Dani to keep an eye on so she and Steve could have gone out together, but he'd gone out by himself. There was nothing much on tv, and in any case, she couldn't settle. It was nearly midnight by the time he came back and then he went straight to bed. Ess followed him, but he turned his back on her. She reached out to touch him. He pushed her away and said that he needed to sleep. After that, she lay sleepless turning over one thing after another in her mind. Dani. Steve. John. Jackson.

It's Thursday at last. It feels as though this is the day she has been waiting for. Esme hardly notices where she's going. It's a bright, breezy day. Sunny with an unexpectedly cold wind. Eventually, she reaches the top entrance of Potternewton Park and goes in. The leaves of the copper beeches rustle in the wind. Glisten in the sunlight. Esme walks down the wide path across the top of the park until she reaches the rose garden where she decides to stop and have a smoke. The air smells fresh. Surprising what a difference being inside the park makes. The air here is completely different from the fume-laden air along the road. Even a smoker can smell the difference.

She reaches into her bag, takes out the tobacco tin and rolls a cigarette. Looks at the green Golden Virginia tin with the pattern that she's scraped onto it. Did it with a coin. Sounds of kids shouting in the playground next to the garden make her think of Dani although her daughter is too big these days for swings and climbing frames. On the brink of adulthood. Childhood gone. She wonders what the two girls are doing and why she doesn't want Dani here with her. The holidays ought to be the perfect opportunity for them to spend time together. That's why she became a teacher in the first place, because of the holidays.

Time to get up and carry on. The grass falls away to her right sweeping down and then rising again to the far side of the park next to Harehills Avenue. In the distance below, she can see a man with five large dogs, none of them on leads. German shepherds and a couple of bull terriers running together. They look dangerous. Best avoid that area and keep to the left. Luckily that's where she's heading anyway, but better sit down and roll another cigarette first. Just to be sure that the dogs are out of the way before she gets down to the bottom. The man lifts his arm and throws a ball high and far. The whole pack race after it, jumping up at each other as they go. Ess inhales, drawing the smoke deep into her lungs. The man and his dogs are moving further away. Why not finish the cigarette and go home? Esme straightens up, puts away her tin and sets off back the way she's come, but when she reaches the park gate, she turns abruptly and walks back in the direction of Jackson's.

The house looks ordinary enough. It's an end-terrace with some steps and an iron railing leading up to the front door. There's a basement, but only part of it is below ground. Some steps lead down to a door and she can hear a dog barking. A young woman walks past and stares at her. She has a child in a pushchair.

'You lost?' she asks. 'Looking for somebody?'

'I'm looking for Mr Jackson,' Esme replies.

'Jackson, you say,' she pulls a face. 'Well, good luck girl. You've come to the right place, Up them steps.'

'Thanks,' replies Esme and starts slowly to climb the steps. The place looks clean and tidy. She reaches the top step and hesitates. The girl with the pushchair is still standing and staring at her. Esme knocks. No reply. She knocks again, louder this time and waits. Still no reply. Ess heaves a sigh of relief and is turning to go when she hears sounds from inside. Someone is coming to the door.

'Well, hello.' Jackson stands in the doorway with a mocking smile. 'I knew you'd come.' Once more Esme half turns to go, but he opens the door wider and stands back. 'Come in, girl. Nice to see you.' Esme steps inside and follows him hesitantly through a narrow hallway into a room that seems to be a combination of kitchen and living room. It's clean but almost empty. 'Sit down,' he tells her. 'Fancy a cup of tea?'

'Is your wife at home?' Esme asks him, looking around. Jackson looks at her and laughs.

'No wife,' he says, 'I'm a bachelor man. This is my own house. Bought and paid for. Don't share it with nobody.'

He gestures with a sweeping hand around the room. 'Come and see.' He leaves the kettle that he was about to fill with water and walks over to a door on the opposite side of the room. 'Come and have a look.' Esme leaves the table where she was standing and follows him across the room. He leads the way down a set of stone steps which obviously lead to the cellar. The dog that she'd heard from outside starts barking again.

'I keep the dog down here,' he announces unnecessarily, opening a door and showing her a skinny, black dog tied up next to a bowl of water and a dirty old bone. You can see its ribs. The dog barks and rushes forward pulling at the chain. 'He won't hurt you,' he tells her. 'He's chained up.'

'Poor dog,' she says.

'Poor? He's not poor,' Jackson replies. 'He gets good food, plenty of walks. Look at his coat. He shines. That dog he shines with health. What do you mean he's poor?'

'Being chained up down here,' Ess replies. 'He's miserable.'

'Ah, girl. You don't know what you talking about. Come and see the upstairs now. I want to show you the bedroom.' Jackson laughs.

This, at least, should have been the signal for Esme to leave, but she doesn't. She follows him back up the stairs, through the living room with the kitchen area and into the hall.

'Come on, girl,' he says and leads her up the stairs. The steps are carpeted and look clean, but there's a damp, musty smell. Jackson opens the door of the room on the left at the top of the stairs and shows her a large room dominated by a huge double bed. Not much furniture, just the bed and a large wardrobe. In the window area, there's a dressing table with three cloudy mirrors and in front of it, a chair. Jackson ignores the chair and sits down on the bed. Pats the space next to him.

'Come and sit down, girl,' he invites. 'You're not scared, are you?'

'Of course not,' Esme replies going to sit down beside him on the bed.

'Now, lay yourself down and feel how nice and soft it is.' Jackson's creased face twinkles at her. His face looks oily, seems to shine. Ess gets up and goes to sit on the chair.

'So it's true,' she says. 'What everybody says about you.'

Jackson looks at her and laughs. 'What's that?' he asks. What do people say?

'That I should keep clear of you. That you're a bad man.'

'Me bad? Well, I don't know about that. What are you doing here if you think I'm bad?' He's right. What is she doing there? Esme pulls herself together as though coming out of a trance and stands up. She picks up her bag and walks hurriedly out of the bedroom back down the stairs. Jackson follows her, chuckling to himself.

'What are you laughing about?' she asks.

'Laughing at you, girl,' he says. 'Laughing at you. I reckon you're scared of Jackson, afraid of the big, bad wolf.'

'Of course not,' Esme replies. 'I don't think you're bad and I'm not scared, but I have to go.'

'What no time even for a quick cup of tea?' he asks as he boils the kettle and pours water onto the tea bags waiting in the cups, then, without asking, adds sugar and milk to each one. She sits down again and rolls herself a cigarette. Offers him one, but he shakes his head and takes a flashy-looking gold cigarette case out of his inside pocket. Draws out two long cigarettes, lights them both and hands her one. She takes it. It's hard drinking the tea because of the sugar and the milk. She sees him watch her struggle not to pull a face.

'Tea not suit you, girl?' he asks and Ess explains that she doesn't usually drink it with sugar and milk. 'Black tea?' he asks, laughing again. 'What's that about then? Who drinks tea like that? Milk and sugar are good for you. You drink it down, girl. Might sweeten you up a bit. Can't do no harm.'

Esme struggles with the drink, then puts it down half-full, gets up and walks to the door.

'Same time next week,' he shouts after her as she walks down the steps to the road below. 'Don't forget, girl.'

She half turns and sees him standing there, laughing.

16

I stand outside Grandma's house and watch my mother drive away. If I had been younger, I would have wept, but recently I had made a vow. I was going to be tough and I've learned how to do it. You act. When you don't feel it, then you pretend and the acting becomes real. I needed to do it when Mrs Richards was shouting at me and it was hard to do, but it worked.

It is essential to keep my mother out of danger. Paramount is the word that Steve would use, the word he tried to teach me while we were playing chess recently, but I already knew it. It's annoying when somebody tries to teach you things that you already know. My thoughts are going all over the place, but what I keep coming back to is the knowledge that I have to keep my mother safe. I can't explain the problem to Grandma or Grandpa, or even to Mandy. If I did, I would have to explain my mother's involvement with John and Jackson. That's impossible. Mum is going to come back with my bike so that I can build it here and Mandy thinks the problem is solved. But it isn't and I'm sure Mum knows that. She knows that getting my bike built is not the problem. It's like a battle between us. Always guessing, a lot we don't say.

I feel in my bag for the stone and stroke it, then look for something to kick but all I can see are some small apples that have fallen too early from the tree. I choose the biggest one and kick it up the path. Aim for the trunk of the cherry tree and miss. The tiny apples are not satisfying to kick.

They're too small and irregular, not heavy enough. I take out my special black egg-stone, place it on the ground and kick hard. It flies accurately towards the old fence post which is almost obscured by hedge but still, my stone hits spot on. Shouldn't have done that. I promised myself never to kick or spoil my stone. I walk over. Pick it up, wipe it and put it back in my bag then look up and see Mandy standing at the back door. She's been watching me.

'Has she gone?' Mandy asks.

I nod.

'Cheer up,' Mandy goes on. 'She'll be back on Friday and then I can help you build your bike. I'm willing to give it a go. Maybe you could teach me and we could both build one. My old bike is too small for me now.'

'It's not because of the bike,' I confess. 'The reason I have to get back is so awful that I can't tell anybody what it is. Not even you.'

'Oh, go on,' encourages Mandy. 'I promise I won't tell anybody.'

For a second but no more, I hesitate and realise afresh that I can't. It would be a betrayal of my mother.

'Oh Mandy, I can't. I really can't. But I do have to get back to Leeds. I've got to find a way to get back.' I look at her and hesitate, then ask if she will come with me but don't expect her to agree.

'Course I will,' Mandy replies instantly and surprise and relief wash through me. 'But how are we going to get there? It's a long way, and we've got no money.'

'We'll have to make a plan,' I tell her and realise that I'm big on intentions and short on successes. It's my usual re-action to any problem – make a plan, but so far none of them have worked. Good job Mandy doesn't know that. I go to sit on the roof of the dog kennel (that Snowy the dog, never used) and try to make space for Mandy to sit next to me, but it's too small. 'Let's go and sit on top of the coal house,' I suggest. 'There's more space there and no-one will hear us talking.'

I lead the way and show Mandy how to climb up onto the coal house roof. Grandpa used to tell me off for that. He said I would damage it, but since he's retired, he seems to have forgotten a lot of his worries. It's a good spot because it's easy to keep a lookout. Grandma and Grandpa are both up the garden out of the way. I tell Mandy that I've already been thinking about it. The first thing that we need to do is to find out the best route to Leeds. I know we have to go up the M1, but I don't know how to get from Grandma's to the motorway.

'Can't see how it's going to help,' Mandy says. 'Even if we know the roads, it's too far to walk and we don't have a car.' That makes me laugh. 'What do you mean we haven't got a car?' I say. 'Even if we did have a car, we couldn't drive it.' I stop and think for a minute. 'Actually, I do think I could drive a car. I've watched. But I think we'd get stopped if I drove because I probably look a bit young.'

'You could wear a disguise,' suggests Mandy.

'Yes, I could, but we still haven't got a car.' By this time, we can't stop giggling. We keep imagining ourselves driving back to Leeds with me behind the wheel in disguise.

'You'd be too small,' Mandy says and starts laughing again. 'Your head would only just show above the wheel.'

'Oh no, it wouldn't. I'm tall and I'd take a couple of cushions.' And we collapse again. Can't stop laughing.

'What are you two giggling about?' We hear Grandma's voice from below but hadn't noticed her come over the lawn. 'And you'd better get down from there before Grandpa sees you. You'll have the roof falling in.' She doesn't sound cross though and adds, 'It's nearly tea time.'

We climb down from the coal house and decide to go down to the stile for ten minutes. It's at the beginning of a path leading into the fields. The stile is excellent for practising balancing acts because it's a double stile made of iron poles that you can stand on if you're careful. One foot has to be placed carefully on each pole, a deep breath, then jump and twist, landing so that you face in the opposite direction. It's hard. It used to be easier when I was younger. Of course, we can practise that only one at a time. Balancing together is hard, too, because there isn't much room and you have to hold your nerve to stop yourself from jumping off. Mandy is surprisingly good at it. 'It's like ballet,' she says. While we are on it together, I have a brain-wave.

'We can hitchhike,' I say as I wobble and fall off.

'Hitchhike?' Mandy asks, keeping her balance. 'Wouldn't that be dangerous?' What about men running off with us?'

'It's not dangerous,' I say. 'I've heard Mum and Steve talk about hitchhiking. I don't think any man would be able to run off with us. We're too fierce. I'd make sure they didn't.'

'How would you do that?'

'I'd think of something,' I say vaguely. 'In any case, there is no other way. Can you think of one?'

'No,' Mandy replies. 'I can't, but the Ripper is out there somewhere.'

'He only attacks in Yorkshire,' I tell her, 'and he doesn't pick up hitchhikers.' I climb back up and Mandy makes space for me.

'How do you know? He might.'

'Then you stay here. I'll go by myself.'

'Don't be stupid,' Mandy says as she jumps down and leans over the stile, folding her body over the pole, lifting her knees and starting to swing. 'How will we know which way to go?'

I tell her that we can find out which roads to take. Not a problem. Hitchhiking is sure to work. My mother used to do it and there were never any problems. How long ago was that Mandy wanted to know? Well, I had to admit, it was quite a few years ago. Was it before you were born Mandy asked? Well, yes, I suppose it was. But it will be fine.

I'm sure it will be easy. All we have to do is to find out which roads we need to take to get to the M1. Once we reach the motorway, there will be no problem at all. We decide that in the evening I shall ask Grandma for the atlas. I know there is one somewhere in the house and we can make notes. Then tomorrow, we shall pretend to be going off to the woods, but instead, we'll go to Leeds. Once we get there, we'll phone to let Grandma and Grandpa know we're safe. The perfect plan.

After this, we go in for our tea and I can see that Grandma is relieved that we're cheerful again. I hope that we get to Leeds quickly tomorrow so that Grandma and Grandpa won't be worried. I don't want to upset them but it's the only plan I can think of, and I'm determined to get back.

17

On Thursday morning we are up early and ready to go, but it's pouring with rain. Bugger. We had the atlas out last night and spent all evening writing down the roads we needed to take. Unfortunately, the atlas didn't have the small roads on the maps so we've got a few gaps. Derby, for instance, is just a black dot on the map, so it isn't clear how exactly to get through it. But we've done our best and are clear at least about which direction we need to set off in. I can remember which way Mum drives when we leave Grandma's. It's Derby I'm not sure about, but we can always ask as well as look at the road signs. I realise, too, that we can't start hitching too close to Summer Lane. We plan to walk as far as we can in the direction of Sealy before we start. The rain is bad luck.

'It's pouring,' Mandy announces hopefully. 'Are we still going?'

'Course we are.'

'Can't we wait until tomorrow?'

'Not possible,' I say. 'But you can stay here if you like. I can do it on my own.'

'Don't be stupid.'

The second difficulty is that Grandma doesn't want us to go off to the woods in the rain. She tells us it's silly. We can do things in the house until the rain stops. Grandpa says that the weather forecast is good for the afternoon. Why not wait until then? But then he sets off up the garden. When I point out that Grandpa has gone out in the rain, Grandma reminds me that he has a shed and a greenhouse. There's no shed in the woods. It will be wet and miserable. And Mandy hasn't got any wellingtons. Her shoes will be ruined. There's no answer to all this so we'll have to wait until the weather clears up a bit.

Miraculously, towards midday, the rain stops. The sun comes out. I begin to feel more cheerful and tell Grandma that we'll be going now. Well, surely not before you've had something to eat, Grandma says, so we stay to eat dinner. The pudding is treacle sponge and custard. Grandma makes puddings every day.

At last, we're off. We can't take our bags, of course, but I've assured Mandy that Mum will come and fetch them for us. Or we might even be able to come back down once I've sorted out the important thing that I need to do in Leeds. I hope that I won't be too late getting there to follow Mum and keep her safe, but it should be fine. Not very likely that she'll be in danger before Saturday. That's the day she goes dancing.

We set off up Summer Lane but when we reach the top road, we turn left instead of crossing over and heading down the Pit Lane towards the woods. I hope no-one is noticing as we set off at a brisk pace in the direction of Sealy. Did think of running, but it might look odd. We walk at a normal pace so as not to attract attention. It takes longer than I anticipated to get out of the village, but eventually, we reach the junction where we need to turn off. I had intended for us to walk further before starting to hitch, but it's already late so we walk a few paces from the junction and start straight away. We stand at the side of the road and hold out our arms like we would to stop a bus.

'Is this how you do it?' Mandy asks, 'Should I keep my arm straight out or wave it up and down?'

'Not sure,' I say. 'But maybe it's better just to hold our arms straight out.'

There isn't as much traffic as I'd expected but still a fair few vehicles. A steady stream of cars and the occasional lorry drive past, but nothing stops. We stand at the side of the road alternately holding our arms still and waving them up and down to see if it makes a difference. It doesn't. Nothing stops, and after half an hour, we're still in the same spot.

'Should we go back?' Mandy asks. 'I'm getting tired of standing here, and nobody is stopping.' Me, too. I'm beginning to lose hope and can't quite believe that nobody has stopped to pick us up.

'Let's just try for another ten minutes,' I say. 'If we don't get a lift by then, we'll have to go back and think of another plan.' At that moment, a police car turns onto the road. 'Don't flag the police car, Mandy,' I shout, but it's too late. The car pulls up just in front of us and a policeman gets out. He looks friendly. Smiles at us.

'Now where are you two heading?' he asks.

'We're going to Leeds,' I tell him.

'Well, that's a long way. Why are you going to Leeds?'

'We live there.'

'And what are you doing so far from home?'

'We've been visiting my grandmother.' I peer up at the policeman who is now standing very close to me. He looks pleasant but I know it's how he's trained to behave. His friendliness is fake. The police won't think it's a good idea for us to be hitchhiking. Still, there isn't time to think up a better explanation.

'And what's your grandmother's address?'

I consider lying, but can't think fast enough so I give the correct one. My spirits sink as I hear the next question.

'Are you in trouble?' the policeman asks. I can at least reassure him about that. We're not in any trouble, I explain, we just want to get back to Leeds.

'And is your grandmother happy for you to be hitchhiking?' the policeman asks. I stop to think before answering. I realise this is not going well, but there is nothing I can do except tell the truth because my brain isn't fast enough to think up a convincing lie. I admit that I haven't told my grandparents what we've planned to do. I explain that I intended to phone as soon as we arrived in Leeds to make sure that they knew we were safe.

At this point, the policeman tells us to get into the car. I feel a bit scared but try not to show it. I've never been in a police car before and see that Mandy is looking anxious.

'Are you taking us to the police station?' I find the courage to ask. Have to sound as normal as possible to reassure Mandy.

'No,' the policeman replies. 'I'm taking you back to your Grandma's.'

'Couldn't you just drop us off nearby?' I ask hopefully. 'Grandma will be angry about this.'

'And so she should be,' the policeman says. I glance at Mandy, but she's not looking at me. 'Don't you know how dangerous it is to go hitchhiking?' By this time, any pretence at friendliness is gone. He pauses. 'And how do you think your grandparents would have felt when they found out you were missing? Wouldn't they have worried about you?' I agree that they would but once again I try to explain that we had hoped to be back in Leeds quite soon. Then the phone call would have been made before Grandma and Grandpa realised we were gone.

'And what if you had never arrived in Leeds?' He is angry. Doesn't like my answers and this is turning out to be a very bad day.

When we get back to Summer Lane, the policeman marches us into the house and things get worse. Grandma looks as though she's going to cry and Grandpa is angrier than I've ever seen him. He tells us to apologise to the policeman and then orders us both into the front room. I can hear him talking but can't hear what he's saying. Mandy looks utterly miserable and I know that the whole heap of trouble is my fault. I try to give her a hug, but she pushes me off and gets her book out. Pretends to be reading. Eventually, we hear the policeman leave and drive away but we aren't called out, so we stay where we are, stuck in the front room waiting to hear what's going to happen next.

After what seems like ages, Grandma calls to us to come out. She tells us that Grandpa has rung Leeds and that Steve answered the phone. Mum was out, but as soon as she gets back, they'll drive down. Grandma seems more upset than angry and I can't bear to look at her. Making Grandma upset was the last thing I wanted and I feel sorry for Mandy. Grandma gets tea ready, but neither of us feels like eating and Grandma and Grandpa are not hungry either. We are all waiting for Mum and Steve to arrive.

Mandy and I go back into the front room but can't settle to anything. We just wait but it's gone half-past nine before we hear the car draw up outside. I look through the window and see Mum and Steve getting out of the car. I'm not looking forward to seeing them and wonder what I'm going to say. Maybe the only thing I can do now is to talk to Steve and explain why I'm so desperate to get to Leeds.

As soon as they get into the house, Mum rushes into the front room and shouts at me.

'How could you, Dani? How could you upset Grandma and Grandpa like that?' and then, 'You might have been killed.' and 'Why did you do it?' She holds me tight but I feel more battered than loved. I listen to her in silence. There's nothing I can say. Eventually, I tell her that I'd like to talk to Steve and she gives me that longsuffering how-can-you-be-like-this look. Mum goes out followed by Mandy who turns around and looks at me with sympathy. Thanks, Mandy. I do appreciate you. After that, I sit quite still and wait. Hear the murmur of voices from next door. Can't hear what they're saying but eventually, Steve comes in. It's getting hard not to cry but I'm still doing my best to be tough. When Steve speaks to me gently, I have to turn away to get my feelings under control. Steve isn't cross. He gives me a minute and then speaks.

'What is it, Dani? What is it that's bothering you?'

'Will you promise not to tell Mum?'

'I'm not sure. It depends on what it is. I might have to tell her.' I take a deep breath.

'It was for her,' I say. 'It was for Mum. I have to get back to Leeds to look after Esme.' I look at Steve who looks puzzled, so I tell him. 'I heard John telling you that Mum was heading for trouble.' I stop, but Steve tells me to go on. I lower my voice and carry on, 'I heard John say that Mum was sleeping around.' I look hard at Steve. 'It's not true, is it?' I look at Steve for confirmation. 'It's not true, is it Steve?'

'No,' Steve says after a second's hesitation. 'Of course not.'

'But she goes dancing and John said she was in danger from somebody called Jackson. I want to be in Leeds so I can follow her and hang about outside the Palace. Maybe I could get in. I look quite old now. If I wear make-up, I could pass for eighteen.' Steve looks a bit doubtful but doesn't interrupt. 'And I was going to follow her anywhere she goes.' Once again, I stop and look at him, but he nods at me to carry on. 'I am going to look after her. I won't be able to stop her going, but I can make sure that I am close by.' I feel a rush of relief as I manage to say all this. At last.

'Oh, Dani,' Steve gives me a hug. 'That's very good of you.' And then he laughs.

'What's funny?'

'The thought of you skulking around outside the Palace on a Saturday night, waiting to rescue your mother.' And then he laughs again. 'Or getting dolled up to pass for eighteen.' For the first time this week, I start to relax. Steve's laugh is infectious and I smile back at him.

'It's strange,' he tells me. 'I had a similar idea myself, but I wouldn't have stood outside. I would definitely have gone in so if you were inside, too, and Esme had noticed us, she would have had a shock. I was going to go this Saturday.' He picks up the cup of tea he's brought in with him and starts to drink it. 'But I've got some good news.'

'What's that?'

'Neither of us needs to go and look after her,' Steve grins. 'She's not going anymore.'

'Not going down the Pally? Not going out dancing anymore?'

'That's right,' Steve replies. 'She came back this evening and told me she'd been for a long walk and decided that the dancing wasn't worth the trouble it caused. She's not going anymore.' I can hardly take this in. The problem has been solved. Perhaps Mandy and I can stay in Summer Lane after all. It doesn't seem possible that everything has been resolved so quickly. That I've caused all this trouble for nothing. For Esme to be safe is what I wanted, but it seems too good to be true. Hardly believable.

Steve says he'll have to go and talk to Grandma and Grandpa so that they know everything is all right now. He tells me to stay here in the front room. Says he'll send Mandy in to keep me company and he does. We try to listen but can't hear what they're saying. I never find out exactly what Steve said to Grandma and Grandpa, but it worked. When Steve calls to us about half an hour later, it seems that everything has been sorted out. We can stay and nobody is angry anymore. Except perhaps Grandpa. Nobody is going to tell Mandy's parents what has happened and Mandy is relieved about that. Says it's better that they don't know.

I am relieved. I can relax again. More or less. I tell myself that I don't have to worry about my mother anymore, but a small part of me does still worry. Mum has told me personally that she's not going dancing anymore and has suggested fetching me back in two weeks rather than three. Mum says that she wants to spend some holiday time with me. I'm pleased about this, but I still feel anxious about what she might do when I'm not there. Don't entirely trust that everything is ok now. It's a good thing that I'll be going back in two weeks. Then I shall be able to check for myself what's going on. I start to breathe again. Heart seems to be settling down. Thought it was going to explode earlier.

18

Thank God for Steve. Esme glances at him as she settles into the passenger seat on the way back to Leeds. He'd been leaning out of the door looking for her when she came back from Jackson's the night before and she'd wondered what was wrong. Her first thought was that he knew where she'd been, but no, he hardly asked. His only concern was for Dani. She and Mandy had been picked up by the police apparently as they'd attempted to hitchhike to Leeds. Dani must be desperate Steve said. She wouldn't have done it otherwise.

Ess had rushed inside to change. Pulled on a jumper, grabbed a jacket and they'd set off immediately. All the way down the motorway they'd worried about Dani, united in their concern for her with the bad feelings of the week suddenly behind them. On the way, she told Steve what she'd decided while she'd been walking back from Jacksons. That she wasn't going dancing anymore. It caused too much trouble. It wasn't worth it.

The truth is that if she hadn't gone to Jackson's, she wouldn't have made that decision, but she feels that it's impossible now to go to the club where both John and Jackson are likely to be. The decision is a relief in some ways and a disappointment in others, but it's clear that Steve is pleased. The old Steve, who is cheerful and loving is back by her side and it feels good. She only hopes that they can find out what's bothering Dani and sort it out. She can imagine what her father must have felt like seeing a policeman escorting the two young girls up the path.

There wasn't much traffic but in their impatience to reach Summer Lane, the journey had seemed endless. When they finally got there, everyone looked miserable although her mother was doing her best to get things back to normal, making tea and trying to chat to the girls. But it was Steve who sorted out the problem. Dani had asked to see him alone and the two of them had talked for over half an hour. When Steve came back into the living room, he was smiling and said that it was all sorted.

He had assured Esme's parents that Dani had acted out of good intentions. He wasn't at liberty to divulge exactly what the problem had been but assured everyone that it was now solved and asked if the girls could please stay as originally planned. Esme's father had needed reassurance. George said that he never wanted the police coming to his door like that again and Ess could understand how he felt. Her father believes that he has failed in his responsibility to keep the girls safe. Failed to look after them properly and that his standing in the community, and more importantly in his own eyes, has been damaged. Eventually, he was persuaded. The girls were told that all was well again, but Esme could see that Dani knew that damage had been done.

At last, everything was more or less back to normal. Her father was still tense, but he would be all right. Esme had suggested that the girls should stay for only two weeks, not three. She explained that she had miscalculated the dates and wanted to spend some holiday time with Dani. Saw her daughter's face brighten as she said this. Her mother, too, had looked pleased. And now she and Steve were on their way home again. It's a pity they couldn't have stayed a bit longer, but Steve had to get back for a meeting with his supervisor.

By late morning they are back in Leeds and after a hasty lunch, Steve sets off for his appointment. Esme heads for the bathroom as soon as the door closes behind him. What a relief to soak in the warm water. It's what she always does when she needs comfort. Has a bath. The house is empty and she's alone at last. She needs to feel clean and to think. Her body looks nice in the water. Slim. Belly rounded but not too big. Nipples showing slightly above the surface moving up into the cool steamy air and then back under again into the warmth of the water.

She reaches for the oil and thinks about the visit to Jackson's. He didn't force her into anything. She'd been sure that he would expect her to have sex with him when he took her into the bedroom, but he didn't. Obviously, he is not that bad a man. She'd moved away when he told her to feel how soft the bed was, and he was fine about it. All he did was look at her and laugh.

There was the half-asked question over whether or not he was bad. What a naive and stupid question. Seems on reflection that she was being flirty rather than serious. A wave of embarrassment washes over her as she remembers how she'd asked the question. What she really wanted to know was why he was sent to prison for GBH. What did he do? If she sees him again, she'll ask him directly. Perhaps there were exonerating circumstances. But nobody has mentioned any and he did get sent to jail. If she does see him again, she will ask, but it would be better not to go.

Still, the British justice system is not colour blind. Perhaps he was discriminated against. Perhaps someone had attacked him and Jackson needed to defend himself. Perhaps he had been defending someone else and that's how the GBH accusation had come about. Esme remembers seeing an Asian guy arrested outside the town hall on election night some years ago. All he'd done was place a placard next to a wall and the police had arrested him. Charged him with being in possession of a dangerous weapon. The placard! That was nothing Steve had said. It happened all the time. Depressing. It had ended her childhood trust in the police.

While she was growing up, the policeman and his family had been part of the community, had lived in the police house halfway down Mount Pleasant Rd where the council houses were. Everyone knew the local policeman but things had changed even there. No police house anymore. Her parents hadn't known the man who brought the girls back.

Esme still can't understand why she wants to visit Jackson again. She should stay away from him, but at least he doesn't seem dangerous. He treated her politely. Once again, she thinks about the fact that he didn't try to keep her against her will. Didn't force himself on her. Yes, perhaps she will go again next week. Just one last time and that will be the end of it. But his laughter makes her uneasy. Somewhere in her consciousness is the suspicion that Jackson really is an unpleasant man. If she goes, she will be careful.

When Steve gets home, he says he'll have to work tonight but suggests that they go out somewhere tomorrow. They haven't been out together on a Saturday night for a long time. Since Dani is in Summer Lane, they could have a night out.

'That's a good idea,' she says. 'Where shall we go?'

'Mozart's *Requiem* is on at the Town Hall,' he tells her and grins. 'Not most people's idea of a fun night out, but then you aren't most people.' She smiles. He knows that Mozart is one of her favourites and she loves the Requiem. When she's feeling depressed, she puts it on and turns up the volume. For her, it's a bit like the Pink Floyd and Hendrix records are for him. She needs either classical or jazz, but she plays the jazz when she's alone. Steve doesn't like it much. He doesn't even like Miles. After they've eaten, Steve goes upstairs to work, and she tells him that she's going over to Suzi's.

Suzi, as usual, is in and smiles as she opens the door.

'How are things?' she asks. 'How's Dani? Is she down in Summer Lane?'

Ess says that she is and then tells Suzi about the trouble with the police and having to go down to sort things out.

'And what was the problem?' Suzi asks, but Ess has to admit that she doesn't know. Dani had been willing to talk to Steve but not to her. And although Steve had assured them that Dani meant well, he hadn't given any details. Esme realises that she hasn't given it much thought. It's not Dani who has been on her mind, although she doesn't admit this to Suzi.

'So Steve rode to the rescue?'

'He certainly did,' Ess replies. 'And at last, Dani looked happy, so I'm sure he did get to the bottom of it. I'm going to fetch them back in a couple of weeks so that I can have some time with Dani before the holidays finish.' Ess notes Suzi's smile of approval at this information and feels irritated.

'What about you?' Esme asks. 'What kind of a week have you had?'

'Mixed,' says Suzi. 'Good with Pete, but bad news from the school.' She goes on to tell Esme that the small remedial classes that she runs are going to be axed.

'Why is that?'

'Rosemary Porter's leaving because her husband has to move to London and apparently, there's no money to replace her. Result is that I've got more teaching with the big class and the support classes can't continue.' Suzi draws on her cigarette. 'It's a mad idea. The progress that the kids have made in the last few months will be wiped out within a few weeks.'

'Have you said that?'

'Yes, of course, but it makes no difference.' Esme feels sympathetic. She knows how hard Suzi works and what good results she has with the kids. 'There's nothing I can do about it,' Suzi says. 'But what about you now that Dani's away? I expect you'll be off down the Pally again tomorrow night.'

'No, I won't. I'm going with Steve to a concert at the Town Hall.'

Suzi raises her eyebrows.

'Why the sudden change of direction? What's happened?'

'Nothing's happened. I've just had enough of reggae dancing.' Ess doesn't think Suzi believes her, but they change the subject and talk about Pete for a while. Esme thinks that Pete neglects Suzi, but she won't hear a bad word about him. Seems so clear-sighted in her view of everyone else but when it comes to Pete, she sees only what she wants to see and it's not what Esme sees. Must be true that love makes you blind.

Suzi goes to put some music on. It's *Blue,* the recently acquired Joni Mitchell LP so they stop talking and listen. It's been out for a long time, but Suzi has only just got it. So good. Ess decides that she'll save up and buy it. Maybe Steve might get it for her for Christmas. Suzi opens a bottle of wine and pours two large glasses. '*Oh, I wish I had a river I could skate away on....*'

***

It feels strange to be setting off for the Town Hall instead of the Pally on a Saturday night. Esme wonders if anyone will miss her. Certainly, John will, but will Jackson notice that she's not there? It will be a relief to stay away. Ess drags her thoughts back to Steve who is sitting quietly beside her. Once the concert starts, the music takes over. She'd forgotten how good it was, how cleansing. Like a redemption. Afterwards, they decide to walk home even though it's a long way. The car has been left at home because of the parking.

Just one thing before they set off. Esme catches hold of Steve's arm and drags him with her to go and stand outside the Art Gallery. It's only just around the corner. There she is. Henry Moore's Reclining Woman. Can't be this close and not go and have a look at her.

'Yes, she's good,' he says. 'Smooth.'

'Smooth?'

The night is clear and lit by the full moon. The city looks beautiful. It isn't late, but the streets are almost empty and the streetlights illuminate the buildings with an orange glow. The sky high above them is black, no stars visible, just the bright moon. Like a picture from her old book of nursery rhymes open at the page where the cow jumped over the moon.

By the time they reach Potter Terrace, they are weary, but Esme is happier than she's been for a long time. She feels uplifted and wholesome. Peaceful. But as they enter the house, she becomes aware of Steve's expectations. She is aware of what the logical conclusion is to such a night but knows already that it won't happen. The perfect night, the night of reconciliation, spoilt because she doesn't want Steve to make love to her. And she doesn't know why.

19

Things are back to normal, but Esme is finding it hard to settle down. Suzi suggests going for a walk along the canal. They've been meaning to go there for ages and at last, they're on holiday with some time for themselves. It's too early for blackberries, but there'll be plenty of nettles and Suzi wants them to make tea, beer and soup.

'Soup?' asks Esme.

'Yes, you can use nettles like spinach leaves and mix them with potatoes, onions and cream. The nettle tea is for Pete because it's good for muscle ache. He's always complaining about his back.'

'Isn't that the squash?'

Suzi grins and puts a couple of bin liners, two pairs of scissors and two pairs of rubber gloves in her bag then passes a large plastic container to Esme to put in hers.

'What's this?'

'Sandwiches and cake.'

They spend the whole day walking and picking, stopping to eat then chatting and picking some more. Esme knows that this should be a perfect summer's day but she can't settle, can't relax. Her mind is elsewhere. She wants to talk about her restlessness, about wanting to get away from Steve, to explore her feelings about John and Jackson. But she can't talk about any of these things to Suzi. She pretends to be having a nice time. Ess doesn't want to spoil the day for Suzi and does her best, but she is relieved when it's time to go home. What a shame that she didn't enjoy it.

Esme writes to her mum and encloses a letter for Dani. Better than phoning she thinks. Easier to hide in letters. She needs a distance from her daughter even though she loves her. A letter is less likely than a telephone call to go wrong and she can't risk a misunderstanding. She knows that things in Summer Lane are all right because her mum rang on Saturday and then again on Monday. On Tuesday her mother said that she wouldn't keep phoning unless there was something to report.

At last, there is time to read. Suzi has lent her *The Women's Room* and Ess has already started it. It's a story about an American woman battling against the expectations of how a woman is supposed to behave and what she's expected to do with her life. It reminds Esme of working in a factory near Grantham while still at uni. She had argued that women should get equal pay and had got the sack for being a troublemaker. Even now with the equal pay act in force, women still do not get their fair share. Their jobs are constantly devalued in comparison with those done by men. It makes her angry but at least things are changing for the better. Shouldn't be too long before there are equal numbers of female MPs, judges, barristers and artists of every kind. Dream on, a cynical voice whispers inside her head. She isn't usually cynical. Optimism usually rises up if given the slightest chance.

Esme is lying on the bed with her book, but she can't concentrate. She's dreaming. Through the window, she can see the tops of the houses on the opposite side of the street and above the roofs and the chimney pots, the sky. The clouds are moving slowly and one of them has some dark edges. Rain for sure. As she continues to stare, the cloud changes into a face. Looks like Dani. No, it's just a cloud with funny edges but as she keeps looking, the cloud changes again. Dani's face turns into Jackson's then slowly vanishes, disappearing back into the grey mass of cloud. Jackson. What's he doing staring at her out of the sky? She has decided not to visit him on Thursday. He makes her nervous. She senses that Jackson doesn't recognise normal boundaries. Kate and John are right about him after all.

On Thursday morning Steve announces that his driving job for the day has been cancelled. What about a trip to Scarborough, just the two of them? They haven't been anywhere together for ages. This should be a lovely thing to do because Ess likes the sea and misses it when she hasn't been for a while. But today it's not tempting. She feels irritable. When Dani was younger, she had regularly put her daughter on the back of the motorbike, and they had gone to spend the day in Scarborough. Esme loves walking along the beach in the wind, but today she doesn't feel like it.

'All right,' she says. 'Let's go.'

'You don't sound very enthusiastic.'

'I know. I feel weary today, but I don't know why. I'll feel better when I see the sea.'

They pack a couple of towels and a thermos of coffee and set off. It would have been nice to take a bottle of wine, but one of them has to drive and it's no fun to drink alone. Coffee will have to do. As Leeds disappears behind them, Esme's mood lightens, and she begins to feel the happy anticipation she usually feels when heading for the ocean. She starts to sing, but Steve smiles and switches on the radio.

'Don't you like my singing?'

'Love it,' he replies. 'I love it.' But he's being sarcastic and the happiness that was beginning to rise within her is squashed.

They arrive in Scarborough late morning and go first of all to buy fish and chips to take to the beach. They've brought their bamboo mat which they spread out on the sand and then settle themselves down to enjoy the sun and the sea. It's lucky that it's only moderately windy but they still have trouble keeping the sand off the food. The coffee tastes good. After they've eaten, they take the things back to the car and then set off to walk along by the edge of the waves. Esme takes off her sandals and the waves wash over her feet. Every so often she stops and squidges her toes into the firm wet sand and watches the dark, grainy ribbons rise between each toe. It's summer, she reminds herself but despite the sunshine, the breeze is cool.

They don't talk much as they walk along and she finds herself thinking about Jackson. He'll be waiting for her in that tidy, musty house with the poor dog still chained up in the cellar. Or perhaps he's forgotten about her but she doesn't think so. Maybe she'll be able to drop around in the evening if they get back early enough. Oh no. What a stupid thought. She had decided that she wasn't going to go. She is definitely *not* going to go. How annoying to waste her time by the sea thinking about Jackson.

It's nearly seven o'clock when they get back to Potter Terrace, and by this time Esme is seriously on edge. She's been looking at her watch every few minutes all the way back and Steve finally asked her what was wrong. Was something happening tonight? Was there something on tv she didn't want to miss?

'Nothing,' she said. 'Just tired of sitting in the car and anxious to get home.'

A light tea is all they need after the fish and chips, but Steve is annoyingly slow and relaxed about it. Esme wonders if he'll ever finish eating.

'Let's have another cup of tea, Ess,' he says as he pushes away his plate. 'It was a good day, wasn't it?'

'Lovely,' she says trying to sound relaxed. 'What are you planning to do this evening? Are you going to work?'

'Well, I ought to, but it's been such a nice day. Maybe we should do something special. It's a bit late to go to the pictures, but we could flop in front of the tv. Shall I see if there's a film on?'

'I wouldn't mind, but I wanted to go and see Kate tonight to ask how things are going with John and Barbara. And I need to let her know that I'm not going dancing with them on Saturday. I should have let her know last week, but I didn't, and she won't be in tomorrow night. I'm pretty sure she has a youth centre meeting on Friday nights.' Esme is gabbling, but Steve doesn't notice.

'Well, you could phone her. No need to go round in person, is there?'

'I'd like to go and see her. I don't think Kate will talk about John on the phone, or at least, not more than a yes he's gone back, or a no he hasn't. She'll open up if I sit and talk to her.'

'That's a shame. It would have been nice to finish the day together.'

'Well, I won't be long,' Esme says and starts to put on her jacket and pick up her bag as she's speaking. She hurries out of the house and soon she's practically running along the street on her way to Jackson's. Slow down, she tells herself. Where do you think you're running to? She nearly adds 'girl' at the end of this. Normally she can't stand men who refer to women as girls, but when Jackson uses it, it sounds friendly, intimate even. But no, she forces herself to be honest. Jackson doesn't treat women as equals. Esme rushes on.

It takes nearly three-quarters of an hour to walk there cutting across the waste ground to the road at the bottom and then through the park into Chapeltown. Esme keeps trying to slow herself down. Why is she in such a hurry? It doesn't matter if she misses him this week. Doesn't matter if she never sees him again. It would be better if she never saw him again. What happened to her decision that she wasn't going to go? One thought chases another and she reminds herself that she'll be going to fetch Dani next week. This is the last possible Thursday.

20

By the time Esme reaches Jackson's house, it's beginning to get dark. She notices with relief that there's a light on in the living room. He's in then. It occurs to her that he might have other visitors and that he didn't invite her to go in the evening. At last her steps slow and she starts to hesitate. The realisation that nobody knows where she's gone creeps into her mind. Steve thinks she's gone to Kate's so if she doesn't return, he will go straight round there. Or ring Kate's house. She thinks Kate is ex-directory but can't remember for sure. While she's thinking about this, the door opens and a woman comes out carrying a toddler. Jackson stands behind her holding a pushchair. It's the same woman who spoke to her the week before.

'Esme!' she hears Jackson shout to her, his voice full of welcome. 'Come on in, girl. Come in. Maureen's just leaving.' As Esme watches, she sees Jackson pat Maureen on the bottom as he carries the pushchair down the steps and sets it up on the pavement. Maureen is, without doubt, the girl who spoke to her the week before. She looks old for her age with dyed blonde hair and a face full of heavy makeup. Maureen is wearing a short, lime green skirt. Same one as last week. The child she's carrying is mixed-race. Maureen puts the child in the pushchair then turns to stare.

'Hello,' Esme says. Maureen looks at her but doesn't reply and doesn't smile. She sets off with the child and walks off up the street. 'What's wrong?' Esme turns to Jackson. 'Is she upset?'

'She's fine,' he says. 'Come in, girl. Come on in.' Jackson leads the way back up the steps. 'How are you?' His voice sounds the same, low and gritty with a mocking edge. Ess follows him in, sits down in the living room and starts rolling herself a cigarette. 'No time for that,' he says taking the tin out of her hands and putting it on the table. 'We got business upstairs.' He takes her hand and leads her like last week into the hall and up the stairs. Esme knows she should leave. Why doesn't she just turn around and go?

The place smells the same as last week, faintly musty. In less than a minute, Esme finds herself sitting, as before, on the single chair in the bedroom, while Jackson sits on the bed. Once again, he pats the bed and tells her to come and sit next to him, but she stays where she is.

'Why did you go to prison?' she asks. 'What did you do?' There's no time for polite chat. She shouldn't be here at all. 'I asked you last week, but you didn't answer.'

'What do you think?' he says beginning to sound irritated. The laughter has disappeared. Once again, she wonders what she's doing sitting in a shabby bedroom in Chapeltown with an unpleasant man like Jackson.

'I don't know. I was told you were convicted of grievous bodily harm. I wanted to hear your side of the story.'

'My side of the story?' he echoes looking at her intently. Esme carries on talking almost automatically as though she is delivering a speech she's rehearsed.

'Most of the time, I think you are all right, but my friends keep telling me that you're not.' He is sitting on the bed in his black leather jacket and she knows, really knows now, that he is not all right. Her mind focuses on his jacket, wondering why he's wearing it inside. As she's thinking this, he takes it off. She watches him. He is annoyed. Not relaxed. Not friendly. Esme can feel him getting angrier. 'Were you really convicted of GBH?' she persists.

'Yes,' he replies. 'And proud of it.'

'What happened?'

'I threw a woman out of a window,' he gets up and points to the window behind the dressing table. 'This window.' There's a pause. 'And I didn't open it first.' Then he laughs.

Esme stares at him and hears what he's saying but can't quite take it in. He's telling her that he attacked a woman. Not a man. Says he's proud of what he's done. He pushed a woman through the window in this room. She imagines the body of the woman on the pavement, the broken glass. The woman could have been killed. Esme wonders how badly she was injured but decides not to ask any more questions. Jackson is still talking. He's not sorry. He's laughing again but he sounds harsh. Says that the woman deserved it and he'd do it again.

'Now you come here, girl,' he orders. 'Come and sit with Jackson.' All kinds of feelings sweep through Esme. Her thoughts are in turmoil, but her body is motionless. She needs to leave. Should never have come, but she can't get up. When she still doesn't move, he speaks again. 'I told you to come here.' His voice has hardened. 'You can't play games with me, girl. Not this time. You come here and lie down.'

Esme comes to her senses with a jolt as though waking from hypnosis. No time to lose. She has to get out. She picks up her bag from the floor and tries to make a joke as she turns towards the door.

'Sit down,' he says again. 'You're not going nowhere.' He catches her arm and pushes her hard. 'Nobody plays with

Jackson. No black girl. No white girl. Now you lie down and get yourself ready for me.' Esme tries to smile as her mind works furiously. She's got to escape, but how can she do that? He grabs her wrist and twists it. Like a Chinese burn.

'Stop it,' she says. 'That hurts.' He laughs.

'Hurts, does it?' he says. 'Oh girl, you ain't felt nothing yet. Now get your clothes off or I'll cut them off you. I've got scissors in that drawer.' He gestures towards the dressing table then gets up and goes over to the door and locks it.

'I've got to get home,' Esme says. 'My husband will be expecting me.' Even as she speaks, she knows that the words are ridiculous. Jackson doesn't bother to reply. He pushes her onto the bed.

'Get everything off,' he orders. 'Hurry up. I don't like girls who keep me waiting. I'm going to teach you a little respect.' Esme starts to feel afraid. She needs time to work something out.

'All right,' she says and forces herself to smile at him. 'Let's take it easy.' There must be some way to slow him down so she can get out of the house and away from this man. Esme sees him relax a little, so she keeps on talking, pretending she likes him, pretending she's looking forward to having sex with him. Pretending she's attracted to him and that she's been thinking about him all week. For a second, the awful thought flashes through her mind that the last part is true. It's only now that she can suddenly see.

'I need a cigarette. I left my tobacco tin downstairs.'

'Here you are, girl' he says sounding more relaxed. He takes out one of his cigarettes and lights it, hands it to her. He waits and watches her smoke. Words dry up and she concentrates on the cigarette. Draw in. Breathe out. Pause. Inhale. Hold the smoke. Breathe out. Pause. Thank God it's a long cigarette, she thinks and almost lets out a hysterical giggle.

'What are you laughing about?'

'Oh, just pleased to be here with you,' she says. 'At last,' and concentrates once more on taking one slow draw after another. It's as though her life depends on the length of the cigarette. She looks at it and tries to hold her fingers steady. It's not going to last much longer.

'What's that?' she asks, turning to look at him as a door bangs downstairs.

'Shit,' he says and pulls a face as they hear a noise from the floor below and footsteps like thunder pound up the stairs. The door handle turns and a woman's voice yells.

'Open the door, Jackson. Do you hear me? Open this door!' Esme watches as Jackson gets slowly to his feet and walks past her, reaches the door. He turns again to look at her, heaves a deep sigh and grins. Then he unlocks the door.

Maureen flies into the room heading straight for Esme, fists balled hard as hammers, aiming at her head, hitting hard. No words. Blows. Pain. Jackson laughing. Esme sees stars. Not just in comics then. There's blood. She tries to shield her face. In vain. Punches keep coming. She doesn't fight back. Something stops her and in any case, Maureen is more powerful. Like a wild thing. Full of fury. Esme can't match it.

Finally, the blows stop. Ess crouches on the floor trying to protect her head. She looks up and sees Jackson still smiling. He doesn't speak. She trembles. Stands. Picks up her bag and manages to leave the room and walk down the stairs. Can't stop shaking but is somehow calm. It's over. She almost laughs, but her mouth won't move. Maureen has saved her. Esme picks up her tobacco tin from the table downstairs and at the top of the steps outside, she pauses. A mistake. A heavy push in her back sends her flying down the stone steps and she lands in a heap on the street. On the pavement outside sits the child in the pushchair. The child is looking at her. Esme stumbles as she walks away.

***

She goes to Kate's. Not sure how she gets there, but somehow, she stumbles through the streets. Can hardly see where she's going. The flesh around her eyes swells to the point where both eyes are almost closed. Her teeth are loose.

'My God, Esme,' Kate says as she lets her in. 'What's happened to you?'

'Jackson's woman,' Esme mumbles. She can hardly speak. 'Somebody called Maureen.' Kate takes her into the kitchen and pulls a chair out. Esme collapses on to it. Kate fetches a bowl and some Dettol and dabs gently at Esme's face.

'Here you are, you do it,' Kate says as Esme flinches, 'but you need to clean those cuts.'

'I'm sorry. I'm so sorry, Kate.' It's too painful to cry and she tries without success to stop her body from shaking. She takes the cotton wool and dips it into the bowl with the Dettol. Can just about see the milky liquid. Starts to dab at her face. 'What can I tell Steve?'

'He'll have to see you,' Kate replies. 'You're not going to heal in half an hour. You'll just have to tell him the truth.'

'I can't do that. How can I do that?'

'You'll have to. How else are you going to explain two black eyes and all those cuts and bruises?'

'I can't tell him the truth. He warned me against Jackson after John came round. I'll tell him it happened on the way here. That a woman attacked me and then ran off. I'll say I didn't know her.'

'And is he going to believe that?'

'He'll have to. That's all I can think of.' She listens as Kate goes into the hall to phone Steve. She hears Kate tell him about her being attacked by some woman and says that although Esme looks awful, the damage is minor. Kate asks him to come and pick her up.

Twenty minutes later, Steve arrives and looks shocked at the state of her. He takes her home and sits her on the sofa. Fetches a blanket to stop her shivering. Makes tea. How did it happen he keeps asking? When Esme tells him she didn't recognise the woman, Steve assumes it was John's wife, Barbara so she lets it be and says no more. He sympathises that she doesn't want to report it to the police. Under the circumstances, he agrees that it might be embarrassing to do that. He is unexpectedly sympathetic and Esme tries to swallow her guilt as she accepts his cups of tea and kindness.

'We'll have to think of something to tell Dani,' he says.

'I should be looking more or less normal by the time we go to fetch her,' Ess replies.

'I have to go to Summer Lane tomorrow,' Steve says and explains that Marsha came round to say that Mandy was homesick. Apparently, Mandy had phoned and asked to go home so he'd told Marsha that he would drive down tomorrow to collect her.

'Oh God,' Esme says. 'Are you fetching just Mandy or both of them?'

'I told Dani she could decide whether or not she wanted to come back. She'll tell me tomorrow.'

'Oh, Steve, please tell her not to come. I don't want Dani to see me like this.'

'I'll try,' Steve says. 'When I spoke to her, I got the impression that she wanted to stay down there for another week, so it might be all right.' He looks at Ess. 'But if she's changed her mind, I'll have to bring her back with me.'

'What can I say?'

'Tell her the truth,' Steve says. 'She's not a fool. You'll have to.'

Esme doesn't say any more. It's painful to speak. She goes upstairs and climbs into bed. Thinks she won't sleep but she does and by the time she wakes up next morning, Steve has already left. She gets herself out of bed and wonders how he'll explain her absence in Summer Lane. Runs a bath. Warm water. Comfort. She can hardly bear to think about Jackson or what happened, but she must. Esme has to understand what a fool she's been so that it can never happen again. Lucky that Maureen came back.

Lucky, she thinks and pulls a face as she struggles blindly towards the bathroom with every part of her body in pain. It strikes her that Maureen was always going to have come back. She wanted to see what Jackson was doing, but her timing was lucky. For Esme that is. Maureen will never know that nothing happened. The realisation sinks in that there is no way she could have avoided the beating. She was in Jackson's bedroom and that was reason enough. To have avoided the rape was luck for which she is going to be forever grateful.

Hopefully, Dani won't come back with Steve. Ess needs to hide away, needs to rest. Doesn't want to think about anything or have to pretend to be all right. She closes her eyes and wishes the bath would last forever. Despite herself, the thoughts come. It's like trying to hold the sea back. Jackson is a pimp. He enjoys hurting women. Why didn't anyone tell her? And the other voice whispers back. *They did tell you, Esme. They tried. You wouldn't listen.*

She reaches for the soap and winces. Runs more hot water into the bath. It's so hot that the bathroom is full of steam. The mirror is misted over and the window. One of her teeth is loose, but it hasn't fallen out and there are no broken bones. She has been lucky. That word again. She lifts the soap to her nose and smells the lemon. Nice, but it stings her skin. Touching her head as gently as she can, she begins to wash her hair using baby shampoo. There are many sore places where the hair is matted with dried blood and some small clumps of hair come loose. She needs to get clean. Carefully, she lies back and rests her head on the end of the bath. Looks at the bruises all over her arms and upper body. Remembers the look of delight on Jackson's face. Two women fighting over him. Two white women. What a fool she's been.

The bathwater is cooling again. Slowly she soaps her legs and her arms. She is thankful for the warmth of the water and the scent of the soap. Her mum gave her the soap. Her mother often gives her gifts of soap. Usually, it's Pears. the soap of her childhood. Red translucent soap almost transparent. She gathers herself together. It is time to get out of the bath. With difficulty, she steps out and reaches for the towel. She can hardly see.

21

It's over a week since Mum and Steve left after all the trouble with the police, but the time has dragged. I'd planned all sorts of stuff with Mandy before we came down here. We were going to go to the local town to check out the cafe there. There's only one, but I thought it looked promising. We'd planned to go to Derby as well. There's a bus, but Mandy's turned awkward. She won't go anywhere. Hardly talks to me now.

'Come on, Mand,' I say. We're sitting on the coal house roof again but keeping a good lookout this time. 'I could say that I'm going to teach you how to fish and we could go and check out what's going on. Have some fun.'

'And where would we get the fish from?'

'We don't need any. It's what I did before you came. Always said I was going fishing. Never brought any fish back. Not a problem. Come on, Mand.'

'No.'

'Why not?'

'Don't want to.'

'Why not?'

'Oh, Dani, shut up. I don't like walking or fishing.'

'Well, we wouldn't be fishing. We'd be checking out the cafe.'

'No.'

'Then what do you want to do?'

'Go for a walk by myself. Get some peace.' As she says this, Mandy jumps down onto the lawn and walks off towards the house. No point in going after her when she's in this mood. Never known her so bad-tempered. I stay on the roof and soon afterwards see Mandy come out of the house and set off down the path.

'Shall I come with you?' I shout, but she shakes her head without turning and walks off. I watch her go.

I'm still worried about Esme. I shouldn't be, but I can't help it. It's because she doesn't want me around. It makes me anxious. On top of that, I'm bored. No bike to build. No bike to ride. Mandy won't go with me anywhere. Thinks we would get into trouble again, but we wouldn't. Going to a cafe is not like hitchhiking. And I've finished *Lord of the Flies* so there's nothing to read. Grandma said she'd try and get permission for us to join the library, but it's not worth it. We'll be going back to Leeds next week.

Grandma's up the garden weeding and Grandpa asked us if we wanted to help, but Mandy pulled a face. It's easy to say no. It was rude to pull a face and I know Grandpa noticed. She's been in a bad mood ever since we got brought back by the police. Says it was all my fault and it was, but it's over now. And she did agree to go with me in the first place. I'd better get down before Grandma sees me sitting here on my own and wonders what's happened.

'Dani,' I hear Grandma's voice calling to me, but I can't see her. Bugger. Too late.

'Yes.'

'Where's Mandy?' I can see Grandma now. She's standing on the yard next to the coalhouse door.

'Gone for a walk,' I tell her.

'Is everything all right?'

'Of course,' I say. 'She just wanted to go for a walk to clear her mind.'

'Clear her mind?' echoes Grandma, and I can see her smile. I feel irritated. Grandma means well, but she thinks we're children. Treats me the same as when I was ten or eleven. Doesn't realise that we're nearly grown up. In some societies, we would already be considered adults with adult responsibilities. Decide to say nothing. No point. I jump down.

'Do you want to come and bake some fairy cakes with me?' Grandma asks and my bad temper boils over.

'No, I don't,' I say and rush off into the house into the front room and shut the door behind me. It slams but I didn't mean it to.

It's not long before Mandy comes back, but she's still in a bad mood. We sit in the front room pretending to read and not talking to each other. It's a relief when Grandma calls us for tea. I've been horrible to Grandma when she was trying to be nice, but she doesn't seem cross. While we're eating, the phone rings. It's Steve, but Grandma's face changes while she listens to him.

'All right,' she says. 'That will be fine.'

'Can I speak to him?' I ask and she passes me the phone.

'Hello, Dani,' he says, 'how are things?'

'Fine,' I tell him, 'but what's wrong? You sound as though there's something wrong.'

'No,' he says, 'nothing wrong but can you put Mandy on? It's Mandy I'd like to speak to.' Reluctantly, I hand the phone to Mandy.

We carry on eating our tea, but we're all trying to listen to what Mandy's saying to Steve. She keeps saying 'yes' so that doesn't tell us much and we can't hear what Steve is saying. Eventually, she puts the phone down and comes back to the table.

'You should have said something,' Grandma says to Mandy, speaking gently. 'I would have arranged for Esme to come and fetch you.'

'What do you mean?' I ask. I feel cross. Does Mandy want to go back? And if so, why didn't she tell me first?

'Come on, I'll tell you what's happening,' Mandy says and we leave the table and go into the front room. Mandy tells me that she phoned her mother when she went for a walk this afternoon. Tells me she wants to go home. Doesn't like it here. Her mother went to see Steve and he's arranged to come down tomorrow to fetch her. I can go back as well if I want to. Can't believe it.

'Why didn't you tell me?' I ask. Mandy shrugs. 'And why aren't you talking to me?'

'I don't like being here. You're always trying to get me to do dangerous things.'

'That's rubbish. What kind of dangerous things?' Mandy shrugs and won't answer me, then she starts talking again.

'I don't want to be here with you. You're trouble.' And then she adds, 'Just like your mother.'

'What do you mean 'just like my mother'?'

'You do stupid things and get into trouble.'

'OK, but what's my mother got to do with that?

'She's the same.'

'What do you mean?' I'm getting angry now.

'Well, she runs around Chapeltown and goes off with men.' I almost slap her.

'No, she does not!' I shout. 'Where did you get that from?'

'Jaffa told me.'

I rush out of the room and go to the only place where I can be private. The bathroom. Lock the door. I was going to have stayed in Summer Lane and let Mandy go back by herself tomorrow, but not now. I'm going back to find out what's going on.

It's all spoilt. Mandy doesn't like it here and Grandma looks upset when I tell her that I want to go back with Steve tomorrow. Once again, I can't explain anything. If I do, I'll betray Mum. I've got to go and find out what Jaffa's been saying. I thought he liked me. How dare he say things like that? I'll kill him when I see him, and I will definitely see him. It will be the first thing I do when I get back to Leeds. I won't let him talk about my mother like that.

It's our last night in Summer Lane. Grandpa has been teaching us to shoot and Mandy liked the shooting practice, but we thought he might not give us a lesson tonight. We're going tomorrow and everybody's upset about it although Grandma's trying not to show it. Grandpa's gone quiet.

The shooting lessons started because he found rats under the shed. First thing he did was borrow next door's dog to flush them out and then he tried to shoot the rats as they ran out. He has an old air rifle and he's not a bad shot. Still, it's not easy because the best time to get the rats out is when it's dark and then you can't see them properly.

In the evenings, we watch and learn. Not allowed to have a go when the dog is around in case we miss and shoot the dog by mistake. Watch and learn, Grandpa says. Watch and learn. Then in the mornings, we take it in turns to shoot at a can that he places on top of a post at the bottom of the garden. Not much like shooting rats in the dark I say but Grandpa tells me not to be impatient. Shooting the can is an important first step. Good practice, he says and Mandy is surprisingly good at it.

Mum didn't seem pleased when I told her about the shooting lessons but that was because she was never allowed to have a go herself. She told me that Grandpa had taught both her cousins (boys!) to shoot but would never let her have a go. Esme doesn't approve of guns. There is never a good reason to use a gun, she says, so there is never a good reason for having one. Nobody should make or sell a gun. That's what she thinks so it's not clear why she wanted to learn how to shoot.

'Awkward,' Grandpa says when I tell him. 'Your mother's always been awkward.' He pauses and looks at me. 'Like you,' he says and grins. Like me?

The change in Mandy doesn't make sense. Just over a week ago, Mandy was having such a good time that she didn't want to go back to Leeds at all. Wanted to move to Summer Lane, she said, a comment that had endeared her to Grandpa. He thinks that Summer Lane is the best place in the world, so he's delighted when anybody else thinks the same. I can't work it out. Mandy has changed her mind about being here. And about me. It can't be just about the police picking us up because she was all right after that. Well, more or less, I suppose. Maybe not quite the same as before if I think back carefully.

Since the hitchhiking, she hasn't really wanted to go anywhere with me, but it's got worse. It's as though she hates me. Won't even talk to me and I have no idea why. She's in the front room and I'm sitting in the living room with Grandma. Grandpa's up the garden again and Grandma's knitting.

'I'm sorry I'm going, Grandma.'

'It's all right, my ducky,' she says and smiles at me. 'It will be nice for you to spend some time with your Mum. I expect she's missing you.'

'I'm sorry I've caused so much trouble this time.'

'It's all right,' Grandma says again. 'I'm sure there was a reason. I'm sure you didn't mean to upset us.'

I get up and give Grandma a hug. She smells nice. Lily of the Valley, her old-fashioned scent. She keeps a little bottle of it on the dressing table upstairs. Grandma always smells of lily of the valley just like Mum always smells of lavender. I like smells. Grandpa smells of tobacco, but Steve doesn't smell of anything. Soap sometimes.

I watch Grandma switch on the tv because she wants to watch *Last of the Summer Wine*. I watch it with her because it's our last night together, but I think it's boring. After that, I say goodnight and go to join Mandy in the front room, hoping that something has changed, but it hasn't. She's still hardly speaking.

I've got nothing left to read so I get out my drawing pad and scribble away making shapes and shadows. I use it to practise my writing and it reminds me that I still can't do it. Still can't write. Not properly anyhow. Mandy's reading some old Readers Digests that Uncle Ted brought round, but after a while, she gets into bed and so do I. I hear Grandpa come in and not much later, the sounds of Grandpa and Grandma going upstairs to bed. I ask Mandy if she's ready for the light off and she makes a noise that sounds like yes. I get out of bed and go to the door where the switch is. After I've put off the light, the room is full of the orange glow coming through the curtains from the streetlight in the lane outside. I stand still looking at the room and hear a car driving past on the top road. Sounds lonely in the night time.

'Night night, Mandy.'

'Good night,' she says. I look at the shape of her in the sofa bed lying curled sideways towards the piano side of the room. Mandy. Once my best friend. Mandy, who doesn't like me anymore.

Next morning after breakfast, we pack up our things. We seem to have quite a lot. I suppose you always do have a lot if you travel by car. I'm looking forward to seeing Mum, especially after what Mandy's said about her. I would never say things like that about Marsha. I'm looking forward to showing Mandy that I'm standing by my mum, but I don't get the chance because Steve arrives without her. He's early, and I rush down the path as soon as I hear the car. I look for her, but she's not there.

'Hello, Steve,' I say. 'You're early. Where's Mum?'

'Hello, Dani,' he grins at me. 'Your Mum's at home. She's got a stomach bug. Couldn't get off the loo this morning, so I had to come without her.'

I'm disappointed, but that's stupid. She can't help having a stomach bug. I wonder privately whether the stomach bug is a hangover, but no point in saying that. My mother has an iron constitution. She's never sick.

We go inside and Steve explains again why Esme isn't with him. I can see that Grandma has got the same suspicions as me, but we don't say anything. Steve says he wants to get moving as fast as possible because he's got a meeting with his supervisor at four, but Grandma insists we have something to eat first. She says she'll get us something quick and goes to get us some bread and soup. It's tomato, my favourite and Grandpa comes in to eat with us.

'Are you ready then?' Steve asks Mandy. He says he's going to put her things in the car so they can go when they've had the soup.

'I'm coming, too, Steve,' I tell him and see that he's not pleased.

'Thought you were going to stay and keep Grandma company for another week,' he says.

'I was, but I've changed my mind. I'm coming home with you.'

Steve nods but beckons me to go with him to the car. Talks to me and says that he thinks I ought to stay because Grandma had been looking forward to having me for another week. I tell him that Grandma doesn't mind and ask him if he's been missing me. Of course, he says. And Mum? Has she been missing me? Of course, he says and then I can see him decide to change what he's saying. He tells me that of course, I should go home with him. He'd just been thinking about Grandma, that was all, but I know it's not true. He doesn't want me to go back with him. I don't know why. All I can think of is that Mum doesn't want me around. If that's the reason, I can hardly bear to think about it.

22

'Bye Mandy,' I shout as we drop her off. I nearly add 'see you soon' but bite my lip and remember not to say it. Steve has got out to help Mandy carry her bags to the house and as he comes back to get in, I see Mandy stand on the step and wave to me. A half-hearted wave. Steve invites me to go and sit in the front with him so I walk around and get in. He looks as though he's about to say something but changes his mind and starts the car instead. We're nearly home now. I'm looking forward to getting there, but he drives straight past.

'Where are we going?' I ask.

'Need to get some orange juice,' he replies. Orange juice? Very strange. Wine, possibly. Beer. Crisps. Nuts. All possible. But orange juice seems extremely unlikely. Steve parks the car outside Victoria Wines. Aha, it is wine, after all, but instead of going in, he turns to look at me. Says there's something he wants to tell me before we go home. My stomach contracts.

'What's happened?' I ask. 'Is Mum all right?'

'She's fine,' he says. 'There's nothing to worry about.' I clench my teeth while Steve tells me that it's nothing serious. Mum has had an accident. Well, actually not an accident. She's been beaten up by John's wife. He tells me that Mum looks awful but that she is fine. Her face will be better very soon. He admits that this is why he tried to persuade me not to come back with him and tells me it's why Mum didn't come down to Summer Lane. She doesn't want anyone to see her looking like this, he says, especially me.

I tell him it's fine and thank him for telling me. But it's not fine. I need to get home as fast as possible. I have to see Mum, but Steve gets out of the car and goes into the shop. Comes out with wine, beer, packets of crisps and surprisingly, orange juice. Didn't know they sold it.

When I go into the living room, she's not there.

'Mum,' I call. 'I'm back. Where are you?' There's no answer so I go upstairs to find her. She's in the bedroom. I hardly recognise her.

'Did Steve tell you what happened?' she asks. Her voice is hoarse and her eyes are so swollen I wonder if she can see me.

'Yes,' I say. 'Oh, Mum.' Tears spring into the back of my eyes, but I stop them. I won't cry. I go to give her a hug but when I touch her, she gives a little cry of pain and shrinks back.

'Sorry, Dani,' she says. 'I'll be fine very soon. You mustn't worry. It's just one of those things.' Who is she kidding? What a stupid thing to say, but she's trying to reassure me.

'Tell me what happened?'

'I was going to see Kate and a woman stepped out from one of the ginnels and attacked me. I was lucky that she didn't have a knife.'

'Who was it? Have you reported it to the police?' I realise as soon as I've spoken that she hasn't. That she won't. That she can't. She's embarrassed. My thoughts race along. I'm still waiting for her answer.

'No,' she replies. I don't ask further.

'Are you coming downstairs? Or shall I get a drink for you and bring it up here?' I stand and look. Don't know what to say or do. Want to hug her, but I can't.

'Yes, I'll come down,' Mum says and I watch as she holds on to the bedside cabinet and slowly stands. 'Go on,' she says. 'Go and put the kettle on. I'll follow you down.'

I make the tea and we sit at the table together. Steve and I eat Grandma's shortbread and cheese scones. Mum says she isn't hungry. We've got a feast, but she can't even manage a crisp. Cheese and onion, her favourite. We've brought some of the first early apples from Summer Lane. Esme loves apples, but she shakes her head. Her teeth are loose, she explains. She'll have to wait a while. She'll be all right soon.

Silence settles for a minute then Steve asks about my time in Summer Lane. There's not much to tell. He asks whether things are ok between me and Mandy. Of course, I say. It was just that she'd become homesick. Mum sits quietly while Steve asks me these questions. She doesn't say anything and after a few minutes, goes back upstairs. Says she's tired.

I look at Steve and wonder if he's going to go with her, but he stays downstairs with me and asks if I'd like a game of chess. It seems like a good idea, but I can't concentrate and Steve is having the same problem. We put the chess set away and switch the tv on. There's a James Bond film *From Russia with Love*. We shout up to Esme, but she doesn't want to watch it. She doesn't like James Bond, but we do.

I am glad to be home. Even with Mum in this state. Even with Mandy gone, it's good to be back. It's nice being in my own bedroom again. I take the black egg stone out of my bag and stroke it, look at it, stroke it, look at it. Stroke it again. I couldn't do that when Mandy was there. To begin with, I enjoyed sharing a room with her. We whispered in bed and giggled. Talked half the night, but it was miserable after we'd fallen out. Except that we didn't fall out. I don't know what happened.

I'm angry with Mandy for speaking disrespectfully of Mum. I won't forgive her. She's right about me getting us into trouble, but it wasn't deliberate. I don't care what she says about me, but I do care what she says about Mum. I have to find out if there's any truth in what people are saying. I used to be a hundred per cent certain that my mother would never sleep around, but I'm beginning to have doubts. Whatever the truth is, Mandy should have stood by me and that means standing up for my mother. But she didn't.

Mum looks terrible. Her eyes are almost closed. Her face doesn't look like hers. John's wife must have been convinced that Mum was having an affair to go and attack her like that. Mum did go dancing week after week and John was there, but there's nothing wrong with dancing and Kate and Murray were there, too.

On my first morning back, I wake up early. As soon as I open my eyes and remember where I am, the first thing I think about is not Mum, it's Mandy. She was my first friend in this new school and I don't know why she's turned against me. The holidays are nearly useless without Mandy. There's no-one to hang about with. And then there's Jaffa. The boy who always stuck up for me and trailed after me around the streets. I took him for granted - what he did for me in class, the nice feeling I got when he shouted out to me across the waste ground or if he saw me do a good kick. Now he's telling tales about my mother. I hate him.

I turn over and try to go back to sleep and forget about it all but fail. I'm awake now. What am I going to do? There's the bike. I'll just have to get on with that. But I don't feel like working on the bike. I need to face my fears. I've got to find Jaffa and ask him what he knows, but I'm scared. And next term is getting closer. I still can't write.

Steve has already gone out. I heard the front door bang just after I woke up. When I finally haul myself out of bed, I realise that most of my clothes need washing. Should have put them in the wash at Grandma's. My jeans are getting close to what even I would call disgusting. I get my other pair out of the drawer. These are clean but have no holes or slashes at all, not even any worn patches. They look new but it can't be helped. I go and shout through Mum's door to see if she'd like a cup of tea but she says no thanks. She's going to have a lie-in.

Downstairs, it's cold and there doesn't seem to be much food in the cupboard. No Weetabix. No cornflakes. The fridge is empty. Hardly any milk. I'll have toast. Shit. No marmalade. I'll have to have jam. The toaster's clogged up again. Bread won't stay down. Millions of crumbs underneath. I give up on the toaster and place it carefully back on top of the pile of crumbs. Put four slices of bread under the grill. Make tea.

It's not very warm in here. It's supposed to be summer, but you wouldn't think so. I put the gas fire on and the downstairs area soon heats up and feels cosy. Mum will say that it's a waste of money, but if she stays in bed for long enough, she won't know. My mother puts it on whenever she feels like it. When *she* feels cold, it's a different matter. No mention of heating costs then.

Half-wish I'd stayed in Summer Lane. Must have been stupid to come back here to defend Mum. I'm not even sure anymore if she's worth defending. What I mean is that I'm no longer convinced that she didn't have an affair with John. The more I think about it - John's visit, Mum's dancing, her always going out without Steve, and now the fact that John's wife was so convinced that she decided to attack her - the more likely it seems that Mum might well have been having an affair.

When I think back carefully, I realise that even Steve hasn't been convincing in her defence. I asked him if Mum was sleeping around and he said no. But he hesitated. It's possible that he doesn't know what the truth is. I wonder how I can find out for sure what Mum does when she goes dancing. I suppose I mean what she used to do. She doesn't go anywhere now. What do people do when they have affairs? How do you find out about what someone's been doing? I go to make some more toast and see that even the bread is going to run out soon. I suppose I'll have to clean up, go shopping and look after Esme. Don't feel like it.

In books and films, there are always clues when people have affairs. Cinema tickets. Restaurant receipts. Notes in diaries. It seems unlikely that Mum's been to the cinema with John or even been to meet him in a restaurant, but it might be worth checking. She's in bed now and Steve's out so it's the ideal time. I take my plate and cup into the kitchen and am about to dump it in the sink when I see that the sink is already full of dishes, so I do the unthinkable and wash up. No choice. The kitchen looks disgusting.

There's plenty of hot water. Steve must have left the immersion on, so that's one good thing. A lot easier than boiling the kettle up several times. I take the dirty dishes out of the sink, but there's hardly any space left on the kitchen counter to stack them. I just about manage it and fill the bowl. Lovely bubbles. *Don't play with the water, get on with the washing up* echoes in my head. Grandpa used to say that to me in Summer Lane, and Grandma would smile and tell him it was all right. *Let her play for a bit* Grandma would say and they would leave me alone, while I dawdled over the sink. Spoilt. Everyone said I was spoilt. It was nice being spoilt.

All the time I'm washing up, playing with the bubbles, smelling the washing up liquid, I'm thinking about whether or not I'm going to go through Mum's pockets. Can't go through all of them because her coat is upstairs in the wardrobe. But the jacket she wears most of the time is down here. Draped over the end of the sofa where she tells me not to leave mine. Yes, I will do it. I'll go and have a look.

I start off just feeling to see if there's any paper in there. Pieces of paper that could be cinema tickets or receipts for dinners. I need to do it pocket by pocket. Get everything out and spread it on the table to have a look. I wonder what I'll say if Mum comes down? Could say that the jacket slid off the sofa and everything fell out of the pockets. On to the table? Ha ha. What else could I say? My mind is a blank. Creative thinking at all time zero. I decide to do it straight away without any more planning and I've just taken the stuff out of the first pocket when I hear a shout.

'Dani. Dani, are you down there?' I jump. Almost believe she can see what I'm doing.

'Yes, Mum' I call up the stairs. Heart pounds.

'Are you still making tea? I've changed my mind. Can I have one?'

'Stay where you are,' I tell her. 'I'll bring it up.' Heart slows down again.

'Thanks.'

I put the stuff back in her pocket. Looks like old tissues mainly, but I did see some bits of paper with writing on. I'll have to make the tea first. After I've taken her a cup of tea, I come down and get the stuff out again. This time I succeed in getting it spread out on the table. There's a comb (slightly broken), half a packet of Polo mints (yuck), several grubby tissues (one with what looks like blood smears on it) and three screwed up pieces of paper. I smooth each of these out only to discover that they're shopping lists.

Why does she keep all this stuff? My own pockets are nearly empty because I don't like them bulging. It spoils the shape. The contents of the second pocket are similar. No comb but another half-finished packet of Polos and another screwed up shopping list. Even the shopping lists are similar. Lists of groceries. No phone numbers.

After I've put the gunge back into the correct pockets, I have a look in her jacket to see if there are any more possibilities. I think I might have hit gold when I discover an inside pocket zipped up. Slowly I unzip it so as not to make a noise. I feel inside. Nothing. It's clean. Not even any dusty bits inside and I feel around the smooth silky lining material. Nothing at all. What a waste of a good pocket.

I'm disappointed not to find anything. At first, I was sure that there wouldn't be anything to find and that's what I wanted, but by this time I was hoping to find at least something. The contents of her pockets suggest an exemplary but boring and untidy life. I should feel pleased that there's nothing there and deep down I do. I've been worrying about Mum getting fed up with Steve, so it's a relief to discover a complete absence of secret love letters, telephone numbers or unexpected items of any kind.

I'm just about to go down to the cellar to get on with the bike when I notice Mum's shoulder bag hanging on the chair. It's where she always sits at the table, but usually, she takes it upstairs with her when she goes to bed. I could look through that. After my experience with her pockets, I think that it might not be worth it but change my mind. I might not get another chance and I ought to be thorough. If she's got a diary or any tickets or receipts, that's where they're likely to be.

First of all, I look in the outside flap section but there's nothing in there except for another comb (this time complete). Then I look in the zipped part just inside the bag at the top. There's some money in there. A five-pound note and some coins (and she always says she's got none and asks Steve for money). The main part of the bag is full of stuff - two pens and a pencil, some elastic bands, a packet of Golden Virginia, three packets of red Rizlas, an apple (bruised), a handkerchief (cleanish) and right at the bottom a small bottle of lavender perfume and a little notebook.

My heart starts beating faster. Why is Mum carrying a notebook with her? It could be a diary. Or an appointments book. Hurriedly I shove everything back into the bag and pull out the notebook. Leaf through the pages. It's not a diary. Just page after page of to-do lists. Make dentist appointment, get Suzi birthday card, wash jumper. On and on.

The little book is nearly full of lists. I read every page, but there is nothing about meeting John or going to cafes, restaurants or cinemas. If Mum has been having an affair, there are no clues here. I push the book back into her bag and go down into the cellar. If I want to find out what Mum's been doing, it looks as though I've got no choice. I shall have to ask Jaffa. Find out what he knows. But even after finding nothing in her pockets or her bag, I'm scared of what he'll say.

23

Esme hears the front door open and looks at her watch. Steve is back early.

'Hello,' he shouts. 'Where are you all?'

'Up here. I'm in the bedroom.' Ess hears him banging about in the kitchen and putting things down in the living room. Not long afterwards, she hears his footsteps on the stairs.

'Hello, Ess,' he says as he opens the door and comes to sit on the bed. 'Where's Dani?'

'No idea,' Esme replies. 'Isn't she in the cellar?'

'No, I just checked.'

'Well, she was here earlier. She brought me a cup of tea.'

'When was that?' Steve asks, looking on the bedside table at the half-full cup of cold tea standing in the messy saucer.

'Not sure,' Ess says and yawns. 'I must have fallen asleep.'

'Suppose she must have gone to Mandy's or round to Suzi's. She might have called up and you didn't hear her.'

'It's only just gone four,' Ess says, peering at her watch. I expect she'll be back soon. I think I'll get up. I'm beginning to feel better.'

Steve touches her gently and tells her that she can get up but isn't to do anything. He will do everything until she's better. He has reorganised his jobs for the rest of the week so that he can stay at home. And he wants to spend some time with Dani. Steve says he's missed her.

Despite feeling slightly better, a quick glance in the mirror reminds Esme that she still looks awful. And everything hurts. As soon as she starts to move any part of herself, it hurts. At least Dani is all right. Her daughter is self-sufficient. Always has some project in hand. As a child, she was the same. Now she is older, Dani is even more independent. Self-contained. Secretive even. Often stroppy but tough and able, Daniela is a girl who can look after herself. She looks older than thirteen. If it weren't for the writing, a problem Ess has conveniently shelved since the holidays started, she would never need to have a moment's worry about her.

Ess swings her legs out slowly and sits on the side of the bed. It's a painful process trying to pull the jumper over her head, so she gives up. She won't bother getting dressed. She takes the dressing gown down from the hook on the back of the door. Together with a pair of leggings and some thick hiking socks, the dressing gown will do fine for sitting around downstairs. Steve laughs when he sees her and tells her she could audition for a horror movie.

Ess tries to smile but it hurts. Her attempts make him laugh even more, so she gives up and stretches out on the sofa with her legs over one end. It's not big enough to get properly comfortable, but Steve grabs a cushion to put under the backs of her knees. Once again Esme is touched by his kindness. Can't understand how she could have been so stupid as to put their relationship in jeopardy. He gets her a cup of tea while starting the curry. Ess reaches for her tin to roll a cigarette and sees Steve look back from the kitchen door. He was about to nag but doesn't. He knows she's promised to give up but now is not the time.

Dani turns up just before five, carrying Esme's rucksack.

'Hi Dani,' Steve calls from the kitchen. 'Where have you been?'

'The library.' Dani replies as she takes out two books and goes to the cellar door to put the rucksack away.

'What did you get?' Esme asks. Her voice sounds strange. She can only speak quietly. It comes out as a whisper.

'Books,' Dani replies and walks across the living room and disappears up the stairs.

'What's wrong with her?' Steve asks as he puts his head around the door from the kitchen. Esme shakes her head.

'No idea.'

Later on, Dani comes down to eat but barely speaks. She disappears again as soon as she's finished eating. Esme thinks it's probably just a passing phase, but the days go by and Dani's mood remains the same. She barely speaks and spends hardly any time in their company. Seems to be avoiding both of them.

Esme's black eyes turn lurid colours, purple and yellow, but the swelling soon goes down and she starts looking like herself again. Steve is spending most of his time looking after her instead of working on his research. Since neither of them is going out, they talk more than they have done for ages. Mostly it is about Dani, wondering what has happened to make her so irritable. She won't talk to either of them.

'We'll find out when she's ready,' Steve says and Ess nods. They know it's impossible to make her speak before she's ready.

On Friday, there is going to be a party for new post-grads, held in Steve's department. He wants to go and wants Esme to go with him, so she decides to ask Suzi to come and babysit.

'Please, Steve, will you go and ask her? I'm embarrassed. You can tell her what's happened to me. It will be easier if you tell her.'

'Easier for who?' he asks but agrees to go. He is sure that Dani will have already told Suzi what's happened, but when he comes back, he reports that Dani hasn't been to see Suzi since she came back.

'Not at all?'

'No.'

At dinner time, Ess tells Dani that they'll be going out on Friday night and that Suzi will come to keep her company.

'No need,' Dani replies.

'Yes, there is,' Esme tells her with some of the old sharpness back in her tone. She's not going to let her daughter rule the household, but she's sad that Dani won't talk to her. This was supposed to be their holiday time together.

***

It's ages since they went to a party. This one is being held in the foyer of the Russian Department. Hardly the best place for dancing, she thinks, but there is music playing and plenty of drinks. Red or white wine, mineral water and orange juice, no beer. The usual. The music is a surprisingly heady mix of jazz and the Beatles. Weird really, but Steve says that all the overseas students like the Beatles and everybody knows the old jazz standards. Songs people know are what work best he says. Ess reminds him that he doesn't like jazz, but he says that these don't count. He likes these. The party is being put on for the benefit of new postgrad students who have arrived over the summer. It's to give them a chance to socialise and settle in before term starts.

Before they leave the house, Esme asks Steve if she looks all right. She watches his eyes sweep down her body.

'I mean my face,' she says and grins.

'Interesting,' he replies with a hint of a smile. 'You look interesting, Ess.' Hmmm, she thinks, *interesting,* that's a convenient word that covers just about everything.

The dramatic purple and yellow patches around her eyes have been expertly hidden with a make-up stick discovered in the local chemist. It covers bruises but was available only in a very pale tint or a very dark one, so she was forced to choose the lighter shade. This evening, instead of her usual healthy-looking freckled tan, Esme looks like a ghost. White face with black mascara and eyeliner for contrast. You can't see the black eyes she got from the beating, but the ones she's applied with the makeup look striking.

'Hi Esme,' she hears as soon as they walk in. 'Haven't seen you for ages. You're looking great.' It is Juliana, an old friend of Steve's, who used to drop in regularly when they lived in the Leeds 6 area. Since they've moved to Chapel Allerton, many of the old friends have stopped visiting. Unless you've got a car, it is quite hard to drop in because there is no direct bus route even though the distance is not that far.

'I could say the same,' Ess grins. 'It's good to see you. You must come and visit so you can see that life goes on even in the outer reaches of the city.'

'Chapel Allerton isn't an outer reach,' Steve jumps in. 'More like an inner hot spot. But Esme is right, you should come and see where we are. It's walkable, you know. We walked it tonight.' This is true, but it isn't an easy walk. They plan to get a taxi home later. Esme helps herself to red wine. She is surprised to see plenty of people she knows and is soon engrossed in conversation.

'Hi Ess,' it is Robbie, another old friend, 'what's with all the talking? Come and dance.' Esme doesn't need asking twice. She jumps up and goes with him to join the mass of people who are swaying about in the middle of the room.

'How are things with you?' she asks. 'Have you finished your thesis?'

'Shhh,' he replies and puts his finger to his lips. 'Don't ask.' They dance to one track after another until the music changes to a slow smooch. *Summertime.* Billie Holiday. Esme excuses herself and goes to get another drink. She finds Steve sitting with a couple of guys she hasn't seen before. They are both black, although one of them is almost jet black while the other guy is medium brown.

'Here's Esme,' Steve introduces her as she joins them. 'This is Joseph,' Joseph is the darker one and he smiles at her and does a mock bow. 'And this is Darius.'

'Hello,' Esme says. 'Are you both new?'

'I am,' Darius says. She feels his steady gaze. He speaks slowly, almost lazily, 'I'm very new.'

'But I'm not,' Joseph says. 'Darius is from PNG. Papua New Guinea,' he expands in response to Esme's baffled face. 'I'm from Leeds. One of those rare beings, a local student.'

'They live in Chapeltown,' Steve tells her, 'just down the road from us. Darius is lodging at Joe's house. Since we're neighbours, I've invited them for dinner, but they're away for the next few days.'

'We're back on Friday,' Joe says, 'and we'd love to come, wouldn't we, Darius?' He turns to his friend who nods, so the invitation is set for Sunday. It turns out that Joe is doing a postgraduate teacher training course, special subject maths and Darius is doing an M. Ed, something to do with psycholinguistics.

Esme is about to ask Darius about Papua New Guinea when she hears the familiar tones of Ella singing *I've got you under my skin* and Robbie turns up to claim her for another dance. She glances back and sees Darius watching as she starts to move. Feels herself admired, but by the time the dance has ended, Joe and Darius are gone and Steve has moved on to talk to Juliana.

Around ten o'clock, the party is beginning to break up. Departmental parties never go on late, but Esme is ready to go home. She is beginning to feel pleasantly drunk and somewhat weary. She leans her head on Steve's shoulder as the taxi whisks them home, but what she is thinking about is the man from Papua New Guinea. For some reason, Kate Bush's song *The Man with the Child in his Eyes* comes into her head. Esme hasn't a clue where Papua New Guinea is. She will have to look it up.

24

I manoeuvre the bike through the cellar door and lift it up the steps outside ready for the first test drive. There's been a lot to do since I got back from Summer Lane, but every day I've worked on it while trying not to think about other things. Can't think about Mandy. Can't think about Esme. Should have gone to look for Jaffa but didn't. Don't know how to ask him about Mum. School's getting closer and so are my writing problems. My demons are closing in.

At least the bike is finished. My first home-built bicycle. Painted blue. Mum bought me the paint. Equipped with a basket I found on one of the tips. A whole packet of Brillo pads and at least half a tin of chrome cleaner have been used to remove the rust. I've polished it until my wrist hurts and my fingers ache from being cramped for so long into awkward positions. It shines. Everything shines. It's gorgeous. With a bit of help from Howard, I finally got the gears in place and now it's ready. It looks like a new bike.

Carefully. Very carefully I push it past the motorbike and steer it gently out of the gate. Taking care, I get on and set off up the street. Brilliant. The wheels turn with ease (well fitted, plenty of oil), and pedalling is almost effortless. Everything is super smooth. Gradually, I increase the speed until suddenly the steering changes and the bike begins to wobble. Wobbles worse and stops. Oh, bugger. The front wheel has pushed up into the fork. Bugger. Shite. Bugger. Can't believe it. I'm sure that I tightened everything properly, but I can't have done. As I get off and turn around, I see Mum and Steve standing in the street, watching me. Mum is laughing, but Steve is looking concerned. He starts running towards me.

'Are you all right?'

'Course, I am. Don't know how that could have happened. I'm sure that I'd fixed everything properly and tightened it all.' I can feel my face beginning to burn.

Half an hour later, I bring the bike out of the cellar for the second time. I'm going to try again. Set off slowly. Steve and Mum are standing outside once more, watching me. Oh God, let it be good. Let it be perfect. And it is. It's smooth, so smooth. It's super good. Super smooth. I pick up speed and power off up the road. Round the block and back again. They clap as I come round the corner and up the road, flying past them. I hold my arms out. Look no hands!

I find myself riding to Mandy's. Hesitate for a moment, but I'm feeling good so I go and knock on her door. And again, louder, but there's no reply. Nobody in. Never mind. I get back on the bike and head for Golden Acre Park. It's quite a long way. I used to go there when I was little. That's where Steve and Mum took me when I first learned to ride. The bike feels so smooth. Goes by itself and I hardly have to move my legs. It's like flying.

On the way back, I remember that I didn't tell Mum where I was going. Better not be too long then, although things have been easier at home since she got beaten up. The shock seems to have changed her. Mum's more like her old self again, doesn't nag me so much and she and Steve seem to be getting on better. Like they did before. Seem to be. I don't trust things.

Still don't know whether Mum went off with John. I've been too scared to go and look for Jaffa. In fact, I've avoided him. I've hardly been outside in case he turned up and I didn't know what to say. He was always hanging about in the past, following me about in a friendly way. Always calling out to me. Blondie. Blondie. I liked hearing him.

Just lately, I changed my mind and decided that I did want to talk to him. Started going out in the hope of seeing him, but no luck so far. I miss him now he's not there and this thought surprises me. But most of the time, it's not like that. Most of the time, I stay inside and don't want to see him (or anybody else) because I'm afraid of what I'm going to find out. Keep thinking about Jaffa. Can't make my mind up whether I want to see him or not. I'm pedalling slowly now. Hardly pedalling at all, but the bike is still going quite fast. Not much traffic. I'm floating.

I think that Mum might split up with Steve and I'm worried about that. They laugh together but Mum is restless. She's like a storm cloud waiting to burst. I can feel it. Steve thinks everything is all right again, but it isn't. On the way back, I turn into Meanwood Park. There's nobody around and I go to sit on the swings. I use my foot to push myself back and start to swing. I look at my bike. It is beautiful. I've done a good job.

I've come to the conclusion that Mum must have had an affair with John. I hope she didn't, but I'm beginning to think she did. Mum is looking for someone else, a new partner. This is what I've been thinking while I've been building the bike. I've been tuning into her thoughts and that's what she thinks about a lot of the time. Steve isn't safe. Mum can throw him out because the house belongs to her. Grandma and Grandpa gave her the deposit money and the house is in Mum's name, not Steve's. She could ask him to leave. (I shudder.) What he wants won't matter. What I want won't matter. Only what she wants. Mum says we have the security of the house, me and her. But it's not secure if it doesn't include Steve. I might lose him. He's my Dad. Well, he's not. But he feels as though he is.

I decide to slow down, hit the ground with my foot and it twists, a sudden stop with a nasty jolt. I swing sideways then push again, harder, swing higher. Jump off from high up. Land well. Better go home. Keep thinking about Mum staying at home these days, how she and Steve talk and watch films together like they used to do. They cuddle up on the sofa and laugh, but something's not right.

I'm on the home stretch now and have a funny thought as I'm riding along. It's about my writing. I've been thinking about it less because of the worry about Mum. I almost laugh. The worries have to line up and wait their turn. It's a nice thought, but it's not true. The writing worries have faded during the summer because I didn't have any writing to do. Soon school will start again. *I might get thrown out.* I try not to think about the writing problem, but I can feel the anxiety creeping back. There will be Mrs Richards for another year unless a miracle happens. In our school, the form mistress keeps the same class for two consecutive years.

'I'm back,' I shout as I glide smoothly to a stop outside our house, turn into the path and lift the bike carefully past the Honda. I go down to unlock the cellar door so I can put the bike away.

'How was it?' Mum asks.

'Perfect.'

'You've done well,' she says. 'I'm proud of you, Dani.' It feels good to hear her say that and I know that she means it. I'm good at putting bikes together. If only I could write as well as I can build bicycles.

It's lunchtime and we sit down to eat. Steve asks me again where Mandy is, and I tell him that she's still away in Manchester. Don't know when she's coming back. He says I must be missing her and I nod. We've just finished eating when there's a knock on the door and Mum goes to see who it is.

'Mandy,' Mum says. 'How nice to see you. Dani's been missing you. How was Manchester?'

'At your aunt's,' I shout to her as she comes in.

'Fine,' she says and grins at me as though she's never been away.

When we get down in the cellar, she looks at the bike. Brilliant, she says. Then she stands over it in silence peering at it as though she has to do an inspection. I watch her. Don't know what to say, but suddenly she looks up at me. Says she's sorry. It's all her fault. She can't explain but will I forgive her? Nothing to forgive I say and ask what she's been doing.

After we've done a bit of catching up, she sits down on one of the old dirty chairs and bursts into tears. Her mum is ill. It's cancer. She makes me promise not to tell anybody. Marsha doesn't want anybody to know. Her mum had told her about it on the day Mandy phoned from Summer Lane. If Mandy hadn't phoned her, Marsha would have rung that evening.

'Why didn't you tell me?' I ask her.

'I promised Mum.'

'But I wouldn't have told anybody.'

Mandy stays silent and shrugs. Eventually, she speaks.

'You didn't tell me why you had to get back to Leeds, did you?' She stops speaking. 'You still haven't told me why you had to get back.' It's true. I didn't trust her enough. And I was right because Mandy has said dreadful things about my mother. I remember that the dreadful things might be true, but I realise that it doesn't matter. What mattered was the unkindness. I still want Mandy's friendship and I'm sorry about her mother, but I won't trust her again. Not like I used to do.

'I was worried about Mum,' I say eventually.

'Why?'

I sit down on the broken bus seat that one of Mum's friends gave us. It wobbles. I push the piece of wood back under the side to stop it moving and start to explain. Once I start talking, I find myself telling her some of my worries. I wasn't going to, but some of it pours out. I tell Mandy that I feel angry about what Jaffa said about my mum. Mandy comes and puts her arm around me and now it's me trying not to cry. Have to remember to stay strong. Pretend, I remind myself, act it out. I've said too much. Could cut my tongue out. I ask her what it was exactly that Jaffa said about my mother.

'Nothing much,' Mandy says. 'He was nice. Told me that he'd heard your mum had run into some trouble. Asked me to tell you he was sorry.'

'You didn't tell me that.'

'No.' Mandy runs her hand over the handlebars and starts to stare at the bike again. Won't look at me. 'I was upset about Mum, but before that, I was cross with you. You got us into terrible trouble and didn't say sorry. I wanted to get at you. Then I was jealous. Your mum was all right and my mum wasn't. I was angry. Don't know why I took it out on you. I'm sorry.' Mandy is still staring at the bike, running her hands over the handlebars, like she's polishing them. 'I've missed you.'

'Me, too.'

25

I'm so pleased that Mandy is back that I don't think too carefully about what she's said. I am awash with relief that I've still got a friend, pleased that it was because of her mum that she wanted to leave Summer Lane and not because she didn't like it there. It matters. I'm relieved to get an apology and any kind of explanation. To begin with, I hardly think about Mandy's mum, but then it starts to sink in that she's seriously ill. Unimaginable to think of losing your mother.

But Marsha is not going to die. Mandy was clear about that. It was only at first, they were afraid. Her mother has got breast cancer, but she can be cured. It's the word *cancer* that frightens people because they think it means death. Mandy says her Mum has had lots of appointments at the hospital and the results so far are good. Now she's waiting for an operation.

I don't know why, but news of Mandy's problems makes me feel braver about my own. It's a relief to tell her some of my worries. I won't tell her everything, of course, but just telling some of it has been a relief. She didn't seem shocked to hear the suspicion about my mum, but she didn't say that it couldn't have happened. That's what I wanted her to say. I want everyone to respect my mother, but I have to find out the truth. Mandy is going to help me. She's arranged for me to meet Jaffa in the park to talk about Mum. I'm pleased, although most of the time I try not to think about it. What a confused mess I am.

Only another week left before school starts. I'm trying not to think about that. Steve and Mum have invited some people for dinner on Sunday so that's good. It means they won't be watching me to see how I'm coping with the thought of going back to school. At least nobody at school will notice how bad things are for me. Except for Mrs Richards of course but she's the one who makes my life bad. Mandy never notices. Just accepts that I struggle with my writing. Doesn't seem to think anything of it.

On Friday, Mum is taking me shopping to get a new school uniform and some shoes. I'm the only one in our class who has to wear sensible school shoes. They are dire beyond belief! Mandy has shoes with kitten heels. I've got my Docs, but they're not allowed in school. I'd like kittens or low platforms, but Mum says they'll deform my feet! No help on the shoe front so I'm not thinking about that, but what I'm not thinking about most of all is that in a minute I'm going to meet Jaffa next to the tennis courts. I'm already feeling scared. Part of me doesn't want to know about Mum. At least it's not raining.

He's already there. I can see him sitting on the bench next to the end court where you sit to watch people play, but there's nobody there. Courts are all empty. What a stupid place to sit. Everybody will see us. It's not private at all. His bike is lying on the grass behind the bench half propped up against a bush. I wheel my bike towards him and say hello. Put my bike next to his. Leaning against the next bush. No space on his bush. Hope it doesn't get scratched.

'How are things?' I ask.

'Good,' he says. 'Fine. You?'

'Fine,' I reply and sit down at the other end of the bench.

'I don't bite, you know,' he says, turning towards me with a grin. 'At least not usually.' I move a bit closer but try not to look at him. We both sit in silence looking at the court where nobody is playing.

'Do you play tennis?' I ask him and feel like biting my tongue out when he grins some more.

'No,' he says. 'Do you?'

Eventually, I start to tell him about my bike, and he gets up to have a closer look. Asks if he can have a go, so I say yes. Off he goes while I sit there minding his bike and staring at the empty court. It's sort of hypnotic looking at a space where something should be happening but isn't. Like staring at an empty tv screen. Thought he'd only be gone two minutes. Hope he's coming back. I peer around anxiously, but this thought has hardly finished crossing my mind when he cycles into view.

'Nice bike,' he says. 'Smooth. How long did it take you?'

'A few months,' I reply trying to make it sound like a couple of weeks. 'Do you build bikes?'

'No,' he says. Ride them but don't build them. I'm busy with other things.'

'What sort of things?'

'I draw. Sometimes I paint, but mostly I draw.'

'Oh,' I mutter as I try to think of something to say in response. Can't imagine Jaffa drawing. That's interesting. Mum used to draw a lot and when I was little, we used to go and look at pictures together. Went to the art gallery in town. Still do but she doesn't do any art herself these days. I know Jaffa reads a lot, but I never thought he would paint or draw. I look at him sitting on the bench. He always seems to be moving or talking. Slouching about. 'What kind of things do you draw?'

'Everything,' he replies. 'At the moment I'm drawing people, although I'll draw anything. Like this leaf, for instance,' and he points to a twig on the bush behind us. 'My grandpa says that you've never seen anything until you start to draw it.'

'Why is that?' I ask. So his grandpa draws, too, and they talk about pictures. I'd never thought much about Jaffa's family or what his life was like outside school. 'I've never drawn my bike, but I can still see it,' I tell him.

'Are you sure?' he asks and grins. Jaffa seems to have an almost permanent grin. So sure of himself. And almost always cheerful. Strange. He goes to his bike and opens up a green satchel affair attached to the luggage rack. Comes back with a little sketchbook and a thick pencil. 'Here you are, Dani. Draw a bike. You know about bikes. Draw a bike.'

I start but soon realise I can't possibly draw a bike. I start with the crossbar and the handlebars but when I try to add the wheels, they're somehow the wrong size. And then the gears don't fit in. I can't make the marks properly because my hand is beginning to hurt and I'm not going to tell him about that, but I begin to realise that he might be right about the bike. When I think about it, I'm not totally sure how the parts fit together. Even though I've only just finished building one, I don't know which parts are longer than others. Or at least, I do know which parts belong in the bike, but I can't draw them as part of one thing. It's even worse than trying to write.

'I can't,' I say. 'I can't draw it. It's because I'm not sure how the length and the width of the pieces fit together. No, that's wrong. I do know when I'm building it, but I don't know how they look with one behind the other.' I pause for a minute. 'I can't explain what I mean.'

'I understand perfectly,' he says, looking pleased. He hands the book back to me, open at a fresh page. 'Now try again. This time, look at your bike and then have a go. Try to draw it while you're looking at it.'

That's a bit easier but I still can't do it. Jaffa has no idea of my writing struggles, but the difficulty is not just to do with how my hand moves. I'm beginning to see what his grandpa means. I'm already answering some of the questions that came into my mind when I tried to draw the bike the first time. Questions about how the parts fitted together when I was just trying to remember but didn't have it in front of me. I look at the bike, then try again but scribble it all out and frown at him.

'It's hard, isn't it?' he goes on. 'Don't worry, Dani. Nobody can do it just like that, but do you see what I mean? When you draw something, you actually start to look at it for the first time. If you don't look carefully, you're not able to draw it.'

'Yes, I agree,' I say, 'but what's the point of wasting all that energy. You could take a photograph.'

'Yes, that's what I said to Grandpa, but he said that taking a photograph is not the same as looking. You still won't have seen the bike.' I consider what he's saying and come to the conclusion that he might be right, but I'm still not sure that it's worth the effort of trying to draw something.

'You might be right,' I say, 'Drawing something probably does help you to see the thing more clearly, but I'm still not sure about taking the time to draw a picture. A story or a piece of music would be better.'

'Why is that?' he asks. He's still grinning, and I realise he's thought about these things before.

'Don't know,' I say and think for a minute, but then suddenly I understand why. 'A story's got time in it,' I say triumphantly. 'A story takes time and things develop. That's what makes it interesting. A picture is just one thing fixed in one spot.'

'No,' Jaffa says. 'A story has only got a little bit of time in it, a day, say, or a year, but a picture has got all the time that ever happened before it was painted, all there in the picture.'

It's interesting, but I can't think about this any more. My mind keeps going back to my worries about Mum. I'm just about to say something else about pictures when suddenly, without knowing I'm going to, I jump into the middle of the conversation with the question that's really bothering me.

'What do you know about Mum?'

'Not much,' he says. 'Just what I heard my aunties talking about a couple of weeks ago. John Hall is Mum's cousin. He's nice. You'd like John.' I shrug and wait for Jaffa to carry on, but he doesn't. He starts making patterns on the ground with a stick that he's holding.

'What were they saying?' I ask and feel my heart start to pound.

'Are you sure you want me to tell you?' he drops the stick and looks at me. 'They might be wrong, you know. It's just gossip.'

'Yes, I want to know.'

'Auntie Joycelyn said that she felt sorry for John,' Jaffa pauses and looks at me. 'She said that your mum asked John to go to bed with her, so he thought he had a chance,

but then she wouldn't have anything more to do with him.'
Jaffa looks at me again and I clench my fingers and hold
on. I know there's something more that he's not telling me.
He's not sure whether he should say it.

'What else did she say?'

'That your mum had started running around with Jackson.'

'How does she know?'

'She knows Jackson's woman, Maureen. Maureen's a
working girl. A prostitute, but she's his main woman.'

'And?'

'Maureen says she caught your mum at Jackson's
house. In his bedroom. So she belted her.'

'Thanks, Jaffa,' I manage to say as I get up, grab my bike
and rush off. I hear him calling for me to wait, but I can't.

26

It is the last day of the holidays. School tomorrow and I'm trying to keep my nerves under control. Act, I tell myself. Act. Don't care. Don't care. Don't care. Don't care about anything. I look for my nail varnish. Joe and Darius, two postgrad students have been invited for dinner. Joe is from just down the road and Darius is from Papua New Guinea. Esme has shown me where it is on the map. It's north of Australia, almost on the equator. Mum seems excited about them coming. A bit odd really because they're only a couple of students. People used to come for dinner all the time when we lived in Leeds 6 but hardly anybody comes now because we don't know many people in Leeds 7. Not yet.

As usual, Mandy isn't available today. It's Sunday so she has to go to the Buddhist meeting. I've been avoiding her since I met up with Jaffa because she'll want to know what he said and I don't want to tell her. For some reason, she's started to join in with Marsha, asking if I want to go with them to the meetings, but I don't. When I first asked Mandy what they were like, she said they were boring. You had to sit still for a long time and not speak. Or chant in a strange language which might be Japanese. I think Mandy is changing her mind about Buddhism and that's why she wants me to go. She will be wondering why I haven't been to see her. I said I had to go shopping with Mum, but that excuse covered only one day. I hope she doesn't think I'm upset because of what Jaffa might have said. Anyway, I'll see her tomorrow at school. School. Bugger. Shit.

Just after lunchtime, Howard turns up. It's ages since I've seen him. Not since I finished the bike. He comes down with me to look at it. He's impressed but seems distracted. When I ask him what's wrong, he just says, 'Woman trouble, Dani' and grins.

'What kind of woman trouble? I ask.

'It's nothing,' Howard says. And he won't say any more, but I wish he would tell me what's bothering him. I don't know much about his life. It's probably because he still thinks of me as a child.

I change the subject and ask if he'd like to have a go on the bike and he says yes. Even with Howard's weight, it's fine. He's not fat but he's heavy. Solid might be the right word. He admires how I've put the bike together, says it's a brilliant job. Likes my cleaning and polishing. He says that if a bicycle or a car is dirty, it shows that the owner doesn't care about it. I nod and wonder what he would think of Steve's car (shared with Mum) which is dirty and messy almost all of the time. Most of all, Howard compliments me on how smoothly the bike runs.

'Not to begin with,' I tell him. 'The front wheel fell off.' Howard laughs and says that there is always something you forget. After he's admired the bike, he has a coffee with Mum but leaves straight afterwards. Esme has been busy in the kitchen for most of the day. She is making a curry, and Steve is going to do pancakes for dessert with a choice of jam, honey, lemon, or maple syrup. Mum insisted on the maple syrup, so Steve had to go and get some. Strange. We've never had it before. Don't even know what it tastes like.

Eventually, the food is prepared and all three of us have washed and changed. I've painted my nails with Devil's Blood varnish. The colour is almost black and it shines with hints of dark red. I've changed from Vicious Violet. The Devil's Blood is better. I did my nails with the violet first but changed my mind and took it off again. I do prefer the shiny black. Every time I look at my fingers, I see the shiny black flash and feel my spirits lift. I'm upstairs reading when I hear Mum call up to ask me to come and have some shortbreads while we are waiting for the guests. There is still over an hour before dinner. She looks at my fingers and shakes her head.

'You'll have to get that stuff off before school tomorrow,' she says. I nod. I already know that so why can't she say something nice for a change. Like how good they look.

'Won't shortbreads ruin our appetite?' Steve asks as he reaches for one.

'Not if you only have a couple,' Mum says. We've just sat down at the table to start on the biscuits when the phone rings. I rush to pick it up.

'Hello,' I say, 'Chinese Takeaway.'

'Stop it, Dani,' Esme says and grabs the phone off me. No sense of humour, that's her trouble. Feel deflated. Both Steve and I sit still and try to listen to what Mum is saying. We want to know who she's talking to but can't hear well enough to figure out who it is or what they're saying. 'OK,' she says. 'See you soon.' Esme puts the phone down. 'That was Joe,' she tells us. 'He says Darius can't come tonight and wanted to know if it was ok if he came by himself. I said yes, of course.'

'Bugger,' Steve says. 'And we've made all that food.'

'It won't hurt,' I say. 'It's curry. It will last all week.' I look at Steve. 'Unless we finish it off tomorrow.'

'You're right,' Esme says. 'It won't go to waste.'

There is a knock at the door. Once again, I'm the quickest and open the door to see a tall black guy in the doorway, but this time I know who it is.

'John!' Steve says, getting up and going to the door to greet him. 'Come on in. How are you?'

I watch as John comes in and is given a cup of tea and offered a biscuit. The atmosphere has changed. As soon as John appeared, I could feel Mum go tense and Steve, too, even though he is trying to sound relaxed. I glance at Mum and notice that she's furiously rolling a cigarette.

'You said you were giving up,' I complain.

'I am, Dani,' she says, as she finishes rolling the cigarette and lights it.

'Steve, can't you stop her?' I ask, but Steve looks annoyed and tells me off for being rude to my mother.

I turn to look at John and see him gazing at Esme as if he can't get enough of her. It's a bit weird. Steve's watching him, too, but my mum doesn't look at John in the same way. I can't imagine them together. Oh no, I tell myself, erase that thought just as I do imagine them together. But erasing something from your mind is not possible. Everything that happens, even a thought, is there forever and can't be undone. It's become part of your past. Part of you. I think all this in the couple of seconds before John starts to speak.

'I've come to see how you are, Esme,' he says. 'I heard that Jackson's woman had belted you up. I'm sorry about that.'

197

Here it comes, I think to myself. That's what Jaffa said. It must be true. It wasn't John's wife after all. It was Jackson's woman who belted her, but I can see that Steve had no idea. He still thinks it was John's wife and can't believe what he's hearing. I see the shock on his face and Steve's crooked smile as he tries to pretend that he's fine.

'Well, yes,' my mother is saying. 'It's true that a woman attacked me, but I have no idea who she was.' I see John look around the room at Steve and me and see that he's trying to work out what's going on. John begins to excuse himself. Says he's sorry. Says he hadn't realised that Esme's family didn't know about it. He gets up to go still apologising, but Steve tells him to sit down and drink his tea.

'Why don't you stay for dinner?' Steve invites him suddenly. 'We have a dinner guest who has just dropped out so there's plenty of food.'

'Are you sure?' John asks, looking surprised and pleased. 'If you're sure,' he says as he sees Steve nodding. 'That would be lovely.'

I think Mum is going to explode or collapse or at the very least tell John that he can't stay, but she doesn't do any of those things. She carries on as though everything's fine except she starts to chain smoke and she tops her glass up almost to the brim. Everybody is drinking, but Esme drinks most. I've never seen her drink like this. She seems to have forgotten that I'm here, so I help myself to some wine, too. It doesn't taste good, but I force it down hoping to get drunk myself. It's hard. If only it tasted better.

There is another knock at the door. Joe this time, so now there are five of us. Joe talks to Mum. Steve talks to John and I'm quiet. Every so often they all manage to talk to each other. I listen. Nothing more is said about Esme getting beaten up. Mum spends a long time talking to Joe about some self-help school that his mother runs. It's starting to get boring and I'm thinking more and more about having to start back to school tomorrow. How will I face Jaffa after what he knows about my mother? How many of the other kids know about her? And how long will it be before Mrs Richards drags me in front of the class to start humiliating me again? I still can't manage the writing. Feel like chopping my hand off.

Eventually Mum says it's late and I have to go to bed, so I say goodnight and go upstairs. As I go, I hear everybody starting to leave. Joe goes first and finally John. I think it's all over and that it could have been worse. I half forget that this is the first time that Steve has been told about Mum's involvement with Jackson. I must have believed what Jaffa told me because I wasn't surprised tonight. I must have already absorbed the shock and accepted it. Poor Steve. How will he cope? And what will Mum say?

I can't hear any more sounds from downstairs and feel relieved. Had thought that the sky would fall in at the point when Steve invited John to stay for dinner, but it didn't. Things went on and everyone was polite. I'm just falling asleep when there's a sound of raised voices from the floor below. I listen, but it goes quiet again. Mum and Steve stop shouting at each other but when I come back the next evening after a visit to the tip, I find that Steve has gone.

27

Esme is back at work. The first day after the long holiday is usually not too bad, but it's the morning after the dinner party. She is struggling to cope with a hangover and not enough sleep. It's hard. The day seems never-ending. After the guests had gone last night, Steve had been grim. Silent. He had said nothing about John's revelation and had fallen asleep soon after he got into bed. Esme had lain awake for hours despite all the alcohol she'd drunk.

In the morning, Steve was gone before she got up. Ess had tried to be cheerful for Dani's sake, but it didn't work. Dani looked worse than Steve had done the night before. Hunched, stressed and miserable. Getting ready to cope with Mrs Richards, no doubt. Ess couldn't think of anything she could do to help.

Somehow she makes it through the day and drives home. She's on the bike today because Steve needed the car. What a relief to get home, she thinks, until she walks in and sees the sink full of last night's dinner plates. Still, at least there is some curry left and some pancake batter. She won't have to cook. What is she going to say to Steve? And what about Dani? Would it be better not to say anything? Esme sighs. That's not an option. She will have to talk to both of them soon.

After dinner, Dani goes off to the tip to look for some more bits for bicycle number two. She didn't look cheerful when she came home from school but said she was fine. Back to the usual, Esme thinks. The best thing to do is to brazen it out with Steve and stick to her original story. That's her plan but when they finally talk, things turn out differently. During the meal, Steve hardly speaks. He goes up to his room straight afterwards, but after Dani goes out, he comes down again.

'We need to talk,' he says.

'All right,' Esme replies and sits down to roll a cigarette.

'I thought you were giving up.'

'I am,' she snaps back.

'Yes, it's like everything else, you say,' he mutters, 'Unreliable. Meaningless...' Steve gets up and comes to sit opposite her at the table. 'It's about time you told me the truth. What did happen the night you were attacked? Seems like I'm the only one in Leeds who doesn't know. How do you think that makes me feel?' Esme looks at him and feels strangely detached. She ought to feel guilty. Afraid. Sorry. Instead, she feels an overwhelming urge to be honest. To get it over with and have everything out in the open.

'Well, the truth is..,' she starts, then pauses and lights her cigarette. 'The truth is that I went to see Jackson, and while I was there, his woman arrived at the house. She beat me up while Jackson watched. Then she pushed me out into the street and I went to Kate's.' Esme stops speaking and raises her eyes. Steve looks stunned. She can see that he had hoped for the lie. Had hoped that she'd stick to her original story. 'You don't understand me,' she goes on. 'I need to be free. I lied because I felt hemmed in. I know you don't mean to make me feel like that. But I do.' Steve gets up and walks across the room to the door leading to the stairs but when he gets there, he turns back and looks at her.

'I think you're mad, Esme,' he says. 'Stupid and mad. You told me that your parents always blamed your bad behaviour on your genes, on the fact that you were adopted. You expected me to sympathise and I did. But I've changed my mind. I'm beginning to think it's true. There must be madness in your family. No sane person would behave as you do.' Steve turns and goes upstairs. Shortly afterwards, he comes down carrying an overnight bag, picks up the car keys and puts on his jacket. Esme watches. Sits and watches. Doesn't move. Feels like a robot. He looks at her but doesn't speak, then goes out and closes the door quietly behind him.

When Dani arrives back empty-handed, about half an hour later, Steve has gone. As soon as Dani comes in, Esme says she's going over to see Suzi. Doesn't ask Dani about the bike bits. Had meant to ask her about school but she can't manage anymore. Esme picks up her bag and goes out. She's shaking.

'Are you all right, Mum?'

'I'm fine.'

'Where's Steve?'

'Gone to see a friend,' Ess replies as she walks out of the house. 'I'll be back soon.'

She walks down the street in a daze. Suzi is the only person she can talk to but when she gets there, Pete is at home. Suzi makes a cup of coffee, but Esme can't talk in front of Pete. She drinks it and goes home again.

'Told you I'd be back soon,' she says to Dani as she walks in. Her daughter looks up and is about to switch off the tv, but Esme can't cope. 'Sorry, Dani,' she says. 'I've got a hangover.' She tries to smile but almost trips in her haste to take off her jacket and go upstairs. 'I'm going to have an early night.' She's still shaking. Can't seem to stop. All evening Esme waits and knows that Dani will be waiting, too, to hear the key in the door, but Steve doesn't come back.

It's not until the following evening that Ess hears from him. He rings to tell her he's got a long-distance driving job going to Berlin and that he'll be back Saturday evening. He asks to speak to Dani and after that, rings off. The rest of the week passes in a blur with Esme's thoughts all over the place. One minute she regrets what she's said and can't wait for Steve to come back, then she changes her mind and thinks that she'd like to be properly free. Whatever *free* means. Not living with anyone, she supposes. Except for Dani, of course. Not being responsible for anyone or to anyone. Except for Dani.

By the time it gets to Thursday, Esme is settling into regret and has decided that she does want to make it up with Steve. She has talked to Suzi who has told her she is risking everything. Doesn't she know what a good man Steve is? Can't she see the gold that's in front of her eyes? Suzi tells her that she, Esme, is the one who will end up getting hurt. Has she thought it through? Esme realises that she's been trying to 'think it through' for months and has got nowhere. Something within her is driving her and no amount of good sense or logic seems to make any difference. And what about Dani, Suzanna asks? How will her daughter feel? Dani will be fine, Esme assures her. So long as her daughter has the continuity of life with her mother, she will be fine. Dani will be able to continue seeing Steve anyway. It won't be a problem.

'But seeing him is not the same as living with him. He's like a father to Dani.'

'No, it won't be the same,' Ess agrees. 'But it will be all right.'

She has to admit, however, that it doesn't feel all right. The empty bed. The empty place at the table. The house without Steve there. Ess decides that Suzi is right. She's been crazy to talk to Steve as she has done. They can put things right at the weekend when he comes back. The week drags on and on Friday evening, she receives a phone call from Joe. It's to confirm the invitation to meet his mother the following afternoon. To talk about the self-help school. At least that will be something to look forward to. A small bright spot in the dismal week.

***

Saturday dawns with sunshine, a blue sky and the promise of a crisp autumn day. It is perfect September weather, warmer than it was in August, although there is a hint of change in the air, a faint chill in the morning, a cool edge to the warmth of the day, hardly perceptible, like a fore-taste of winter. The chill in the air makes Esme think of Bonfire Night and the weather you get at the beginning of November even though that's nearly a couple of months away. And there is the smell of leaves.

Suzi is going to keep an eye on Dani, while Ess goes to Joe's in the afternoon. An expedition is planned. Suzi is going to take Dani and Mandy to look for abandoned bicycle bits and says she knows of a couple of tips on the other side of the city. The boot of Suzi's car has already been cleared and old sacking laid down ready for whatever they find.

All week, Ess has felt miserable about Steve, but she tries to put these thoughts out of her head as she sets off to meet Joe's mother. Her spirits lift as she walks over the rough ground and across the road to head down into Chapeltown. Perhaps Darius will be there. She tries to push the man out of her mind. How foolish to even think about him. She only met him once. Her thoughts turn back to Steve. They will be able to talk tonight when he gets back from Berlin. He will surely be ready to forgive her by then. She will apologise, of course, and she hopes that all will be well again.

Ess is walking to Joe's through the ginnels. Funny how everyone has their own local word for ginnel. In South Derbyshire they're jitties and Murray, who comes from down south, calls them alleyways. There are leaves everywhere. The tobacco tin is in her bag, but she hasn't had a cigarette all day. Soon she will give up completely and that will make both Dani and her mother happy. Steve, too They all nag her about smoking. Steve, surprisingly, is more understanding than you'd expect, given that he's a non-smoker. She ought to give up. She gets out of breath more easily than she used to do. The last time she went swimming, for instance, she could hardly manage a couple of widths unlike in the past when she could swim all afternoon. As these thoughts about how smoking is damaging her health pass through her mind, she thinks of the tobacco tin and begins to long for a ciggie.

Twenty to two. Esme slows her pace. Doesn't want to arrive early but when she reaches the house and checks the address, it is still not quite two o'clock. Best to walk around the block a couple of times. There is hardly anyone around. A man mowing his lawn and a well-dressed couple walking along the street hand in hand. After walking around the block three times, it is, at last, the appointed time, so she walks up the long garden path to the front door and rings the bell.

'Hello, Esme. Come in.' It's Sheldine, one of Joe's sisters. It turns out that he has three sisters and since he is the only boy, he's been spoiled.

'Not by Mummy,' Joe insists. 'She has always been strict, but my sisters look after me.'

'When he behaves himself,' Sheldine says. 'Come and sit down. Mummy will be down in a minute. Would you like a cup of tea? Or coffee?'

'She'd like a coffee,' Joe replies, glancing across at Ess who looks surprised. 'I remember from last Sunday at your place,' he says. 'You said you preferred coffee.' Esme nods a thank you and looks around. Polished wood floor. A piano along one wall and some leafy pot plants in the large bay window. There's one that Esme can't identify and a couple of fig trees. The room is spotless, elegant and well used. Esme wonders who plays the drum kit that stands in one corner then turns back towards the piano, feeling a strong urge to have a go.

'Who plays?' she asks, gesturing towards the piano.

'Geraldine mainly,' Joe says, 'but we all play a little.' He walks over to the piano, lifts the lid and runs his fingers over the keys. 'Gerry's out at the moment. She's the eldest and was supposed to be a boy, so she got named after Daddy. She's a solicitor,' he adds. 'Got her own practice in town.' He sounds proud.

'Hello there,' Esme turns as she hears a deep, rich voice from behind her. An imposing woman stands in the doorway, heavy in stature but not fat. 'I'm Lillian.' Esme stands and turns as Lillian walks towards her, half smiling. 'Joseph said you wanted to meet me.'

'I'm Esme,' she introduces herself, 'I'm a secondary school teacher. French, German and English.'

'Well, Esmerelda,' Lillian replies, 'I'm pleased to meet you.' She sits down and continues. 'Come and sit over here and tell me about your school. It's what I believe in, you know. Education.'

'No, not Esmerelda. It's just Esme. But me, too. I believe in education. Joe told me that you run a self-help school.'

'Yes,' Lilian says. 'Many of our children don't do well at school. They don't usually get the help they need.'

'So that's why you started the Saturday school.'

Lilian nods and Sheldine brings in a tray with a pot of tea, a can of coffee and a plate full of cakes. The four of them sit and chat. While they talk, Esme is aware of the way Joe looks at her and wonders where Darius is but doesn't like to ask. Lilian has offered to arrange a tour of the school for Esme on the following Saturday. It runs in the mornings finishing at midday. Sheldine says she will show her around.

'I would be happy to come and do some teaching,' Esme offers, 'if you need anyone that is.' She pauses. 'Not for pay, of course.' Lilian laughs and thanks her but says that it is a West Indian self-help school, so they have their own teachers. That means black teachers and Esme feels excluded. She tries to keep smiling but feels hurt that her offer has been so speedily refused. At this point, the door opens and Darius stands in the doorway. A young woman is by his side.

'Come in, Darius,' Joe calls. He turns to Esme and says, 'Meet Helen. She's my little sister.' Esme watches as Darius and Helen walk into the room. She looks at Darius and feels his eyes meet her own. Feels herself blush.

'Hello, Esme,' Helen speaks as she comes over and Esme turns towards her. 'Joe told us about you and how interested you were in Mummy's school. Pleased to meet you.' Esme smiles and is about to answer when Darius starts to speak.

'Hello, Esme,' he says, as he puts Helen's coat with his own over one of the chairs. 'I've been in London. Helen's studying there, so we came back together. How are you?'

Esme feels herself blushing and rushes to tell him that she's started back at school then asks if his course has started and how he is liking Leeds. Her words fall over themselves. He says yes, and fine in answer to her questions, but what she is noticing is the slow way he speaks as though each word is weighed and the intense way he looks at her. She remembers the party. Ess notices how good-looking Helen is, how she moves and speaks. For possibly the first time in her life, she catches herself feeling a twinge of jealousy.

Lillian invites Esme to stay for dinner, but she has to refuse. Dani will be waiting for her and Steve is due back soon. She picks up her bag, says goodbye and leaves, then almost runs until she finds somewhere out of sight of the house where she can roll a cigarette and light up.

28

I'm with Mandy in Suzi's car driving round the tips while Mum has gone to Joe's. It's Saturday, the day Steve is coming back after being away all week. All week! Suzi and Mandy keep talking to me about this and that, but I can't concentrate. Not even on going to look for bicycle parts. I want Steve home, properly home. I want everything to be all right again.

It's been a miserable week. I've been thinking about what I heard last Sunday. That Mum did go to Jackson's and got beaten up by Jackson's woman. That means that John was right in the first place when he came and warned Steve that Mum was in danger. He said she should stay away from Jackson, but she didn't listen.

I'm starting to believe that all the stories about her are true. When I listened to John, it was clear that he was telling the truth and as soon as he realised that Steve didn't know, he stopped. John didn't come to upset the family. I'm beginning to like him despite everything. Very strange. I'm sure now that what Jaffa told me was true. It's hard to accept. I can't bear to think of Mum going first with John and then with Jackson. Can't bear it. And now that Steve knows, or at least suspects, he has left the house. Been gone all week. Said he was doing a long-distance driving job, but it's never happened before. He's never been away all week like this.

Mum stuck to her original story and said that she didn't know who her attacker was, but nobody believed her. Steve left on Monday so he certainly didn't. I wanted to talk to him. He was there for dinner but when I got back from the tip, later on, he'd gone. He rang in the week and spoke to me but it was impossible to talk because Mum was there. He told me that he was coming back tonight. I can't wait. I've been counting the days.

'Are you dreaming again, Dani?' I hear Suzi ask. We're out again inspecting another tip. 'What about this piece here? Will this be any good?' I look at the piece Suzi is showing me. It looks like a front fork and it might be all right. The next bike is going to be for Mandy and then the one after that, I am going to sell.

'Yes,' I say. 'Yes, thanks. That looks all right.'

'And what about this?' I hear Mandy yell. 'Look what I've found.' It seems to be almost a whole bike intact. The front wheel is buckled, but that could be replaced. On closer inspection, however, it becomes clear that the frame is bent. What a shame.

'I don't think I can use it,' I say, 'but let's take it anyway and I'll have a good look at home. I think we'd better stop after this. If we gather any more, there won't be enough room in the cellar.'

It's late afternoon when we get back to the house and Mum is already in the kitchen, cooking. Smells good. It's a baking smell like a pudding or a cake. There is no sign of Steve yet but I hope he gets back soon. Suzi comes in to help bring all the bicycle bits into the cellar and stays for a cup of tea. I scrub my hands and after that, sit next to the window so I can keep a lookout for Steve.

'What are you cooking, Ess?' Suzi asks. That's what I was wondering but didn't like to ask. Mum has been on edge all week.

'Blackberry and apple pie,' my mother answers. That's a good sign, I think. It's one of Steve's favourites. 'We're having spaghetti bolognese to start with,' Mum says, 'but I can't start that until he comes.'

I like both the spaghetti and the pie, but I don't care what it is except that it's something Steve likes. It's something that's been chosen for him and it means that Mum cares about him. I wish he would hurry up and get here.

As soon as Suzi finishes her tea, she leaves and the house goes quiet. You can almost hear the silence hanging between us. Mum and I have hardly spoken all week. There's nothing to say. I turn on the television but can't see it from my place at the window, so I get up and turn it off again. Go back to keep a lookout for signs of the car. It takes hours. Literally. More than two hours before Steve gets back. I've waited so long, staring out at the road that my eyes have glazed over. I almost miss it when the car finally pulls up. I watch Steve get out.

'He's here,' I shout to Mum, but she hardly looks up from her book. She turned the food off ages ago and I'm starving. 'He's here,' I shout again as I open the door and rush outside. Steve is getting out and putting his bags on the pavement. He looks tired but pleased to see me and puts everything down to give me a hug. He asks me what school was like this week and how Mrs Richards was. Mum hasn't asked me once about Mrs Richards. Not once. All week she's hardly spoken. She's been in her own world. That's what they used to say about me. That I was in my own world. Locked in. Now it's Mum. I think she's forgotten I exist.

It's such a relief to have Steve home and asking about what's happening in my life. I start to tell him the good news that Mrs Richards is no longer my form mistress when I notice that he's not listening. It's the only good thing that's happened all week and it's a brilliant piece of news but nobody cares. I nearly shout at him and rush off upstairs, but I hang on. Somehow, I hang on.

I watch as my mother smiles and says hello, but she doesn't go to hug him. Steve stands in the doorway. Looks unsure about what to do next. Things are not all right and my mood sinks. Esme walks into the kitchen to start the food again. She tells Steve that she's cooking spaghetti, but I can tell that Steve has been hoping for a different kind of welcome. He seems to slump as he carries his things inside and goes up the stairs.

'Down in a minute,' he says but doesn't sound cheerful. I don't know what to do. Should I follow him upstairs? I hesitate so long that eventually, he comes down again and by this time the food is ready. We sit down to eat and I barely taste it. I try to ask him about Berlin and he answers but doesn't say much. Just keeps looking at Mum.

It's obvious that I'm not going to manage to talk to him tonight, so I give up and decide to go to bed. Maybe they'll start talking after I've gone and sort things out. Perhaps I'll be able to listen and find out what's going on. There are so many questions that I can't ask. That I daren't ask. I say goodnight and go to sit on the top step just outside my room. I sit there for ages. Listening. Gradually getting cold, but the only sound that floats up from downstairs is the sound of the tv. I try tuning in to their thoughts but they both feel blocked off. I can't get in.

On Sunday morning, I'm downstairs for breakfast and it's nearly eight but there's no sign of my mother or Steve. That's normal for a Sunday but I keep waiting for them to get up. To come down and talk. Eventually, I go down to the cellar. I want to do something with the bicycle bits we collected yesterday, but on closer inspection, none of the pieces matches any of the others. I can't get started. Keep hoping that I'll be able to talk to Steve. I need to talk to him alone because it's not possible to say anything when Mum's there. Is he coming back to stay? Has he actually left? What is happening? I had my weird dream again last night, the one that comes every so often. After that, I can never get to sleep again. It's the dream about my dad, my first dad.

In the end, it is my mother who gets up first so I decide to try and talk to her while she eats her breakfast. It's a waste of time. She's as ratty as she has been all week. It's not possible to say anything. Finally, I hear Steve getting up and eventually, he appears. He gives me a lovely smile, the same old smile but he doesn't sit down at the table. Says he has to catch up on work. Gets a coffee and takes it upstairs.

The rest of the day is the same. Waiting around. Hoping to talk to Steve. Mum says she's got to get on with her school work and Steve still doesn't come down. Howard drops in just after lunch and I take him downstairs to show him the latest bike project, but after looking at the pieces we gathered yesterday, his advice is to dump most of them. Start again he says. This is disappointing although he promises to go looking with me next weekend. He will help me if I haven't found any better pieces by then.

Steve stays upstairs all day. When he finally comes down, I follow him to the car and ask if he's ok. Yes, fine, he replies but he's had a lot of work to catch up on after driving all week. He'll be back tomorrow, he says, but doesn't say where he's going or why he's not staying. He doesn't ask about my week or how I'm feeling like he usually does. Doesn't ask if I'm all right. Doesn't ask about my assignments.

Neither Mum nor Steve has asked about my homework. Something that I would normally have considered a miracle but it doesn't feel like one this week. I do have a homework assignment that I have to give in tomorrow. It's the first one this term. Slowly I drag myself upstairs to my bedroom so I can have a go at it. For hours, I keep trying to start writing. More than one hour anyway, but my hand cramps worse than usual and my thoughts are on Steve. In the end, I pull up my sleeve and bite into my arm. When the pain kicks in, I manage, at last, to forget about the homework. And about Steve.

29

Another week. Monday morning isn't easy. I have to go without my homework because I didn't do it but my new form mistress doesn't get angry like Mrs Richards did. Miss Smith just asks me what's wrong. Nothing I reply, but she still doesn't get cross. I'll do it next time, won't I, she says, and I nod. Jaffa's there at the back of the class and I notice him now. Can feel him looking at me. I hope he hasn't talked about my mum to the other kids.

All day I keep thinking about Steve and wonder if he's still living with us or not. I'm going to have to ask my mother to tell me what's happening. And Mandy's not here. Hope her mum's not worse. She was feeling worried last time I talked to her. Said that her mum kept saying it would be all right but her dad had taken time off work and that was a bad sign. And then I think about Steve again. Just can't concentrate.

At the end of the day, I walk out of school with relief. I'll be brave tonight. I'll ask Mum what's happening. I'm walking down the road when I hear Jaffa calling me and I turn around. He's right behind me.

'I've got something for you,' he says and looks almost shy. Very unlike Jaffa. 'This is for you,' he says and he's standing close, so I have to look up at him. He hands me a large brown envelope. A4 size. Then he rushes off. Also not like Jaffa. I put the envelope in my bag and hope that it's not something awful about Mum. I shall wait until I'm by myself to have a look at it. By the time I say thank you, he's gone.

Normally, I'd go to the library because it's Monday or to Mandy's to see what's happened to her, but today, I just go home. I was going to sit and wait for Mum but when I get there, she's already home. She smiles at me and asks me to take my jacket off and sit down. Says she wants to talk to me. This is not normal.

'What about?'

'I want to tell you what's happening between me and Steve,' she says and my heart starts thumping. I sit down at the table and look at her. I don't say anything. I wait. Mum rolls a cigarette and lights it. 'Do you want a cup of tea?' she asks. 'Or an orange juice?' I don't think my mother has ever offered me an orange juice in the afternoon before. It's usually reserved for breakfast, doled out in small quantities and diluted.

'No thanks,' I reply.

'I'm sorry, Dani,' she begins and I fear the worst. Steve's going. She's going. I'm going to be taken to Grandma's and left there. It will be goodbye to my friends in Leeds. She's stopped speaking again. She's smoking not talking. 'I'm splitting up with Steve.' There she's said it. I knew it was coming but I'd hoped and hoped that it wouldn't happen. 'He still loves you,' she goes on. 'He will always love you.'

'But he won't be here,' I say. 'He won't be part of our family anymore. You told me Steve was part of our family.'

'Well, he is part of our family, but no, he won't be living here anymore.'

'I want him here,' I say. 'I don't want him to go.' But even as I say the words, I know they're useless. It doesn't matter what I want or what Seve wants. It matters what Esme wants.

'I'm sorry, Dani,' she says again and comes to give me a hug but I shake her off.

'You're getting rid of Steve,' I shout at her. 'Are you getting rid of me as well? You don't want me, do you?' I've said it but I didn't mean to say it.

'Oh, Dani, of course, I want you. I'll always want you. Your place is with me. I'm your mother.' Mum looks upset. She was calm before but she's nearly in tears now. 'Don't you know how much I love you?'

'Me, too,' I say. We hug each other but I've had enough. Need to be on my own so I pick up my bag and go upstairs. Sit on the bed, take out my stone and without thinking, start to stroke it. I remember the envelope from Jaffa but can't bear to open it. Not yet. I'm still sitting stroking the stone when Mum calls to tell me that Mandy's here and is coming up. Mandy's smiling so she, at least, must have some good news.

'Where were you today?' I ask her.

'At home. Mum was due to get her results from the hospital. She said I should go to school, but I couldn't force myself. I did go to school this morning but couldn't make myself walk through the gates. Went back home.'

'And what were your Mum's results?'

'Good,' she says, but I already know. I can see it in her face. I'm so pleased for her.

'What happens now?' I ask.

'Mum has to have a small op and chemotherapy,' she says, 'but she'll get better. The cancer hasn't spread.'

I tell her how pleased I am and then I tell her that Steve is leaving. That Mum is throwing him out. That I won't have a dad anymore. Well, he's not my dad anyway, she reminds me, and he'll still love me, won't he? He'll come and see me. She's sure he will. I suppose she's right. I'm going to have to cope. She is right. Steve will still love me. I do know that he will. Mandy talks to me for ages and I start to cheer up. She makes things seem normal again and that's what I want more than anything. I want things to be normal. Eventually, she goes but she'll be at school tomorrow. She'll see me there.

Finally, when I'm alone, I take out the envelope from Jaffa. I'm going to have to face everything. I'm beginning to think I can do it. Maybe things are not quite so bad as I thought. Mandy doesn't think so. She's reminded me that my mum loves me, that Steve loves me and that she's my best friend. She says lots of kids have parents who split up. It's not so bad. Parents are people, too and have their ups and downs. Mandy says parents have their needs as human beings. They're people as well as parents. Well, it sounds reasonable, but it doesn't feel good.

I know she's right. I can think it, but I can't feel it. I decide that I'll try. Mandy says that I will have to accept it. There's nothing I can do. She says that's what the Buddhists teach. Acceptance. I'm not sure I can do it. I usually try to change things that I don't like, not accept them. But I realise that what she's saying makes sense. There are some things that I can't change and this is one of them. I will probably be able to accept it for about five minutes until I feel angry and miserable again. Then I'll stop accepting and try to change things again. Listening to Mandy helps. Talking to Mandy helps. I feel slightly better than I did earlier. I think I can face losing Steve from our family. In some ways, he's already gone.

So now I'm holding the envelope from Jaffa. I open it carefully. There doesn't seem to be much inside. Just a piece of paper. I take it out and see that it's a drawing. I turn it over to look at the back, but it's blank. No message. I turn it back again and look at the picture. Done in pencil. Thick pencil. At the bottom, it says *Girl with Bike* by Jaffa Johns. It's a drawing of me. The only colour is the blond of my hair, but it isn't a colour. Just light and bright. Thick. Don't know how he's done it. It's my hair that looks dramatic. In places, you can see the individual strands. My hair looks fab.

At first, I think that it's not very good, but then I change my mind. You can see that it's me. That's probably quite hard to do. I'm facing forwards. My eyes are staring straight out of the picture, so now I'm sitting here looking back at myself. My face seems more important than my body and my right hand is resting on the bike. Some parts of it don't look the same as the one I've made, but other parts do and some of the details are spot on. The basket, for instance, and the handlebars. The bike in the picture is definitely my bike and, as he showed me the other day, it's not easy to draw a bicycle. I look at my face again and confirm that yes, it does look like me., I'm beginning to smile just a little bit.

A strange warm feeling goes all the way through me as I look at the picture. Jaffa's drawn it for me. He's spent time looking at me. He's spent time thinking about me. In a little while, I'm going to hide it in my exercise book, but for now, I can't stop looking at myself and the bike that I've built.

30

It's Sunday afternoon and I can see him sitting on the same bench as last time. He can't see me because I'm walking along the path that's hidden from his view. Pushing my bike. I think about the picture that he gave me and I wonder what the news is about my mum. Will I believe it? The answer to that is probably yes, I will, although a few weeks ago I wouldn't have. Not at all. I see a nice kickable stone and angle my foot towards it without thinking. I walk past the bushes behind him and hurry onwards heading home. I want to go and talk to Jaffa, but my legs won't go there. I get on my bike and am nearly home when I circle the block without meaning to and head back up towards the park. If he's still there, I'll go and meet him.

'Hello, Jaffa.'

'Dani,' he says. 'I thought you weren't coming.' I smile at him and go to sit down. Not so far away as last time. Don't want him laughing at me again. Or thinking I'm scared of him. He looks at me and I can see the question in his eyes. I know what it is, so I give him the answer.

'Yes, I like it.' I look up, straight into his dark brown eyes. 'Thank you for doing it for me.' He grins and jumps on to his bike.

'Let's go for a ride,' he says. I get on my bike and follow him as we head out of the park.

'Where to?'

'Meanwood,' he shouts, and we glide along pedalling on the uphills, freewheeling the downs. Not much traffic so we're soon there and I follow as he turns into the park and dismounts. We walk along in silence pushing the bikes. Leaves everywhere. Some scattered across the path, plenty on the grass, some in dark, wet piles near the bottoms of trees. It's cold today and a bit windy.

'How are things?' he asks. I shrug but don't answer. Funny, if it were somebody else, I'd have said 'fine' but with Jaffa, I feel that I can be honest. He glances at me and carries on, 'Haven't heard any more about your mum, Dani. Nobody's talking about her now. Not to my knowledge.' I feel myself start to relax. That's what I was waiting for. News about my mum. What people are saying. We carry on walking, kicking up the leaves here and there.

'What are your brothers and sisters like?' he asks.

'Haven't got any. What about yours?'

'I've got an older sister called Annie, but she's grown up, married, got two kids. Lives in Hunslet. And a little brother called Granville.'

'Are they nice?'

'I reckon,' he replies and grins at me.

'And what about your mum and dad?' It's Jaffa's turn to shrug but after a while, he starts to talk.

'Mum's all right,' he says, 'but Dad's awful when he's been drinking.'

'Does that happen often?'

'More and more,' Jaffa says. 'I wish he'd leave.' Is that really what he just said? That he wants his dad to leave? And here I am, desperate for Steve to stay and he's not even my proper dad. I tell Jaffa that we're back to front. He wants his father to leave, but his dad doesn't seem as though he's going to and I want my dad to stay but Mum's going to kick him out. At least that's what she told me. I expected Steve to be gone already, but he's still at home. Maybe there's hope.

'I want to show you something,' Jaffa says, and I'm immediately on guard. Start feeling apprehensive. The girls at school agree that when a boy says he wants to show you something, you run. You don't wait to find out what it is, you run. It means he wants to have sex with you, and he might force you into it. I look around and calculate how quickly I could jump on my bike and get away. Jaffa bends down and picks up something from the ground. 'Here,' he says, 'Look at this.' He shows me a leaf. I relax again and look at it. Looks quite ordinary as far as I can see. Dark red mostly with a blotch on one side. 'What do you think?' he asks. I look more closely, but it still looks ordinary. A boring leaf. 'Imagine you're going to paint it,' he says. 'Look carefully and imagine that.' I look again and try to imagine painting it. Start to see different colours. 'Look at the browns,' he says, 'and the shape of the veins. That's where the lifeblood runs.'

'It's beautiful,' I say and mean it. 'But it's not perfect.' I've never looked so closely at a single leaf.

'That's what makes it good,' he says. 'That's what makes it interesting.'

'I've got a special stone,' I tell him and take it out of my bag. I never show it to anyone. I don't know what's come over me, but I know he won't laugh and he doesn't. He takes it in his hand and strokes it, turns it over, examines it.

'Wow,' he says as he hands it back to me. After that, he throws the leaf into the air but it won't fly just flutters down back to the ground. We head for home.

As soon as I get in, I go to the stairs door to call up to see if Steve's in. He always works upstairs but he's not there. Instead Mum calls to say she's coming down.

'Hello, Dani,' she says. 'Where have you been?'

'Out,' I reply and go into the kitchen to look for something to eat.

'Where to?' Mum asks and, 'Who with?'

'Nobody,' I say and decide not to bother looking for food. I come out of the kitchen and head for the stairs.

'Stay down here,' Mum says. 'I want to talk to you and dinner will be ready soon.' I turn around and sit down on the sofa, waiting to hear what she's got to say. What is it this time?

'Where have you been?' she asks for a second time. I don't reply and then she asks me what homework I've got. Am I ready for tomorrow?

'Haven't got any,' I tell her and hear her sigh with frustration. She knows it's not true, but there's no point in telling her about my homework. I can't do it and that's that. My writing was bad before but since this new term has started, it's got worse. I keep trying, but I can't manage to write without making a mess all over the page. My new form mistress is much nicer than Mrs Richards. Mrs R was a bully, but Miss Smith is kind and fair. In the end, however, Miss Smith's kindness doesn't make as much difference as you might think. I still can't do it and not being able to do it makes me feel stupid. And now Mum's starting on at me again over my homework. I can't stand it, so I decide to go upstairs. Maybe Steve will come back later. Or maybe he won't. Nobody tells me anything.

'Is Steve coming back tonight?'

'I don't know,' my mother replies and I pick up my bag and go upstairs.

This morning my mum went over to see Suzi and I knew she'd be gone for ages, so I phoned Grandma. Sunday mornings are a good time to ring Grandma because she's always in the house, cooking dinner instead of up the garden, helping Grandpa. I know she can't change things, but it helps to talk sometimes. My two big worries are Steve leaving and not being able to write. I'm getting into trouble at school more and more. I must be stupid. Everybody who is intelligent can write but not me. Even with Grandma, I feel ashamed. I can't talk about the writing, but I do tell her about Steve. That Mum said he would be leaving but one week later, he still hasn't left. That's a good sign, isn't it? Grandma listens but doesn't say much. I wish she lived closer, so I could chat to her from time to time. Can't pop into Summer Lane from Leeds or at least, not without a hundred mile trip down the M1.

When I get upstairs, I sit on the bed. I get my book out but can't concentrate. It's Monday tomorrow. I get my bag and take my stone out and stroke it. Then I go to the hiding place at the back of the fireplace where I keep the exercise book for practising my writing. Not that it helps. I've almost stopped doing it. Underneath the cover (cream wallpaper with faint pink roses, embossed) of the exercise book is where I keep the picture from Jaffa. I had to fold it in half to make it fit there, but it's safe. I take it out and stare at it.

My hair is blonder and thicker in the picture than it is in real life. I look at myself holding the bike that I've made. It's not accurate but it is recognisable and the more I look at it, the more I like it. What is odd is that the image in the picture is beginning to take over from the reality of what my bike actually does look like. When I think about it now, I tend to see the bike in Jaffa's picture. It is not quite the same as the real bike so that I'm almost surprised when I go down to the cellar. The bike in the picture shines more than the real one. How did he do that? Make it seem shiny? Some of the details are entirely accurate. Like the bell for instance with a dull patch on one side.

And then there's me. I like looking at myself because I look different. Have to admit that I look better than I do in real life. Is that how he sees me or is it the only way he can draw? I see something new in it every time I look. This time I notice that he's given me little tiny earrings, but you can only see one. My ears are pierced but usually, I wear studs. In school, we're not allowed to wear earrings. He must have looked hard at me. I like the earrings in the picture. After a few minutes, I put it away again. It is just possible Mum might come up and the picture is a secret. I haven't even told Mandy.

It's time to have a go at my homework so I try. Look at my watch to check the time that I start. I grip the biro hard in an effort to control it, but the marks I make are laughable. I try again. And again. The bin in my bedroom is nearly full of failed attempts and my exercise book is getting terribly thin. Hardly any sheets left in it. I keep trying. Bite my tongue as I concentrate. Look at my watch again. I've been at it for nearly an hour, but I still can't do it. Can't get my writing small enough. Can't manage to write at all. I pull up my sleeve and bite my arm until the pain takes away my worries. I do it until all I feel is the pain. Relief.

31

Esme is struggling through the week. After she told Dani on Monday that she and Steve were splitting up, she's gone back to not being sure. She's sitting in the staffroom in her usual place at the long table next to the window surrounded by exercise books. On Thursday, she has to start the after-hours drama club so she needs to think of a good play that will be doable and also popular. On top of that, there are three staff members absent and only one supply teacher. All three absentees have English lessons that need to be covered and Esme is required to fill in for them all week. Whenever she does have a moment to think, she divides her time between worrying about Dani, thinking about Steve and, although she shouldn't, trying to figure out how she can see Darius again.

Darius. Ess doesn't understand why she wants to see Darius. She's only met him twice. Briefly each time. It's crazy to keep thinking about him. And he comes from Papua New Guinea. Only in Leeds for a year. She must be mad. Steve says that she *is* mad (although he didn't say it in relation to her thinking about Darius). Says the madness is in her genes. That it's her bad blood because she's adopted. Normal people don't behave as she does. Maybe he's right. It doesn't make sense the way she feels. Steve has been good both to her and to Dani for years. He is kind, intelligent and reliable. Darius, on the other hand, is a huge unknown with obvious disadvantages. And she doesn't even know if he likes her. When she saw him at Joe's, he seemed to be with Joe's sister, Helen.

Thoughts of Steve come crowding back and Esme realises that she is still wavering. One minute she wants him to stay, but when he's there again, she changes her mind and wants him to go. When she told Dani that she and Steve were splitting up, it felt like a relief but now she's hesitating again. Not easy for Dani to cope with, Esme realises, but she's doing her best to find a way through this.

'Esme,' she hears Jenny calling to her. 'You're late. What's wrong with you? You're supposed to be with 7G.' Esme sweeps the pile of exercise books off the table into her bag and hurries off to the classroom. She's teaching on automatic pilot and she's teaching as little possible. Can't concentrate. Instead, she gives the kids written exercises to keep them occupied while she sits at her desk and daydreams. But this strategy backfires because after the class has finished, she finds herself drowning in the extra marking all those exercises have generated. Back in the staffroom, she spreads out the piles of exercise books ready for marking then sinks once more into her thoughts.

It's disturbing. More and more, she finds herself thinking about Darius, but in a different way from how she was drawn first to John and then to the dreadful Jackson. Oh God, what a summer. With them, she'd been curious and restless but had always felt herself in control. Ironic, considering the fact that she'd lost control of the situation with both of them although in different ways. She tries to get her thoughts clear. What she means is that she had felt in control of her feelings. She had liked them, but she didn't need them. Yes, it was true that she wanted them to like her and want her. But not too much. Esme didn't want to have a permanent relationship with either of them, didn't want to be burdened.

Yes, that's the right word *burdened*. She had wanted a casual friendship with possibly a little sex, but she didn't want to have to look after these men. That's what women always seemed to end up doing. Looking after people. She was curious about what kind of lives they led, what kinds of worlds they inhabited. Worlds that were close to hers but different. Interesting. She was using the method her French teacher had recommended many years before when the girls in her class were setting off on an exchange visit to Lyons.

'Get yourselves a French boyfriend, girls,' she had said (although afterwards, the teacher insisted that she had been joking). 'It's the quickest way to find out about another culture.' Esme suppresses a smile. A teacher would be disciplined these days for saying something like that. Might even lose her job. Those girls who tried it (including Esme) thought that it worked fine. Up to a point, of course. Relationships could be dangerous. You took your heart in your hands.

Ess goes to make herself a coffee and manages to spend half an hour marking, but then her mind wanders again. She always boasted that she was never jealous. It used to be true, but with Darius, a man whom she has only just met, she finds herself feeling suddenly possessive. She doesn't want him to be with Helen. Or any other female. Esme wants him to be with her. As she admits these thoughts, she is almost shocked. She doesn't know him. And what about Steve? Ess already has a partner, so why shouldn't Darius be with Helen? Or anyone else. Esme tries to put him out of her mind and forces herself back to the exercise books.

Back at home once more, Ess heaves a sigh of relief. Another day gone. It is easy to put off talking to Steve because most of the time he isn't there. He is either upstairs working or he's out. Mostly, he's out, which is highly unusual for him and she knows that Dani is missing him, but there is nothing she can do about it. Steve is booking as many driving jobs as he can and in between times says that he is either working or with his friend, Paul. Hardly seems to have any appointments with his supervisor. When asked how he can fit in so much driving, he doesn't answer.

The week passes in a daze. Ess still hasn't decided which play to do with her after-hours kids but the general session she has with them goes well. A nice bunch. At the end of Friday, she is exhausted and decides that fish and chips would be good for a change so she won't have to cook. Dani usually loves fish and chips but nothing pleases her at the moment. She spends her time slamming doors and flouncing about the house. Says that she isn't slamming them and that they are closing like that by themselves. And when accused of flouncing around the house, Dani's face sets into even grimmer lines.

32

Will be all right to turn up to the Saturday School in the jeans she usually wears when not at work? Esme decides against it and chooses a fairly formal jacket and skirt. She adds some gold hoop earrings which are mostly hidden by the dark hair that falls well below her shoulders. Her fringe needs cutting but she doesn't like it too short. It will last a bit longer. Ess regards herself in the mirror and thinks she looks ok. Wonders briefly what she would look like if she dyed her hair red. Esme's hair already has some dark red tints (that only she can see according to Steve) so it might look all right. She laughs at the thought. It would make a change. She might try it.

'I'm off now,' she calls up to Steve and goes downstairs.

'You're leaving early,' Dani says.

'Yes, I'm going to walk.'

'All the way to Roundhay Road?'

'It's not that far. I need the exercise.' She doesn't really. Apart from the smoking, Esme is lithe and fit. Always rushing about. She likes walking, but today, it is grey and cold, totally different from the previous week when she'd set off for Joe's. Last week the sun had shone. It was warm, but this morning it seems as though winter has arrived before its time. The wind is icy.

It takes longer than she thinks, but it's not difficult to find the school which is housed in a dilapidated Victorian terrace set back from the road. Esme has arrived at break time and the coffee area is where Sheldine takes her first.

'This is the best place to get to know the students,' she says. 'You can chat to people and start finding out what goes on.'

Sheldine takes Esme to join a group of girls who were laughing at something a minute ago, but who now turn quiet and polite. The age range is enormous. Little ones sit next to adults all mixed in together. It seems more like a church club than a school. When lessons start after the break, Shelly takes her around to each of the classrooms and Esme asks how the classes are organised.

'When someone new arrives, we let them visit the classes and decide which one they'd like to join,' Shelly tells her. 'Each class operates at a different reading level. The classes are for reading and writing. We don't do maths, yet.' They are now back in the drinks area and Shelly is making another cup of coffee. 'Mummy says that Joseph should come and teach maths, but he says he hasn't got any time this year.' She laughs, 'Mummy says he should make the time.'

'So the new students decide which class they think is right for them after they've seen what the class does?'

'More or less. They are asked to do a short test to find out their reading level. They are given the result, but it's their own choice after that. The system breaks down sometimes when we get too many people wanting to join the same class, but we usually find a way around it.' The atmosphere in the place is impressive. With little or no pressure from the teachers, all the students seem to be highly motivated. Ess comments on this.

'Yes,' Shelly says, 'but everyone's problems are the same. It's low self-esteem. All the students want to learn, but most of them think they won't be able to succeed. It's not easy to get them to believe in themselves. Especially when the message they get in the other school is frequently the opposite.' It is getting late, and Esme has to get back. As she is leaving, Sheldine asks if she and her husband are going to see Benjamin Zephaniah. 'He's on at the Trades Hall tonight,' she says. 'It will be good.'

Esme doesn't hesitate.

'I'd like to go,' she says. 'I didn't know Zephaniah was on, but I'd love to go.' Furious calculations whizz around in her head as she wonders how she can manage to get Suzi to look after Dani, but she really would love to go. 'I don't have a husband,' she tells Sheldine, 'I'm a widow, although I live with a friend called Steve.' She pauses and slows down a bit. 'I would like to go,' she repeats, but I'm afraid Steve won't be able to come with me because he's working tonight.' Esme hesitates. 'Would it be all right to go by myself, do you think?'

'No need for that. You can go with us if you like. Come to the house around seven and we can go together. You'll be able to buy a ticket at the door.'

'That's kind of you,' Esme says as she leaves. 'Thanks for telling me about it. And thanks for showing me around.'

'It was a pleasure,' Shelly replies and gives her a warm smile and a pat on the arm. 'See you later.'

It is still windy, and it's starting to rain as Esme leaves the school. She's come without raincoat or umbrella so she's soaked by the time she reaches the bus stop even though it is only just over the road. Ess does want to see Zephaniah but wonders how she is going to manage it. Steve won't be there to look after Dani. She will have to ask Suzi and hopes that Suzi hasn't planned to go out this evening. Esme likes Zephaniah's poetry. Well, she thinks she does. Hasn't heard that much of it, but it would be good for teaching purposes. And she hasn't been to any poetry readings for years so she ought to go. And, well, Darius might be there.

She hurries back and goes straight to Suzi's house to ask her to babysit, but Suzi isn't keen. Tells Esme that she should stay in more with her daughter. Dani is in need of some attention. Esme knows that Suzi is right and starts to feel guilty but then reminds herself that she is going to spend all the rest of the weekend with her daughter. Dani is always mooching around at the weekends because Mandy isn't available.

'I didn't know Zephaniah was on, but we're teaching his poetry at school,' she says crossing her fingers. (Would Suzi be aware that schools had a set syllabus for literature and that it was unlikely to include contemporary West Indian poets?) 'Do you know his work?' she asks and Suzi shakes her head. 'It's performance poetry. It has to be spoken out loud so it would be brilliant to hear it spoken by the poet himself. A pity I can't tape it, but I would need permission to do that.'

'I'm not sure,' Suzi replies. 'What about Dani?'

'Yes, Dani would love it, but I wouldn't be able to take her. They wouldn't let her in.'

'I mean, what about Dani wanting to spend time with you?'

'We're going to spend the whole of tomorrow together,' Esme says and after a bit more persuasion, Suzi reluctantly agrees. Esme heaves a sigh of relief and goes home to tell Steve and Dani that she is going out to listen to poetry tonight.

'What about me then?' Dani asks. 'Am I staying in by myself?'

'Of course not,' Ess tells her, 'Suzi's going to come round.' She notices that Steve is looking at her with that critical look in his eye that is becoming increasingly familiar but he doesn't say anything.

'That's all right then,' Dani says. 'At least there's somebody who likes spending time with me,' and she leaves the room, slamming the door behind her. Ess goes to the stairs door and calls after her.

'Dani, come back here. What do you mean by that?' There is no reply. The bedroom door slams.

Esme sits down and rolls a cigarette. She has just lit it when the phone rings. It's Joe saying that he will come and collect her at a quarter to seven. It isn't safe for her to walk alone in the evenings. Esme starts to protest, but Joe reminds her about the Yorkshire Ripper and says that his mother has insisted that he fetch her. Reluctantly, Esme agrees. She looks at Steve who has listened to her side of the conversation and sees him raise his eyebrows then frown as he, too, turns to go upstairs. What has happened to her views that women should 'reclaim the night'?

***

The Trades Hall is packed. You can hardly move through the sea of young, white lefties. You can count the number of black people on one hand and all except one of them are in the group with Esme. Joe, Shelly, Darius and Helen. The only other black guy is working behind the bar. So, five altogether not counting Zephaniah himself.

They are late so there's no time for talking before the performance starts. But oh God, Esme thinks to herself as Zephaniah starts his act, she is glad that she's here. He speaks with passion. His poems are clever but what you feel most of all is Zephaniah's warmth and energy. One minute he's mocking the tabloid press and in the next, he's switched into the personal with a poem about his mother. Holds the audience in thrall. When he stops for the break, it's like being released from a spell. Suddenly they are their ordinary selves again, needing drinks or the loo. Joe goes off to get drinks for everyone. Darius touches Esme on the arm and asks if she will follow him outside. He leads her into the foyer.

'Can't talk in there,' he says and hesitates. 'I wanted to ask you something.'

'What's that?' Esme asks, feeling her heart begin to beat faster.

'Shelly said you weren't married to that guy you live with. Steve.' He stops and stares at her. 'Is that true?'

'Oh yes,' Esme falls over herself in the effort to distance herself from Steve. Judas, her brain shrieks even as she speaks. 'We're not married. Just very good friends.' Then she, too, hesitates and adds. 'We were more than friends, but we are separating.' Once more, she stops and looks up at Darius, 'He's a very nice person. It's not easy.' What has she said? Where is her loyalty? Where is her courage to tell the truth?

'So would you be free to go out with me one day next week?'

'Oh, yes,' Esme replies and then drops her eyes. 'Yes, I would.'

'What about Sunday?'

'You mean tomorrow?' Esme asks.

'No, not tomorrow. I'm busy for the rest of this weekend. I meant a week tomorrow. We could meet in town for a coffee.'

'Yes, of course,' Ess replies. 'I have a daughter, Dani, so I'll have to see if I can get a babysitter, but it should be all right.'

'I'd like to meet her sometime,' Darius says. 'Will you ring me then? When you know?' Esme nods. She has Joe's number and feels flustered and tongue-tied. Unheard of for her, she thinks, as she follows him back inside making their way through the crush of bodies to get back to the others. What is the matter with her?

Joe has fetched the drinks. They are busy discussing Zephaniah's performance and comparing him to Linton Kwesi Johnson. Esme can think of only one poem that she remembers by Johnson. *Inglan is a bitch.* Powerful and rhythmic. In some ways like Zephaniah's poems, but more aggressive. Kwesi Johnson, like Zephaniah, uses dialect to underline the difference between 'us' and 'them'. Esme realises with a sinking feeling that she is part of 'them' but doesn't want to be. The *Inglan* poem is about a Jamaican immigrant working for poor pay and being treated like shit. Esme wonders if John would like it. She has never discussed books or poetry with him, so she doesn't know what he likes but suspects that he doesn't read much. The only thing he ever mentioned was the horse racing section in *The Sun*. But you don't have to be a great reader to enjoy Zephaniah's poems. All you have to do is listen. But John is not here so she can't ask him.

'What do you think?' She hears Darius speak and is about to reply when she realises that he is speaking to Helen.

'I like him,' Helen says, 'but he hasn't done my favourite yet.'

'Which one's that?'

'*Pen Rhythm*,' Helen replies.

'I don't know that one,' Esme says. 'What's it about?'

'About the words in the poem being immortal,' she replies, 'not susceptible to disease or death like people are. The rhythm carries them out into the world. You can't kill them. They can't die.'

Darius nods and Helen goes on to explain that their whole family likes Zephaniah although Mummy only likes some of his poems and doesn't like Kwesi Johnson's poems at all. When Darius asks why, Helen says that although Mummy is an activist, she is also conservative. Lilian likes the royal family, for instance, and thinks that it is possible to overcome prejudice through education. It is Lilian's way of saving the world. Education. And she doesn't approve of bad language. Or even dialect. Geraldine agrees with Mummy, Helen says, but she, Joe and Shelly love Linton's poems. They like some of them more than Zephaniah's. And they think that something more powerful than education is needed to change society.

'Like what?' Darius asks, but Helen just smiles and shrugs her shoulders. Joe is starting to speak again, but the second half is about to begin so they settle back to watch and listen. Zephaniah combines anger against the world out there with warmth for the people he is addressing in here and Esme can feel the hall throbbing to the rhythm of his words, throbbing with ... with what? With hope and good fellowship. With hope for a better future? The man radiates warmth and hope.

It is over all too soon and Darius accompanies Sheldine and Helen, while Joe walks Esme home. They chat about this and that but Esme is thinking of Darius. She is going to see him again. Alone. He likes her. Esme invites Joe in for a drink before he sets off back, but he says that he has to be going. She says goodbye and turns to go in. Steve and Dani are sitting on the sofa watching tv and laughing, but as she enters, it's as though an ice block has entered the room. Steve excuses himself and goes upstairs.

'Don't go, Steve,' she hears her daughter plead before turning to Esme and saying quietly, 'I hate you, Mum. I hate you. I wish you hadn't come back.' And she, too, leaves the room and pounds off up the stairs.

33

I have survived the week. Every day I had to write. Can't bear to think about it. I used to like going to school. Yes, once upon a time, I did. Doesn't seem real. Was that me in another life? This life is much harder.

Steve's here after not having been at home for most of the week. He's upstairs working. Again! And the understanding is that we don't disturb him while he's up there so I'm hanging about down here. Waiting for him. I'm still hoping that he won't leave and I've decided to ask him what's happening. Is he going or not? I ought to ask Mum, but I can't because I know she wants to get rid of him. She already told me that. It was weeks ago, but he's still here so maybe they've made it up. I wish I knew. This Saturday she's gone to the West Indian school that Joe's mother runs. It's on Roundhay Road and she set off early so she could walk there. It's pouring now so she'll probably come back on the bus.

While I'm waiting, I decide to go and do some work in the cellar. I'll hear when Steve comes down. Haven't got started on the new bike because the pieces don't fit together. Need to make a list of parts that I still need. That's all of them. Ha ha. I do that and decide that my first bike could do with some more chrome cleaner on the handlebars. I've just got started on that when there's a knock at the door. I go up to see who it is.

'Mandy, come in.'

'Come round to mine. We can have the place to ourselves. Everybody's out.' I think of Steve and hesitate but, with a bit of luck, he'll be here all weekend and won't leave without seeing me. He said yesterday we could have a game of chess tonight when he gets back from his afternoon job so it should be safe to go with Mandy. I'm sure he'll be here later on.

Mandy's attic is warmer than our cellar and there's nearly always some crisps but not today.

'Sorry,' she tells me. 'Ate them all last night. Got some biscuits.' I ask about Mandy's mum whether there's any more news. No, Mandy tells me. It's the same as before. Just a small op and then chemo afterwards. No date yet for the op, but they said it would be soon. Mandy asks me about Steve. I shrug and attempt a smile.

'Has he already gone?'

'No. He's still in the house, working upstairs.'

'Does that mean he's staying?' she asks, but I shake my head.

'Don't know.'

'And what about Jaffa?' she asks me, grinning.

'What about him?' I don't want to talk about Jaffa.

'Larry saw you with him in Meanwood last Sunday.' Bugger. There are people everywhere.

'What did he say?'

'Said you were walking along talking to each other and didn't see him. He waved and shouted to you both, but you didn't hear.' That's a surprise. Don't remember seeing anybody in the park at all.

'Met him to talk about Mum,' I tell her.

'And is there any news?'

'No. Jaffa thinks she's not going out anywhere in Chapeltown at the moment. Nobody's seen her for weeks. And in any case, he said, it was just gossip.' This isn't news but Mandy doesn't know that. At least I don't think she does. Esme hasn't been out without Steve since she was beaten up by Jackson's woman. 'I'm sure nobody has seen her lately,' I say. 'If they say they have, they're lying. Mum's not been out anywhere except to school.' I'm permanently angry with my mother these days, but I wouldn't tell anyone. Not even Mandy. Especially not Mandy.

'Ok, so why did you spend so long with Jaff?'

'Didn't,' I reply. 'Just tested the bikes and talked for a few minutes.'

'I like him,' Mandy says. 'He's clever,' she giggles, 'and sexy.' I can feel myself starting to blush which is annoying. I've become so good at acting when I need to and it usually works, but I don't know how to control the heat that rises to my face at times like this. I've been trying all week not to look at him. Not easy since he's in the same class as me for nearly everything, but I'd hoped to get a message from him. Instead, there has been nothing. Maybe he was upset because I wouldn't look at him all week, but I don't think so. Perhaps he thinks I don't like him, but once again I don't think so. Now it's too late to do anything about it. I want him to know that I do like him. It's important. Now Mandy is saying that *she* likes him and thinks he's sexy. She's not mentioned him before. I think of the way he looks at me and start to blush. Again. Damn.

'Dunno. Haven't noticed,' I say. 'I'm not interested in boys.'

'Don't believe you. What about Vee Jay?' I did tell Mandy once that I half-fancied the lad next door. He's good looking and about eighteen. Jaffa's our age. Fourteen tops. I thought he was too young, but I've changed my mind. He's a lot better than Vee Jay. More interesting. And Mandy's right. There is something sexy about him. At first, I thought it was the way he walked but now I think it's his eyes. The way he looks at you. He always looks interested. Suppose it's because he draws. He must have got into the habit of looking closely at people. Mum used to draw but I never noticed her looking at people like Jaffa does. But what I like best about him is that he's beginning to feel like a friend. He's easy to talk to.

'Haven't seen Vee Jay for ages. Think he's got a girl-friend. Saw him with somebody last week. What about you?' I ask, desperate to switch the conversation as far away from Jaffa as possible. Thank God Mandy doesn't know that he drew a picture of me. People probably don't even know that he draws.

'Well, there is somebody,' Mandy admits. 'There's a boy who goes to the Buddhist meetings. When it's time for meditation I've seen him looking at me. Don't know where he lives though. He doesn't go to our school.'

'What's his name?'

'Breally,' she says. I try not to laugh. 'Breally!' I repeat. 'How can anybody be called Breally?'

'Well, he is, and he's gorgeous. I'm hoping he's there to-morrow. Used to hate going to the meetings, but I'm changing my mind.'

We've finished the packet of biscuits. Hardly noticed that we were eating them. 'There are some apples,' she says and goes downstairs to fetch them. 'And look what I've found.'

I look and see that she's brought two apples and a packet of chocolate digestives. The best kind. Not own brand.

'Hope Mum wasn't keeping these for anything special,' she says as she opens the packet and we get stuck in. 'We can eat the apples afterwards. Have you done the local history assignment yet?' Mandy asks with her mouth full.

'No,' I reply. 'Have you?'

'Nearly finished it,' she says. 'What are you doing yours on?'

'St Matthews Church,' I reply without thinking. Well, it will do as well as anything else. 'What about you?'

'I'm doing the library,' she says, then hesitates. 'Do you want any help, Dani?' She knows I've been getting into trouble with my assignments lately.

'No, thanks,' I reply. 'Everything's under control.'

***

Mum comes back from her visit to the Saturday School and tells us that she's going out again this evening. Steve looks cross but has to go to work. Says he'll be back later on. I shout at her but don't mean to. Mum doesn't seem to want to spend any time with either me or Steve. She didn't have to go to the Saturday School, she could have stayed at home. And she doesn't have to go out to listen to poetry tonight, however brilliant Benjamin Zephaniah might be. (Never heard of him and I'm sure she's never mentioned him before.) She could stay at home with me and be there when Steve gets back. Mum could stay and talk to me to-night and tell me what's happening with her and Steve. She's said often enough that she wants to talk to me so what's happened to that? Or we could watch a film together. But no, she's going out again. Has arranged for Suzi to come round and sit with me until Steve gets back. As soon as Suzi arrives, my mother leaves. Gone.

'What do you want to do tonight?' Suzi asks. 'Have you got any plans?' I shrug.

'Tv?'

'Ok,' Suzi says and settles herself down on the sofa. 'Your call.' At least I won't have to talk. Suzi's good like that. Doesn't nag me. She's brought half a bottle of red with her and offers me a little. Don't like red wine but decide to accept. Hope it's not the same kind they had at the dinner party. Maybe I'll be able to get drunk. I like old films and *North by Northwest* is on. I like Hitchcock. I get myself comfortable on the floor with cushions behind my back against the sofa. Steve gets back just before it finishes and is good at not speaking until the film's over. Steve notices my wine glass but doesn't say anything. Just gets himself a beer. I didn't get much wine anyway and it's all gone now. Suzi drank almost all of it. She doesn't stay long once Steve is back. No sign of Mum, thank goodness. I am hoping that she won't come back until very late. I don't want her to disturb my time with Steve.

'What about the chess?' Steve asks after Suzi leaves. 'Do you want a game?'

'Not tonight,' I say. I know I won't be able to concentrate.

'Good,' he says. 'I was hoping you were going to say that. What about *The Goodies*?'

'OK,' I say. Not my favourite programme, but not too bad.

'They're on in ten minutes.'

That means I've got ten minutes to talk to Steve, but I'm suddenly silent. Don't know what to say.

'What's happening with you and Mum?' I finally manage to ask and watch Steve start to look uncomfortable.

'I don't know,' he replies and I feel my spirits sink. At least he's here now. I switch the tv on and sit down once more with my back against the sofa. We can watch tv together. We are just getting settled when Mum arrives. Steve takes one look at her, picks up his beer and says goodnight.

'Don't go, Steve,' I shout after him but he's already gone. I turn to my mother. 'I hate you.' I see the pain in her face and I want to make it worse. 'I wish you hadn't come back.'

I pick up my glass and take it upstairs leaving her alone with the Goodies. She switches it off before I get to my room and a sort of silence, broken from time to time by the closing of a door or the boiling of a kettle, settles over the house. I hear my mother go upstairs and shortly afterwards both she and Steve go down again. It's quiet after that. They must be talking to each other again. Relief.

I'm still not tired so I read for a while and finally put out the light. Just as I'm drifting off to sleep there's a sound of breaking glass. Maybe they've got drunk and decided to do the washing up together, I think and suppress a giggle. But there's no laughter from downstairs.

34

As Esme walks in from her evening of poetry, Steve and Dani get up and leave the room, one after the other. Dani says that she hates her. Says it quietly and somehow that makes it worse. Esme trembles and goes to make a cup of coffee then hesitates and switches off the kettle. She has to talk to Steve. They've put off talking for long enough and Dani is becoming increasingly stressed. Ess knows that the uncertainty over whether or not Steve is staying or going is distressing for all of them.

Her mother has written to say that Dani has rung more than once and talked about Steve. Does Esme know how upset she is? It's unusual for her mother to write such a letter. She has never written like that before. All of them need an end to the uncertainty. Esme goes upstairs and asks Steve to come down. She tells him that they have to talk. At first, he looks as though he is going to refuse but he changes his mind, closes his book and comes down-stairs with her

It would be good to have a glass of wine, but it is too late to go and buy any. The Off License will be closed, and they don't have anything to drink in the house.

'I wish we had something to drink,' she says as she sits down at the table.

'I've got a bottle in the car,' Steve says. 'I'll get it.' Ess fetches a couple of glasses.

'When did you get back?' she asks.

'About an hour ago,' Steve replies. 'Suzi left just after I got here. They'd been watching Hitchcock. Dani didn't want to play chess, so we were going to watch tv.' He opens the wine and fills their glasses. 'Dani asked me what was happening between us.'

'And what did you say?'

'I told her I didn't know.' Ess looks concerned but doesn't answer, so Steve changes the subject. 'Was it good at the Trades Hall?'

'Yes, you would have liked it.'

'And who walked you home?'

'Joe,' she replies, 'I invited him in, but he said he had to be getting back.

'Well, he's got *some* decency, then.'

'What do you mean *he's got some decency*? He walked me back. Out of politeness.' She raises her glass and drinks then reaches for her bag and takes out the tobacco tin.

'I thought you were giving up,' he says, and she sighs.

'Steve,' she says. 'We've got to stop getting at each other like this.'

'I'm not,' he replies. 'I'm just reminding you of what you said you were going to do.' He drinks and reaches for the bottle to refill their glasses. 'But I suppose you're right. We do need to talk. I can't live like this, and Dani doesn't like me being away.'

'No,' Esme agrees. 'She doesn't but we can't bring her into it. We've got to sort matters out between ourselves.' She draws on the cigarette. 'It used to be so easy between us, Steve, but now all you ever do is criticise me.'

'That's not fair,' he says. 'You've lied to me and run off with other men. First John, then Jackson.' A pause. 'And now there's Joe, too.'

'No,' Esme says. 'There is no Joe, too. He walked me home. That's all.'

'Well, you seemed pretty desperate to go out tonight,' Steve says. 'Just like the times when you went off dancing week after week.'

'Yes, you're right. I did want to go out tonight.' She hesitates, 'And yes, it is like the times when I wanted to go out dancing. I'm feeling stifled.' Steve is a decent man, has always treated both her and Dani with kindness. She doesn't want to hurt him, but she needs to be honest. 'I want us to have an open relationship.'

As Esme says this, she watches Steve's face and is reminded of a time long ago when she was with a different man, with Dani's father. She had wanted the same thing, a free relationship, but she hadn't told him. She'd gone ahead and done what she wanted. Started a relationship with someone else, with Howard actually. Her relationship with Howard had not developed, but there had been disastrous consequences.

She stares into her wine and remembers. How ever much you want to, you can't undo the past. This time, she promises herself, it *will* be different. She will tell Steve honestly what she wants. She won't deceive him anymore. She shouldn't have played around with John and with Jackson. Thank God Steve doesn't know what happened.

'Do you mean 'free' as in 'free to sleep around'? Steve asks.

'Yes,' Esme replies. 'Yes, I suppose I do.'

Steve drinks then puts down his glass and looks at her, 'And you said he walked you home out of politeness.' Esme is about to argue again but she hesitates. Let him think what he wants.

'So, what do you say?' she asks. 'To an open relation-ship?' Ess finds herself rolling another cigarette even be-fore she's finished the one she is smoking. The tobacco is running out.

'I can't believe you're saying this. It's an insult.' He pushes the hair out of his eyes. 'I love you, Esme. And I love Dani, too, but I'm not a doormat to be trampled un-derfoot. What kind of a fool do you think I am?' and then 'How come you love me so little?' He finishes the wine and puts his head in his hands. Ess wants to hold him and com-fort him but she stops herself, stays where she is. Steve gets up and walks into the kitchen. He throws his glass into the sink and the sound fills the house. Splinters fly onto the worktop and some land on the floor.

'I'll leave tomorrow,' he says. 'After I've talked to Dani.'

***

When Steve talks to Dani, Esme isn't there. Nothing was said at breakfast and Ess thought that he'd changed his mind. It is Sunday morning so she decides to go over and see Suzi. She shouts down to Dani, who is in the cellar as usual, to say where she's going, but when she gets back, there is no sign of either Dani or Steve. On the table, there is a note saying they've gone for a drive.

Esme gets the lunch ready. Fish fingers with tomato ketchup and chips. One of Dani's favourites, but they don't return. Eventually, Esme eats alone. It is time she got on with the marking. Normally, Esme does it on a Saturday to get it out of the way, but she was out almost the whole day yesterday. It's the last thing she feels like doing, but it has to be done.

Once the table is cleared, she forces herself to get the books out and start. Every time there is a sound outside, she looks up and stares out of the window. It's almost impossible to concentrate. First of all, there is 7G's German homework. The assignment was to write a paragraph about their mother or father. Esme sighs. Unbelievable how many mistakes can be made in one paragraph. Choosing which mistakes to point out and which to let slide is not easy. It takes over an hour and a half until 7G's books are finally finished, but Steve and Dani are still not back. Now for 9B's English homework.

By six o'clock, Esme is beginning to get both worried and annoyed. Steve could at least have rung to let her know when they were coming home. At just gone seven, she hears the car draw up outside and looks out. Yes, it's them. It looks as though Steve is not coming in, but Dani is still sitting in the car. Hang on. Ess forces herself to stay in the house. Don't they know how worried she's been? Another five minutes and they are still in the car. Esme is just going to go out when the car engine starts up and they drive off again.

Clearing up the broken glass had been the first task of the day. Ess had got up early to make sure that Dani didn't see it. What a long, exhausting day. Mostly waiting for Steve and Dani to come back. She's still waiting. When will Dani have time to do her homework? Have they already eaten she wonders? By this time Esme has delayed dinner for so long that she is feeling extremely hungry. She still can't bring herself to finish cooking the dinner before they get back, so she makes herself a bowl of Weetabix. And then another. And then a cup of coffee. Finally, at nearly ten o'clock, the car pulls up again and Dani crashes through the door, slamming it behind her.

'I've been waiting for you for hours,' Esme starts, but her daughter walks straight past her without speaking. 'Don't you want any dinner?' Esme calls after her, but there is no reply. She follows her daughter up the stairs, but Dani is lying face down on the bed, sobbing.

'Don't touch me,' she says. 'Just don't touch me.' Esme goes into Dani's bedroom and tries to sit down on the bed.

'I'm sorry,' she says but gets no further.

'I said don't touch me,' Dani repeats. 'Just get out and leave me alone.'

Ess goes back downstairs and makes a fresh lot of fish fingers and chips. Takes them upstairs on a tray with a glass of orange juice and a bottle of tomato sauce, but the door to Dani's bedroom is closed. Esme puts the tray on the floor then tries to open the door, but it has been wedged shut from the inside.

'Your dinner's outside,' she calls through the door. 'I'll leave it on the landing.' There's no response so she goes back down, makes coffee and sits at the table. You can feel the misery filling the house. Steve gone. Dani distraught. Esme tries switching the tv on, but it doesn't help. Eventually, she picks up a book and goes to lie down. The bedroom feels empty. Does she really want him to be gone? Has she done the right thing? Ess thinks she has, but it doesn't feel good.

Mother and daughter go through the motions of daily living. Esme goes to work and Dani goes to school. Her daughter hardly eats and hardly speaks. Steve rings to say that he will come and fetch his things on Thursday, the day she gets back late from school. He will look after Dani until

Esme gets back and then he will go. Where is he staying, she asks? At Paul's, he says and gives her the address and phone number in case she needs to get in touch. Dani already has the number, he says.

On Thursday, Esme gets through the day and the after-hours drama session on automatic pilot. Then she rushes to get home a little earlier than usual, but Steve does exactly as he said he would and leaves as soon as she arrives. She watches Dani's face as he leaves.

The only thing that keeps Esme going is the thought of seeing Darius on Sunday. It shouldn't be, but it is. It will be the first time she's been alone with him. He has already rung and they've arranged to meet in a coffee bar in Chapeltown. No need to go into the city, he said. They could have a coffee and then go for a walk. Would that be all right? Fine, she'd replied.

Getting Suzi to babysit has turned out to be impossible. Suzi is angry with her. Not so much because of splitting up with Steve but because of not spending more time with Dani. No matter how much she tries to persuade her, Suzi refuses. Esme considers ringing Darius to change the date but instead finds herself ringing Steve and asking him if he will spend time with Dani on Sunday. Of course, he will, he says. He'll come and pick her up in the morning and take her out for the day. Esme feels a terrible pang of guilt, but she knows that Dani will be happy to spend the day with him.

Late on Friday, the phone rings. It's her mother.

'What's wrong?' her mother asks without preamble. 'I spoke to Dani earlier and she tells me that Steve has left.'

'Yes,' Esme says. 'I'm afraid that's right. I can't explain on the phone, but we're just not compatible anymore.'

'Compatible?' her mother almost snorts. 'What's that supposed to mean, Esme? Anyway, we're coming to see you. That's what I'm ringing to say. Your father and I are coming tomorrow for the weekend.'

'Oh no,' Esme says, the words spoken before she can stop them. 'I'd love to see you, Mum,' she gabbles, 'but could you come next weekend instead? I'm working tomorrow and Steve's taking Dani out all day on Sunday.'

'Working on a Saturday?'

'School work,' Esme says. 'I've got some tests to prepare for next week and they're going to take hours.' She looks around for a cigarette and tries without success to roll one while holding the phone. 'There's no point in coming if we won't have time to talk.... but it's kind of you, Mum.'

'All right,' her mother replies. 'We'll come next weekend instead. Will you be able to cope until then? And will Dani?'

'Of course,' Esme says. 'It feels awful at the moment, but it will be all right soon.'

'Dani doesn't sound all right,' her mother says, 'and neither does Steve.'

'Has Steve been in touch with you?' Esme asks, starting to feel angry.

'He wanted us to have his contact details,' her mother replies. 'Didn't say a word against you. I do hope you can patch it up, Esme.'

'Oh, Mum, you don't understand. I'm so sorry about all this. I'll try to explain when I see you.' Ess picks up her tobacco tin again and stares at it in desperation. Tries to roll a cigarette with one hand and fails once more. 'I'm sorry, Mum, I have to go now. I'll ring soon.' Esme is about to put the phone down when she remembers to add, 'Thank you for ringing, Mum. Thank you.'

35

Steve's been gone for a whole week but he came today to take me out and we're on the way to somewhere. It's Sunday and Mum's going out again. She just wants to get rid of me. I sit next to Steve in the passenger seat and fiddle around with the tapes in the glove compartment. Make up my mind, stick a Jimi Hendrix tape into the cassette player and turn up the volume. Steve half turns to look at me but says nothing. For a time, we are quiet just letting the sounds of Hendrix slide through the air. I wonder how hard it would be to play the guitar.

'Where are we going?' I ask after a while.

'I thought we could go to Scarborough,' Steve says, 'and go paddling.' *Paddling*?

'OK,' I say and he turns to look at me.

'Don't you want to?' he asks. 'I thought you might like that.'

'It's all right, Steve,' I say. 'I don't mind.'

'You don't sound very enthusiastic.'

'It's because going to Scarborough is a treat,' I tell him.

'And you don't like treats?'

'No,' I say, then look away from him and stare out of the window, holding on to my face to keep it under control. 'I don't want treats. I want life to be normal. I want you to come home.' I hear Steve sigh and watch him turn his attention to the road in front of us. There isn't much traffic. No wonder on such a grey day. Nearly the end of October. *Paddling*!

'Do you want an ice cream?' he asks after we've arrived, parked the car with no trouble at all unlike during the holiday periods, and are walking towards the beach. *An ice cream!* He is trying hard. How old does he think I am?

'No, thanks,' I say and grin at him. He is doing his best to cheer me up. There aren't even any ice cream vans in sight. All packed up for the winter, no doubt. He is carrying a large bag that he's brought out of the car. When we reach the beach, I discover that it contains a thermos flask, two plastic mugs, a bottle of coke and a couple of bananas. There is a large towel, too, that he says we can share after we've been paddling. I don't recognise the towel. It's not one of ours and it gives me a funny feeling.

We sit down for a bit on the cold, damp sand and stare out at the sea. There is a family with two small boys and a dog walking along the beach. Otherwise, the place is deserted. The father keeps throwing what looks like a red rubber bone for the dog who goes mad each time trying to retrieve it. It's hypnotic watching them. I keep thinking that a ball would be better.

'How was school this week?' Steve asks. I shrug in reply. What can I say? School is getting harder and harder, but what can Steve do about it? What can anybody do? I feel as though I'm being swept out to sea, out to disaster. Life is out of control and nobody can save me. Grandma has rung every day to ask how I am, but I can't tell her. In any case, it is impossible to talk on the phone because my mother might come in.

I did think of trying to talk to Suzi but the one time I knocked on her door, she wasn't in and I didn't go back. Anyway, what could she do? Solving my problems involves getting Esme to change her mind and performing a miracle on my ability to write. Both beginning to feel impossible.

I've thought of running away but that wouldn't work either. The only place I could run to would be Grandma's and I remember the last time I tried travelling between Leeds and South Derbyshire without permission. I don't want to get picked up by the police a second time. The distress it would cause Grandma and Grandpa wouldn't be worth it. Even if I got there, I would probably just be sent back and in any case, I don't want to be there. I want to be somewhere far away, where nobody knows me. In a place where I don't have to write, and where the bad dreams about my dad finally stop. A place where I can start again. But I'm trapped. Too young and no money.

'Did Mum ask you to take me out today?'

'Yes,' Steve says. 'She did. But I wanted to spend the day with you anyway, so I was pleased.'

I know he is telling the truth. He does enjoy my company, but what about Esme? My mother seems more interested in going out with other people than in spending time with me. I've tried to talk to her more than once during this last week but every time it ended in a row. Always the same pattern. My mother starts off being concerned about me, but as soon as I say anything about Steve coming back, she closes down and then she gets cross. And now Mum has gone out again. She told me she was going to see Darius, the man from Papua New Guinea, the one who didn't come to dinner when Joe came. I wonder how she's got in touch with him when she never goes out. Something Steve shouted at her when they were having a row comes into my head.

'You're completely heartless,' he told her. 'You pick men up all over the place, one after the other as they take your fancy. You say a few sweet words, lead them on and then drop them without a second thought.'

Heartless. Was he right? I remember other people describing my mum as *all heart*. Who is right? I don't think Grandma would describe Esme as heartless, but then maybe Grandma doesn't know her very well. Only knows one side of her. Doesn't know how she behaves sometimes. The worst thing I've heard Steve say and the most worrying thing was when he told Mum she was mad. He said it was in her genes, so if it's in hers, it must be in mine. Am I going to go mad and act like Mum? I shiver. It's cold in the wind. Too cold to sit on the sand so we get up and go to walk by the edge of the sea.

'What's it like at Paul's?' I ask. Steve shrugs and says something that sounds like ok. I stop for a minute, then continue walking. Eventually, I manage to ask, 'Is there room for me?' I grin and try to make it into a joke.

'No, Dani.' Steve picks up a stone and lobs it into the waves. 'Your place is with your mother. You have to stay with your mum.' I don't ask again. I turn away so he can't see my face and I'm glad of the wind that whips the strands of hair in front of my eyes. I pick up a pebble and spin it to make it bounce on the water. Suddenly I have an idea. I feel in my bag and bring out my precious stone, the jet black shiny egg-stone that I've carried for years. One last look, then I hurl it as hard as I can into the water.

'What was that?' Steve asks.

'Nothing,' I reply.

'It was a good throw,' he says, and we walk on.

36

What to wear? Jeans or skirt? Which earrings? Esme heaves a sigh of relief and starts to relax. Steve has picked Dani up as promised and there is plenty of time before the afternoon. She ought to be finishing her marking but can't concentrate. The exercise books are spread out on the table, but Darius fills her mind. She goes upstairs and tries on the denim skirt that she got ready last night. The light blue one (she's got two). Not quite right somehow. She takes it off and puts her jeans back on. No, they look too ordinary. They are old. Don't fit as well as they ought to. It is time she bought some new ones.

Three times now she's seen Darius. Once at the party, once at Joe's house, and once on the club night to see Zephaniah. Each time it's been as though the air was charged, as though her body had been put on special alert. Ess has been thoroughly aware of Darius every time he's been anywhere near her. Didn't matter whether or not she was looking at him and she is certain it was the same for him. The connection is like an electrical charge. A series of jolts. Since their first meeting, Ess has been aware night and day of Darius's existence and that knowledge has heightened not only her physical senses but her mind. It is as though she has moved on to a different plane - which she never wants to leave.

When she is forced to attend to her daily tasks, she can't help but feel irritable. What she longs to do is to gaze into space and do nothing but think about Darius. She knows this is stupid. Moonstruck teenager is the description that comes to mind. She has never been like this with anyone else but she can't help it. It's as though she is under a spell. The music from the party plays in her head. *I've got you under my skin.*

Esme still can't make up her mind about what to wear. Darius usually wears jeans and a leather jacket, she thinks. Usually? She's only seen him three times. Once again, she stares at her own jeans which are getting worn out. They don't fit as well as they once did. The skirt would be better. She puts it back on and looks at herself in the mirror. Yes, she looks all right. Ess goes downstairs and makes a coffee. Sits down to read but can't settle. She is reading Doris Lessing's *Briefing for a Descent into Hell.* It's about people preparing for lives on earth.

The book seems to speak directly to her. Such a relief and such excitement to find a writer who shows her a world to which she can relate and characters who inspire her. And the book feels like a wake-up call, a reminder that she should be doing something good with her life, her precious life. The people in the book have a concern for education and for changing the way children are taught. It makes her think of school, of her pupils, of her responsibilities as a teacher. Of the possibilities of being a teacher. In the story, there is a group of people who have known each other in previous lives and who have been given a briefing together before their current life on earth started. They have a joint mission to change things for the better. When they meet each other in their current life, they feel a connection that they can't explain. In their new lives, it is like having a shared memory that they can feel but can't access clearly. That's how she feels about Darius. He is a total stranger, yet it feels as though she has always known him.

Just before it is time to set off, she changes her mind yet again and puts her jeans back on. At least they feel comfortable and she adds a smart jacket and her favourite gold hoop earrings. The large ones. She doesn't look too bad. Esme walks along and wonders what she'll do if he isn't there when she arrives, but as she gets close to the cafe, she sees him approaching from the opposite direction. Darius looks taller than she remembers and darker. Esme thought she'd feel awkward with him and wouldn't know what to say, but it isn't like that at all. They stare at each other as the distance closes between them then they laugh. Darius touches her arm lightly and steers her inside.

'Two coffees,' he orders, 'and two slices of apple pie.' He turns to Esme, 'Cream or ice cream?'

'Ice cream, please.'

'The coffee is awful,' he confides when they're sitting down, 'but the apple pie is homemade. You'll like it.' He is right on both counts. Darius tells her that they have good coffee in Papua New Guinea. It grows there, but most of the people prefer instant. What about apples, she asks? No, he says. Only imported ones. No apple trees. It's the wrong climate. That would be no good for her she tells him. She is an apple addict. Is that right, he asks, as he looks hard at her? She doesn't know whether he is commenting on her apple addiction or her statement that PNG would be no good for her. They always call it PNG he says.

After they've eaten the huge slices of pie and drunk the coffee, he leads the way outside and they go to the nearby park. It is late autumn. Most of the trees are already bare but there are still heaps of leaves everywhere. It's windy and her hair keeps blowing in her eyes. That's lucky she thinks to herself. It will keep her face hidden. As they walk around the park, she hears him humming an old pop tune *I'm the urban spaceman, baby.* So that's what he is Esme thinks and laughs. She seems to remember that it was by the Bonzo Dog Doo-Dah Band and that the song had a funny ending. She can't quite recall what it was. Esme tries to kick a pile of leaves towards him but they scatter haphazardly.

'I like the autumn,' he says. 'We don't have seasons like this at home.'

'No seasons at all?' Esme asks.

'Just the wet and the dry season.'

They find a bench near the rose garden. One rose still blooms. A single solitary rose. Surprising since it's the end of October, cold and windy. The petals are cream with a faint pink tinge. She's sure that it's the Peace rose. Her father grows roses. Has done ever since she was small and presumably for years before that. The Peace rose has a soft heady scent that she's often bent down to smell in Summer Lane. Esme tells Darius about her father's garden and about the flowers that he grows. She gets up and goes to smell the heavy bloom. A couple of petals fall. It's nearly over. Yes, she is sure it's Peace.

They talk a little about where Darius comes from and the course he is doing. His university is paying for him to do his masters here. In PNG, he teaches in the Education Department. He is thirty-one. Just one year older than she is. After a while, she asks Darius what kept him busy the previous weekend.

'I write,' he says. 'It's what keeps me busy most of the time, although I ought to be spending more time on my studies.'

'What kinds of things do you write?' she asks.

'Poetry mainly,' he replies. 'The kind of writing that doesn't earn any money.'

'Have you had anything published?'

'Just one small book,' he replies. Esme says she'd love to read his poems. Could she buy a copy? Of course not, he says. He will get one for her.

Soon Esme finds herself telling him about the troubles of the week, about Steve leaving and about how upset Dani has been. Esme discovers that she can't stop looking at him because when you talk, he listens. Listens carefully and looks into your eyes.

'I'm sorry,' he says. 'I'm very sorry.' They are quiet for a while.

'Tell me about you,' Esme says. 'I want to hear all about you. From the beginning.' Darius laughs and looks at her. Esme feels transfixed by his gaze as though she is being hypnotised.

'That would be hard,' he replies. 'It's a long story. I'll tell you another time.' They walk on in silence, gradually becoming aware of the sounds of the park: a dog barking, some kids shouting, the sounds of their feet kicking the leaves.

Before she knows it, it is time for her to go. Steve will be bringing Dani back at six, and it's already gone five. She can't let her daughter come back to an empty house. Darius walks her home, and Esme is acutely aware of him walking beside her. She is waiting for his touch. When they reach her house, he says he won't come in. That's a relief because she doesn't want Darius there when Dani comes home. It is too soon for her daughter to meet him. Before he turns to go, Esme lingers, hoping that Darius will hug her or kiss her. She wills him to put his arms around her. But he doesn't. He just gives her another intense look before he turns and walks away.

37

Things blow up at school. It isn't just the old homework problem. Miss Smith has turned out to be much kinder than Mrs Richards. So long as I can manage to scrawl a few untidy sentences for my homework Miss Smith accepts it and even complimented me once on one of my answers. The problem is that the few untidy sentences take me hours and in class, I don't have all that time.

We have to write in class several times a day and I can't manage it. Everyone else writes quickly, and over and over again, I am left with no notes, nothing in my exercise book. If it weren't for Mandy, I wouldn't even know what the homework was because I can't write it down fast enough. But as I said, it's not the homework that's the problem, it's the classwork.

On Thursday, there is usually a spelling test. Miss Smith is fond of spelling tests and has decided that we'll have one every week. She says that the general standard of reading and writing is terrible these days and blames this deterioration on excessive watching of television. I knew the test was coming and had thought of bunking off to avoid it but decided it was too risky. So I went to school as usual ready to go through with it. We write on loose pieces of paper and then mark each other's tests.

Last Thursday, Mandy gave me six out of ten (even though none of my answers was correct), but this week she's away. Mandy was fine yesterday, so I keep expecting her to turn up. Maybe she's gone to the dentist or something and forgot to tell me, but lunchtime passes and she's still not back. Don't know what to do. I could walk out of school but that would cause problems. Had better go through with it. The test starts. Miss Smith dictates one word after another and then we swap papers. Karen marks my test and gives my score as zero. Nobody else gets 0 out of 10. Miss Smith says nothing but at the end of the lesson, she walks around and collects the papers of everyone who has got less than five. Just before the afternoon break, I'm called to go to the staffroom. My heart starts to thump. What if they throw me out of school because I'm too stupid to be here?

The first good sign is that Miss Smith doesn't seem cross although perhaps that's a *bad* sign. Anyhow, I calm down a little bit. The teacher asks me to follow her into an empty classroom and tells me to sit down. I expect her to start shouting like Mrs Richards always did but instead, Miss Smith holds out my test paper and asks me what's wrong. Why am I having trouble writing? Could I try writing some words now so that she can see what the problem is? I hunch over the desk and grip the biro as hard as I can.

'I just want you to write a couple of sentences for me,' Miss Smith says gently. 'I'd like to see how you hold the pen when you write.' I hunch myself around the paper still more as though I'm surrounding it so that it can't get away. Nearly laugh at this image despite all the stress. 'I think your sleeve is getting in the way. Maybe that's what's hindering you,' Miss Smith says as she leans forward and peers at my arm. 'What's that on your sleeve?' I see where she's looking and notice that my arm must have bled through the cardigan.

'It's nothing,' I say. 'Must have caught it on something.'

'Pull your sleeve up and let me have a look,' Miss Smith insists.

'It's nothing,' I tell her and wince as I quickly yank up my sleeve and then pull it down again.

'Oh, Daniela,' Miss Smith says. 'Your arm looks very sore. Take your cardigan off and let me have a proper look.' I have no choice so I hastily pull off my cardigan and hunch over the paper once more, taking as much care as possible to hide my right arm. Miss Smith is determined to have a look. 'Show me your arm,' she says again and I hold out my left arm for her to inspect. 'No, Dani. Show me the other one.' Reluctantly I stretch out my right arm and she looks shocked.

'How did this happen?' Miss Smith asks me.

'Don't know,' I say and try to grin. 'It's just that biting my arm sometimes helps with the writing.'

I get sent off to the first aid room and Miss Smith tells me to come back and see her after my arm has been dressed. When I get back, she asks who is picking me up after school so I explain that I only live just down the road. I don't need anyone to pick me up. It's Thursday, Mum's late day. I explain that my mother teaches an after-hours drama group on a Thursday so I go to Suzi's until Mum gets home. Miss Smith says that she will ring my mother to make an appointment to come to the school tomorrow and that she will go with me to Suzi's. Oh no, I think. This is worse than having the police escort you home. Everybody will wonder why Miss Smith is going home with me. But there is nothing I can do about it.

After Miss Smith takes me back to Suzi's, I am coddled like a sick child and none of them seems to realise that there's nothing I hate more. I am not sick and I am not a child. Suzi sits with me in our house after Miss Smith has left and waits with me until my mother comes home. Normally, I would have watched tv at hers or gone round to Mandy's. It's as though I'm about to drop dead or commit suicide or have a weird fit or something. They won't leave me alone. When Mum does get back, she hugs me as though I've just returned from the dead and then they both try hard not to whisper about me. Can you imagine?

38

On Thursday afternoon, Esme is summoned to the office to take a call from her daughter's school. She can hardly believe what she is being told. That her daughter self-harms. That Dani's right arm is a mess and at risk of infection. Is she not aware of this? An appointment is arranged for the following day at 10 am for her to go to the school to discuss the matter. Teaching the last class and then the drama club seems to last a lifetime and when she finally gets home, there is a very serious-looking Suzi waiting for her.

Suzi can't tell Esme any more than she already knows. Just passes on what Miss Smith has said about the situation and emphasises that Miss Smith is very concerned. The teacher has assured Dani that she is not to worry about her writing.

'I wish you'd stop talking about me as though I don't exist,' Dani mutters as Suzi passes on this information to her mother. Suzi walks over to the sofa where Dani is sitting and gives her a hug.

'I'm sorry,' Suzi says to her. 'Of course, you exist. We're just worried about you that's all.' Esme does indeed feel terribly worried. She turns to Dani.

'Why did you do it?' she asks but Dani just shrugs her shoulders and leaves the room. Esme hears her going up the stairs, not banging loudly as she usually does. Her daughter's steps sound slow and tired. Esme turns back to Suzi.

'Let her go,' Suzi says. 'She probably needs some time by herself.'

'What can I do?' Esme lowers her voice and looks at Suzi. 'I've got to do something.'

'Well, the first thing is not to whisper about her,' Suzi says. 'Let's do something ordinary and put the news on.' Once the news is on, Suzi speaks again. 'It seems to me that Dani has two major problems.' Suzi stops speaking.

'Which are?' Esme prompts.

'Well, one is her writing,'

'Yes,' Esme says.

'And you know what the other one is.'

Esme does know. She waits until Suzi has left and before she starts cooking, makes two phone calls. The first one is to Steve. She tells him what has happened and asks if he will come over and help her sort things out. Esme has decided she will ask Steve to come back. Whatever she wants in life, she can't have her daughter distressed to the point of self-harm. Esme agrees with Suzi that the self-harm will have come more from the misery over the family breakup than from worry about her writing. Steve says he'll be over in half an hour.

The second phone call is to Joe. Since Joe is a student in the Education Department, he will surely know of someone who could help with the writing difficulties. Dani can't be the only person in the world with this particular problem. There must be some way of helping her. Esme explains in as much detail as she can about the writing problem and says that it is getting worse. Can Joe recommend someone in the Department who might be able to help? There is a short pause before he replies.

'The best person to help with the writing problem is Darius. He's an expert on that sort of thing.' There is another pause. 'I'll ask him and get back to you.'

In less than half an hour, Steve arrives. Esme asks if he is in a hurry and on finding out that he isn't planning to rush off, she starts to cook. It doesn't take long.

'Dinner's ready,' Esme shouts up the stairs to Dani. Silence.

'Do you want me to go and tell her?' Steve asks and Esme nods. A few minutes later, he comes back down and tells Esme that Dani doesn't want any food. They will have to eat without her. Steve asks Esme to tell him what has happened at the school so she explains once more that Dani has been biting her arm. Miss Smith told her on the phone that Dani's arm looked awful and in danger of infection. It was dressed by the nurse at school so Esme hasn't seen it.

'I've been thinking,' Steve says. 'I think I'm willing to give it a try, Ess.'

'What?' Esme asks.

'Your suggestion of an open relationship,' he says. Esme listens but finds it hard to believe what she is hearing.

'You mean that you would do that for Dani?' she asks him. 'It's not fair, Steve.'

'No,' he replies. 'It's not for Dani. It's for me.' Steve looks at her. 'I miss you, Ess. Life feels empty without you.' His voice softens. 'I need you.'

'I was going to ask you to come back,' she says.

'For Dani's sake?' Steve asks and for a couple of seconds, Esme remains silent.

'Yes,' she says. 'For Dani's sake.' Steve slumps. For a minute, he had begun to look cheerful, but now his face darkens again.

'And what do you think of my offer?' he asks. Esme goes and puts her arms around him.

'I think you're one of the most wonderful people on the planet,' she says. 'Come home, Steve, and let's see how we can sort things out.' Esme takes a drag on her cigarette. 'I've missed you, too.'

'I'll go and get my things then,' Steve says. 'And I'll pick up a bottle of red on the way back.' He stops and looks at her and sees that he doesn't need an answer.

While Steve is gone, the phone rings. It's Darius, saying that he thinks he might be able to help but isn't sure. He would need to talk to Daniela about her writing and she would have to be willing to work with him. If she is coerced, it won't work, he says. And if she is willing to discuss her writing, he would prefer to see her alone. Darius offers to meet her on Saturday morning at the self-help school, where he has an office. Would Esme ring him before then to let him know what Dani has decided? Darius asks Esme how she is. Fine she tells him, but he doesn't ask to see her again. Ess can hardly believe it. She was sure that Darius liked her. More than liked her. She sits down and finishes her cigarette. Then she goes upstairs to tell Dani that Steve is coming home.

Next morning, Esme feels apprehensive when she goes to the school to discuss her daughter's problems. The meeting takes place in the headmaster's office and Miss Smith is there with him. Although the teacher is friendly and trying to help, Mr Rowley is full of disapproval. As soon as Esme explains that she has recently split up with her partner, Dani's father figure, she sees his eyes almost light up as though everything is now clear. Of course, Dani self-harms because she comes from an unconventional home where the parents are not married. It's now a broken home and this is clearly what one would expect from such a situation. Mr Rowley doesn't state such an opinion explicitly, but he doesn't need to. Esme hurries to add that her partner has now returned to the family home, but this information seems to make no difference to the headmaster's assessment of the situation. Not judging by his face at any rate.

Dani's problems with writing are discussed and once again Esme is blamed. Why didn't she bring these problems to the school's attention? In vain, she tries to explain that her daughter made her promise not to say anything to the teachers. The headmaster shakes his head and looks meaningfully at Miss Smith. There will be two outcomes he informs them. Daniela will have to see the school psychologist and will be immediately referred for remedial writing lessons.

'I have already organised writing sessions for Daniela with someone from the university,' Esme tells them, 'and I know she won't want to see a psychologist. That will upset her even more.'

'Well, that can't be helped,' Mr Rowley replies. 'The appointment will be made and a letter will be sent. You will be welcome to attend with her, Mrs Hoffman.' Esme can see that there is no point in arguing further, but Miss Smith is looking at her sympathetically.

'We can work with you to support Daniela's writing sessions with the university,' Miss Smith assures her and asks Esme to send her the details. Ess is about to ask once more that Dani not be required to see the psychologist, but the headmaster stands up to signal that the meeting is at an end. There is no more to be said.

When Esme relays the information from the meeting to Dani, her daughter's reactions are even worse than she expected.

'How could you?' Dani says when Esme tells her that she has to go and see the school psychologist. 'First I'm bad, now I'm mad.'

'What do you mean, first you're bad and now you're mad?'

'First of all, I don't do my homework, so I'm bad,' her daughter replies. 'And now that I've bitten my arm, you've all decided that I'm mad.' Dani can hardly contain her anger and frustration. 'Well, I'd rather be bad. There's no way I'm going to see a psychologist. It's only a small bite. It's not as though I've tried to commit suicide. Or killed anybody.'

'I told your Headmaster that it wasn't necessary,' Esme tells her daughter, 'but he wouldn't listen, so there's nothing I can do about it. You'll just have to go.' Esme looks at Dani. 'I'll come with you,'

'What about Steve?' Dani asks. 'If I go at all, I want Steve to go with me. Not you.'

'OK,' Esme replies. 'I'm sure Steve will go with you.' Esme reaches for her tobacco tin, all attempts at giving up shelved for the time being. She wonders whether to tell Dani about the writing sessions or if it would be better to leave that news for another time. Esme decides to risk it. 'There's something else,' she goes on.

'What's that?' her daughter asks.

'I told the school that we'd got your writing problems in hand because I'd asked somebody in the Education Department at the University to hold some sessions with you,'

'Oh, no.' Dani says. 'Haven't I got enough to deal with already? How could you, Mum! How could you do that to me!'

'I had to say something, or the school would have found someone to see you about your writing. It's up to you. You'll have to face it with someone, Dani. I'm only trying to help.'

'Yes, you've been helping for months. For years.' Dani shouts. 'And look at how much good it's done.' She is close to tears. 'I can't bear any more of it.' And she grabs her bag and runs out of the house.

'Dani!' Esme stands on the doorstep and calls down the street. 'Dani. Come back.' Esme leaves the house and runs after her, but her daughter is too fast. There is no way Esme can catch her once she has started running. Esme goes back to the house and rings Suzi. Asks if she will come and wait in the house in case Dani comes back while Esme goes to look for her. If only Steve were here, Esme thinks to herself, but he is out on a driving job. Won't be back until late tonight.

The first place to look is Mandy's but Dani isn't there. Where else could she be? Mandy says she doesn't know. Dani is on foot and she has no coat. She must come back soon. Esme trudges around the neighbouring streets up and down the ginnels, but there is no sign of her. Eventually, she goes back to the house, hoping that Dani has already returned.

'No sign of her,' Suzi says. 'Come in, Ess and have a cup of tea. She'll be back soon.'

'It's gone eight o'clock,' Esme says. 'It's dark and it's cold and she's got no coat on. If she's not back by nine, I'll have to call the police.'

'Let's hope she turns up before then,' Suzi says. 'Dani won't thank you for getting the police involved.'

'But it's not safe,' Esme says. 'What about the Ripper. He's still out there somewhere.'

'He doesn't target girls as young as Dani,' Suzi says trying to offer some comfort but Esme doesn't bother to reply. She sits down at the table with the curtains open peering outside and chain-smoking. At ten to nine the door opens and Dani walks in.

'Thank God, you're back,' Esme says and goes to hug her but Dani pulls away. 'I was about to phone the police.' Her daughter gives her a terrible look but doesn't reply. Dani collapses onto the sofa and Suzi goes to get her a drink. 'And where have you been?' Still no reply. 'Where have you been?' Esme asks again. 'I've been everywhere looking for you.'

'For God's sake, Mum,' Dani mutters. 'Just walking about. I needed to walk.'

'It's not safe,' Esme tells her. 'I've been worried sick. The Ripper's out there somewhere.' A couple of minutes later, Steve comes back and Suzi makes a drink for him, too.

'Why did you run off?' Steve asks quietly as he sits down next to Dani.

'Mum's arranged for me to go and see a psychologist,' Dani manages to reply. 'She thinks I'm mad.'

'No, I don't,' Esme interrupts but Steve shushes her.

'Let Dani speak,' he says. Dani looks up and shivers.

'There's worse,' she says, pulling herself together and trying to look fierce.

'What's that?' Steve asks but Dani can't say any more. She buries her head in her hands and starts to shake. Esme goes over to try and comfort her, but Steve gestures to Esme to leave her alone. 'It's enough,' he says. 'She's had enough for one day. We can talk some more tomorrow, or whenever she's ready.'

'Do you want some food?' Suzi asks her, but Dani shakes her head as she gets up and leaves the room. Esme hears her climbing slowly up the stairs.

Suzi leaves soon afterwards and Esme and Steve sit down to a bowl of soup. Neither of them feel like cooking. It's out of a tin. Esme tells Steve what happened at the school and how Dani had run off when she'd told her about having to go and see the psychologist.

'What did Dani mean when she said there was something worse?' Steve asks.

'It must be the writing sessions,' Esme replies and explains that she'd told the school that she'd arranged for Dani to see someone from the University about her writing.

'And have you?' Steve asks.

'Yes,' Esme replies. 'I asked Joe to recommend somebody, and he did. The first session is arranged for tomorrow morning. I'll have to ring and cancel.'

'Who did he recommend?' Steve asks. Esme looks at him and hesitates.

'Darius,' she says.

39

I'd been dreading the thought of having to go back to school after having been escorted home by Miss Smith. Was sure everyone would be looking at me and whispering but amazingly nobody seemed to have noticed. Maybe they thought that Miss Smith knew Suzi and was going to visit her. Maybe I was saved because Miss Smith went with me to Suzi's house and not to mine. Who knows? Somebody asked if I'd got into trouble over Thursday's test. A bit, I told them and that was that. No more was said.

Worse than that was the fact that Mum went to school yesterday morning to talk about me and came back to say that I've got to see the school psychologist. After that piece of news, she told me that she'd arranged for me to have writing sessions with somebody from the university. Writing sessions! When she knows I can't write! On top of that, the somebody turns out to be Darius so you can imagine what Steve thinks of that. He knows that Mum fancies Darius. How could she!

Steve has been called back into the house to help 'save me' and I reckon that Steve coming back is the only good thing to have come out of all this. It was sheer bad luck that Miss Smith noticed my arm. I had hoped nobody would find out. It would have healed up by itself before long. What a terrible fuss they're all making. I live in fear that the whole school will find out. I'll be considered mad by everybody and whispered about forever. It seems as though Steve's words are coming true and both my mother and I have been marked out as mad. The thing is that there's only Steve who thinks that there is anything wrong with Mum, whereas I am being officially labelled mad by the school. I wonder if I shall ever be regarded as normal again. It's what I want more than anything. To be left alone and seen as normal. A normal, ordinary student.

It was so bad last night that I took off for a while to walk myself back to sanity but while I was out Mum went looking for me and that included knocking on Mandy's door! When I got back - and it still wasn't even nine o clock - Mum and Suzi were both sitting waiting for me, head in hands, about to call the police. The police!!! Anyhow, I've told Mum that I'm not going for the writing sessions and I'm not going to see a psychologist, so we'll have to see what happens next. I couldn't even sleep properly after all that and when I finally did go to sleep, it wasn't for long. I woke up in the middle of the night because I had the dream again, the nightmare about my first father trying to kill me. That dream always wakes me up. I can never dream it to the end and it's coming more often. Perhaps I *am* going mad.

I'm still in bed going over all this and not even properly awake when the realisation hits. It's Saturday and Grandma and Grandpa are coming today. Help. I'd forgotten all about them. They are due to arrive at the station just after lunchtime. They're coming for the whole weekend and I've arranged to meet Jaffa in the park tomorrow afternoon. Will they be gone by then? I've got no way of letting him know that I won't be able to make it. In any case, I don't want to tell him that I can't make it. I want to see him. He won't treat me as though I'm ill. Or mad. He treats me like an intelligent human being and he's my friend. I realise that I'm starting to trust him and I'm looking forward to seeing him. What can I do? First off, it's essential that my mother doesn't tell Grandma about my arm, or about the psychologist. That's the first thing. I'd better get up and talk to Mum before she does anything else to make my problems worse than they already are.

I pray that Esme hasn't rung Grandma to talk about me. I pray with pounding heart as I rush into the bathroom and out and get dressed as fast as possible There are sounds from the kitchen so I know that both Steve and Esme are already up. I'm pleased Steve is back but I don't know if it is permanent. No point in asking Mum because she's always changing her mind. I remind myself once more that my mother can't be relied upon, so I mustn't start believing that Steve is back for good. I remind myself that it's likely that he will get kicked out again. Better face reality although I can't help the hope that keeps creeping back. When I open the stairs door into the living room, Esme and Steve are sitting at the table eating breakfast. They both turn to look at me, peering at me as though I'm a freak.

'Good morning, Dani,' Steve grins at me. He behaves more normally than Mum but since the arm business, they both treat me as though I'm ill. 'You're up early.' There's no time to think about that at the moment. I've tried to tell them that I can't bear to be treated like a sick, mad person but they don't listen. Don't seem to understand. 'Treated like what?' they ask, and then, 'We love you, Dani, we just want you to be all right.' Anyhow, there's no time for that now. I turn to Mum.

'You haven't said anything to Grandma, have you?'

'Oh my God, they're arriving this afternoon.' My mother turns to Steve. 'I'd forgotten about them.'

'Did they ring yesterday?' he asks.

'No, I haven't heard from them since Wednesday,' my mother says. 'They were supposed to be coming on the two o'clock train and I said we'd meet them at the station.'

'Better ring to check that they're still coming,' Steve suggests. 'They won't have set off yet.'

'I'm sure they'll be coming. They would have rung me if their plans had changed,' but Esme picks up the phone and dials the number. I can hear both sides of the conversation. Yes, of course, they are still coming, Grandma says. Is it all right? Yes, Mum replies and says that we are looking forward to seeing them, especially me (?!). We shall be at the station to meet them.

'So, you haven't said anything to Grandma about me?' I ask again.

'No,' my mother says. 'I'd forgotten they were coming.' I can see that Mum is looking at me and wants to reassure me. She understands that I don't want anybody to know about what's happened. 'I won't say anything to anyone, Dani,' she says. 'Only Steve and Suzi know about the school problems. We won't tell anyone.' I believe that she means it, but she's already told Joe and Darius, so how many other people will she tell and think that somehow they don't count? I wish I could rely on her. She does love me but she's always talking about me and I can't stand it.

'And what did you say when you went to Mandy's looking for me?' I ask. My mother looks at me.

'I didn't say anything,' she says.

'You must have said something. You can't just knock at the door and when somebody opens it, stand there and say nothing. I want to know what you told Mandy. She wasn't even at school yesterday.'

'I didn't say anything,' Mum repeats. 'Only asked if you were there.'

I feel relieved if it's true and I hope it is. I'm dreading the thought of people asking me what's wrong. Even the thought of it makes me feel sick. Makes me feel like a freak. If anybody asks, I'll have to pretend that I'm in trouble over my writing. The kids might believe that after all the hassle I've had with Mrs Richards. But Miss Smith has been all right. I'll have to think things through. Essential that nobody knows about me being sent to see a psychologist.

I decide to go down to the cellar to work on the bike. I can be by myself and think things through. Still don't know how I'm going to let Jaffa know that I might not be able to meet him tomorrow. But if Grandma and Grandpa leave early then I might still make it. I'm not seeing him until half-past two. I go back upstairs and ask Mum when Grandma and Grandpa are leaving tomorrow. She gives me a funny look and says she doesn't know. What do I want to know that for?

I don't feel like going to call for Mandy in case she starts asking questions about Mum going round last night. Mandy would be sure to ask me what's wrong. In any case, Mandy was still off school yesterday so she might be ill. If Mandy had been there on Thursday, none of this would have happened because she would have given me a respectable mark for the spelling test.

I can hear Steve and my mum rushing around upstairs getting ready for Grandma and Grandpa. They had said they would have to go shopping and clean the house, especially their bedroom which Grandma and Grandma would have for the night. The two of them always move up into

Steve's workroom when my grandparents come to stay. They said that the living room needed cleaning, too, but they haven't asked me to help. More of the 'poor Dani, we'll have to look after her, can't put any pressure on her' kind of bullshit. Normally I would have felt pleased about not being included in the cleaning duties, but this morning, it feels awful. Just one more sign that they think I'm not all right. I know they're not cross with me, so they must think I'm ill. Mentally ill.

Things start to feel more normal at lunchtime when my mother starts to nag at me about the state of my bedroom, but there is no time left for any more cleaning. I did go out this morning but not to Mandy's. I roamed around the streets hoping to bump into Jaffa so I could tell him that I might be late tomorrow. Or might not be able to make it at all but I didn't see him. Didn't see anybody. Don't know where everybody was this morning. There's usually somebody hanging about, but the streets were nearly empty. Maybe it's the end of the world. Ha ha.

Steve says that Esme should stay at home while just he and I go to the station. Otherwise there won't be enough room in the car on the way back. I feel relieved to get away from Esme for a little while. When I'm alone with her, she keeps asking me what's wrong and now she's started asking me how I'm feeling. How I'm feeling! Steve and I are at the station in plenty of time and eventually, according to the arrivals board which we scan until our eyes hurt, we see that the train has arrived.

I stare into the crowd of people approaching the barriers. They are all blurring together, hardly look like individuals at all and then I see them separating into lines ready to show their tickets. At this point, the mass of humans starts changing into separate people and at last, I spot them. It's almost as though it's not them but just look-alikes. It is strange seeing Grandma and especially Grandpa in Leeds standing in the queue waiting to show their tickets. Grandpa is all dressed up in his best suit. I'm not used to seeing him looking like this. He looks out of place among all the rest of the people in their ordinary clothes. He belongs in Summer Lane dressed up for Chapel or in the garden, working. I prefer seeing him in the garden in his overalls. Not here. He looks as though people might knock him over and he wouldn't know what to do. Grandma is dressed up, too. She is wearing a blue hat that I haven't seen before. It must be a new one. Rare for Grandma to get a new hat. It's been a dreadful couple of days and suddenly I feel like crying as I run to hug them when they come through the barrier.

'Steve's back home again now,' I tell them and notice the smile of satisfaction that appears on Grandpa's face. When we get back to the house, Grandpa says that what he wants most is a cup of tea and after that, he wants to see my bike. I'd forgotten that they hadn't seen my bike yet. It took months to build. I thought it would never be finished but now that I've started the second one, I've started taking the first one for granted. The first one feels as though as it's been there forever.

'I'm on the second one now,' I tell him. 'The new one is for Mandy.' Grandpa comes down with me to have a look and I can see that he is impressed with my workspace as well as my bike. He hasn't seen it before. It is quite a while since my grandparents last visited. I think it was just after we first moved in which must be nearly a year ago.

'I never knew you were so tidy,' he says to me and of course, I'm not. My bedroom, for instance, is a tip, but I explain to him that I have to know where my tools are and all the bicycle parts. Grandpa agrees but says that he hadn't expected me to have everything so well organised. Then I take the finished bike outside and ride it around the block so Grandma and Grandpa can watch and admire. They always admire everything I do, but I can tell that they are genuinely impressed with my bike building skills.

The day passes quickly and soon there is only Sunday morning left because it turns out that they have to leave for the station just after lunchtime. Grandpa doesn't like getting back late and they've arranged for Uncle Ted to pick them up at the station in Sealy. It is Grandma's turn to come down to the cellar with me to have a look at my workshop. After she's admired it, Grandma asks me how I'm feeling. She means about Steve. Do I feel better now that he is back? I say that yes, I do. No point in telling Grandma about my fears that he might not stay. I know what Grandma would say if I did say that. She'd smile and say that nothing in this life is permanent; everything is temporary. But it's not true. Grandma and Grandpa are permanent. Their house in Summer Lane is permanent. They've lived there forever.

Grandma asks me about school and how I'm getting on with my writing. I don't mind Grandma asking these things because she's gentle and if I don't reply, she doesn't try and force me to speak. I don't talk about my writing but decide to mention that I'm a bit worried that Mum might throw Steve out again.

'I hope she doesn't,' Grandma says.

'Do you think she will?' I ask.

'I don't know,' Grandma says. 'But if there's another argument, Dani, or another separation, you must ring me. I hope it doesn't happen, but you can always ring me.'

'I can't,' I tell her, 'because Mum's always around and I can't speak when she's there.'

'Then go to a phone box,' Grandma tells me. 'You can reverse the charges. It'll be all right.' The thought of being able to make private phone calls to Grandma feels comforting. I find myself starting to tell her about the writing sessions that Esme has arranged with the man from the university.

'And how do you feel about that?' Grandma asks.

'Terrible,' I tell her. 'I don't want to go.' Grandma looks at me and I can see that she's thinking it over. 'I'm scared of failing and looking like a fool.' Grandma nods and is quiet for a minute.

'I can understand that,' she says. 'I used to feel like that about my maths when I was at school. I was put into the remedial class and at first, it felt awful. I was called out of the main class every Friday afternoon. I hated the way everybody looked at me.' Then she added, 'but it worked.'

'What worked?' I ask.

'Being put in the remedial class,' my grandmother says. 'I learned how to do some of the maths that I hadn't been able to do before and at the end of the year, I did so well in the exams that I got a scholarship.'

'Wow,' I say. 'I never knew you got a scholarship, Grandma.'

'No,' she replies and looks thoughtful. 'You wouldn't have known because I wasn't allowed to accept it. It's a long story. I'll tell you another time.' Grandma has never talked to me like this before. I realise that she is telling me something important to her that she doesn't usually talk about.

'So do you think I should try the writing sessions?' I ask, but without waiting for a reply, I carry on, 'But my writing won't be like your maths. I'm not going to do well and win a scholarship. I keep failing with my writing. I've tried so many times and I know I can't do it.' I stop and look at her. Grandma is sitting on the bus seat and I'm sitting opposite on the wobbly stool. 'I've tried so hard, Grandma. Nobody knows that I've practised secretly, but I still can't do it. Even Mum thinks I'm lazy. I know she does. Even Steve doesn't know how hard I've tried.' I look at my arm feeling an instinctive urge to bite hard but I go for my nails instead, then realise what I'm doing as I see Grandma looking at me. 'Steve is sympathetic, but nobody understands that I can't do it. Mum just thinks I should try harder.' Grandma waits for me to say something else, but that's it. There's nothing more to say.

'Well, maybe the sessions won't help. And maybe you won't do well with your writing. But you could give it a try.' And then Grandma stops speaking, too.

'I'll think about it,' I say and we go back upstairs.

40

He's there on the same bench, in the same place, but he's sitting slumped. Maybe it's not him. Jaffa doesn't sit like that. Jaffa sitting. Jaffa walking. Jaffa leaning against a wall. You can always tell it's him. Unmistakable Jaffaness. Always. A sort of confident slouch.

He staring downwards. Doesn't even look up as I approach.

'Hello, Jaffa. What's up?' He does look up then and I get the trace of a smile.

'Hello, Dani, how are things?' He looks down again. Sits bent over.

'What's the matter?' I ask again and sit down next to him.

'Mum's in hospital,' he says. 'Dad came back drunk on Friday and they had a row.'

'What happened?' I ask. 'Were you there?'

'Yes. I watched from the top of the stairs. I was trying to keep Granville in the bedroom but I couldn't make him stay there. I wanted to go down and rescue Mum but Granville clung onto me, begged me to stay with him. He hid behind me and held on. Wouldn't let me go.'

'And what happened?'

'They were shouting at each other, then Dad pushed her. She hit her head on the wall and collapsed. I went down too late. I didn't rescue her.'

'Oh, Jaffa.' I want to offer comfort, to tell him that it's not his fault but instead, I ask, 'Is she still in hospital? Have you seen her?'

'Yes, she's in Leeds General. I've just come back from there. Annie's with her. Dad's disappeared.'

'Will she be all right?'

'Don't know.' I reach out and put my hand on his arm without thinking but pull it back. Feels like a shot of electricity. He turns to look at me and smiles. Almost like the old Jaffa. 'Don't be kind, Dani,' he says. 'I've got to stay strong.' I know what he means. Know exactly what he means. 'And don't tell anybody,' he says. I shake my head. Of course, I won't. 'How are things with you?' he asks. 'What happened on Thursday? Did you get into trouble with Smithy?'

'It's my writing,' I say suddenly. 'I can't write, Jaffa and I've got to go and see somebody.' What have I said? I am shocked. I have never told anyone. I don't want anyone to know. Not even Jaffa. What made me speak? 'Please don't tell anybody,' I beg him. 'Please, Jaffa.' He looks at me and I know that he won't. He holds out his hand and I take it and we sit close, holding hands, not speaking. It's like a pact, a wordless promise.

'I've got to go,' he says. 'Only came out to tell you what's happened. I've got to go and look after Granville until Annie gets back. He's on his own in the house.'

'Jaffa,' I say and he turns to look at me before jumping on his bike, but I can't think of the right words. Can't think of any words at all, but it's all right. We don't need any.

'See you, Dani.'

'See you,' I repeat as I watch him go.

When I walk into the classroom on Monday, I see that Jaffa's already at his desk and I catch his eye. We look at each other just briefly. Seconds only but it's enough. We don't speak but he knows I'm there for him. And I know he's there for me. The day is easier than I had expected. I've managed a couple of sentences for homework and nobody mentions what happened last Thursday. I'm beginning to think that everything's back to normal when Miss Smith asks me to go and see her at lunchtime, so I start to feel apprehensive again. I go to the classroom and she is surprisingly kind. Not only is she kind, but to my surprise, she asks me how I feel about going for counselling.

'I don't want to go,' I say. 'I'm not mad.' I attempt a smile. 'I don't need to go.'

'Nobody thinks you're mad,' Miss Smith tells me. 'Counselling wouldn't be any good for mad people. They would need something else.' She smiles at me and explains that the psychologist would listen and then give me some advice.

'No, thanks,' I say. 'I've had too much advice already. I'm sick of advice.'

'All right,' Miss Smith replies. 'I'll get the appointment put on hold to give you time to consider it. It won't be of any help unless you decide that it might be useful.' I thank her and tell her that I don't think that I'll change my mind, but that I'll give it some thought.

'Is there anything else that's bothering you?' Miss Smith asks. Well, there's the worry about Steve and the worry about Jaffa's Mum and most of all, the worry about whether to go and have the writing sessions. There's the risk that I'll have 'stupid' stamped officially on my school records. I know they would use different words, but it would amount to the same thing. I can't talk about any of these things. Not even to Miss Smith who is being very nice to me. She's still a teacher. In the end, she'll talk to Mum and they'll make decisions about me. Make my decisions for me and I don't want that. I'll do my best to find my own solutions. But there is one thing Miss Smith might be able to help me with.

'There is something that's bothering me,' I tell her. 'I don't want anyone to know about all this.' I look at her to see if she understands what I'm trying to say. 'About my arm, I mean.' I can't tell if she understands or not. 'It was only a few bites. It wasn't anything serious, but people wouldn't understand.' It is Miss Smith's turn to go quiet. Then she speaks.

'We have to let the other teachers know,' she says. 'Because they need to be aware that you are feeling sensitive at the moment. They need to know that there should be no pressure put on you.'

'I just want to be treated like everyone else,' I tell her. 'I don't want to be a special case.' Miss Smith looks sympathetic.

'I understand that, Daniela,' she says, 'but sometimes we all have need of a little help. You need to learn to accept it.' I frown in response, not happy with what she's saying. Miss Smith continues. 'But of one thing you can be quite sure.' She waits for me to look at her. 'The teachers have been told about your problems in the strictest confidence. No-one else will be told.'

'None of my classmates?' I ask.

'None of your classmates,' Miss Smith confirms. I feel a huge sense of relief and am about to leave when she speaks again. 'There is one last thing,' she says. 'Will you let me know how you get on with your writing sessions?' My mood plummets again. There is no choice then, I think. I nod and turn to go.

***

The week has passed and at last, it's Friday. School has been better than I expected although I feel worried about Jaffa. There's hardly been a chance to speak to him, but we manage to look at each other from time to time and I'll see him on Sunday (he dropped me a note). I hope his mum's getting better, but when I saw him near the gates yesterday, he looked at me and shook his head. Not good news, I think, so I hope Granville's all right and that their dad hasn't come back drunk. Less than 48 hours till I see him on Sunday. It's funny. I miss him all the time now. It's easier to talk to Jaffa than it is to Mandy although I've known Mandy for ages. It shouldn't be like that, but it is.

As far as my writing goes, the teachers have largely ignored me. I've been left to get on with things at my own pace although I've had to report to Miss Smith every day at twelve, just for five minutes. But it isn't too bad. Things at home seem to have gone back to being how they were before Steve left. Well, not quite. There is a tension between Steve and my mother that seems to come and go, but mostly things are all right. Better than they were before anyway.

By Wednesday, I had decided to give the writing sessions a go. On two conditions. First of all, I asked for Steve to go with me and stay there throughout the session. The second condition was that I should be allowed to stop going at any time if I didn't think it was working. Surprisingly, Mum agreed to both conditions, and Steve said he would go with me. The person I'm going to see is still Darius, the man from Papua New Guinea, the man my mother went to meet on the day I went with Steve to Scarborough. Darius is supposed to be an expert in writing problems. It has been arranged that I will go for my first writing session on Saturday morning. That's tomorrow. I think about the session and I miss my stone. I have flashes of regret that I threw it into the sea. I miss it terribly. There's nothing to stroke.

41

I feel nervous. How am I going to write when I know I can't? What is this man going to think of me? If he calls me stupid, what will I do? I didn't sleep properly last night. Kept waking up every few hours. When it was time to get up, I felt exhausted. I ask my mother if she will ring to postpone the session because I am so tired, but while my mum hesitates, Steve says that I ought to go. Putting it off won't help. He says that I will only feel worse if I don't go and that even if I can't keep my eyes open, it is still better to go.

I get there with Steve soon after nine and meet Darius. He doesn't look like a teacher because he is wearing jeans and a light brown leather jacket. And he's black. We don't have any black teachers in our school. Still, he's a consultant. That's more important than a teacher so maybe he's more frightening than he looks. I can't work him out. I look at Darius again and see that he is looking straight at me with an interested look that makes me feel self-conscious but also acknowledged. When he speaks, his voice is deep and smooth with a slight accent. It is a voice that makes you want to listen. But it is when I start to speak myself that I begin to think that he might be all right because he listens. Darius looks at me, he listens and he takes me seriously.

I watch as he greets Steve and offers him a cup of coffee and a table in the corner where he can sit and read the newspaper. I notice that Darius doesn't discuss the writing session with Steve. Instead, he turns back and speaks directly to me. He starts by telling me about his work with some of his previous students. There was a university student who used to have problems with his writing, although mostly, he tells me, he has worked with students in school. Writing problems are common all over the world, although some kinds of problems are more common than others.

The first thing he asks me to do is to tap on the table.

'I'll sing,' he says, 'and then you tap the rhythm.' So he does that and I tap out the rhythm. 'Was that hard?' he asks.

'Not at all,' I reply. 'I've thought of becoming a drummer. I like rhythms, although it's hard to keep all the beats even.'

'So let's make it harder,' he says. 'I'm going to tap on the table, **one** two three, **one** two three, **one** two three. With a heavy beat on **one** each time, and all the beats even in length. Listen.' Darius taps on the table. **One** two three. **One** two three. 'Now you do it,' he says. I grin and do as he asks. My beats were nearly even, although when he asks me to keep going, it starts to get harder to keep all the beats an equal length.

'That always happens,' Darius says. 'As you said before, it's hard to keep the beats even.'

The next thing he asks me to do is to read him a paragraph.

'Well, there's nothing wrong with your reading skills,' he says and smiles at me.

'I know,' I say. 'That's why everybody tells me I'm lazy. If I can read, then I must be able to write.' I hesitate. 'But I find it very hard.'

'Don't worry,' Darius says. 'I'm sure I'll be able to find out what the problem is and then find ways of helping you.' I begin to feel slightly hopeful because he sounds so sure of himself. 'There's only one thing that is necessary,' he says.

'What's that?' I ask.

'You have to want to do it and you have to work with me.' Darius stands up and walks over to the blackboard. 'It won't all be easy,' he says, 'and it will take time.' I nod, but I'm not sure. I'm going to wait and see what comes next. The next thing turns out to be that I have to copy a sentence. I notice that he gives me lined paper and a thick pencil, which makes it easier. This isn't too hard. Then he asks me to write a sentence about him.

'What kind of a sentence?' I ask.

'Oh, anything,' Darius replies. 'You could describe what I look like. Or you could say that you don't like me.' He looks at me and grins. 'Or that I've got a deep voice. Just choose one thing to say and write it down. Just one thing.'

Oh dear, I think. This is much harder. This is the kind of thing I can't manage. When I have to concentrate on my thoughts, I can't manage to write. I can't concentrate on both. I press the pencil on to the paper and start to write his name.

'How do you spell 'Darius'?' I ask. Can you write it for me? Darius writes his name on the board, so I copy that, but then I get stuck again. Start chewing the pencil, but Darius tells me to stop.

'That's fine, Daniela,' he says. 'I think I know what the problem is.' I feel amazed.

'Well, what is it?' I ask. 'And can you make it easier for me to write?'

'First of all,' he says, 'do you know why you can copy a sentence, but when you come to write down your thoughts, you get stuck?'

'I think it's because I can't concentrate on both the writing and the thinking,' I reply.

'Precisely,' Darius replies. 'That's excellent. You've analysed the problem perfectly.'

'But why does it happen?' I ask. 'Other people don't have that problem.'

'Plenty of people have much worse problems,' Darius comments, 'but you're right. Most other people don't have the same problem that you do. Although it's not that uncommon.' He stops for a minute. 'It happens,' he explains, 'because the muscles in your hands are not well coordinated with the signals from your brain.' Darius pauses again and searches for words to explain what he means. 'The muscles in your hands still work,' he says. 'And your coordination problem is manageable. You can tap beats, for instance. Some people with the same problem can't do that.' I look at him and listen intently. 'The coordination problem between your hand and the messages your brain is sending means that you have to work much harder than other people just to form the letters on the page. Which in turn means that there's no space in your short term memory for your thoughts.' He looks at me. 'Are you following this, Daniela?'

'I think so,' I say. 'But if that's the case, how can I ever manage to write?'

'Oh, it's easy,' Darius says and grins. 'We just find a way to make the physical act of writing easier.' He stops again. 'Or bypass it.'

'And how am I going to do that?'

'Well, first of all, there's the typewriter,' he says. 'I think that if you learn to type, it will be easier for you than trying to make the shape of the letters with a pen or pencil.' I listen, but it doesn't sound as easy as he says.

'And what about bypassing the act of writing?'

'You can record your thoughts on to a tape recorder,' Darius says. 'Or your answers to exam questions.' He is silent again and looks at me. 'If necessary, your thoughts can be written down later.'

'That's a lot to think about,' I say. 'Is there a name for the problem that I've got?'

'Yes, we've done a lot in this first session,' Darius says. 'That's enough work for today. Do you want to come again next week, and I'll show you how to start using a typewriter?'

'Yes,' I say, 'but even if I can learn how to type, and even if I can record thoughts or exam answers, it won't be any good because I won't be able to do that at school.'

'I'm sure you will,' Darius replies. 'I'm sure the school will be happy to work with us to solve the problem.'

'And what is it called?' I ask. 'What is it called this writing problem that I've got?'

'Dysgraphia,' Darius tells me. 'It's called dysgraphia. The more common problem with writing is dyslexia, although that's a very broad term. But dyslexics have trouble with their reading and that's obviously not the case with you. People who have dysgraphia don't have reading problems and usually, like you, often have high IQs.'

'How do you know I've got a high IQ?' I ask.

'It's obvious,' Darius replies and smiles at me. I try to shrug off the compliment but can't help smiling.

'Most people call me Dani,' I say.

'OK, Dani,' he replies. 'See you next week.'

42

Esme sits at the table and waits.

This morning Steve had set off with Dani for the first writing session, but it had hung by a thread. Dani nearly didn't go. Ess could hardly believe it. Her daughter was terrified. Shaking. How could Dani be so afraid of going for a writing session? It was hard to understand. Ess went to hold her and tried not to tremble in sympathy.

'Why, Dani, why?' For a while, Dani just turned away. Didn't reply. Tried to get herself under control. Suddenly she turned back.

'It's because I'm stupid,' Dani had screamed at her. 'Don't you understand? It's because I'm stupid. Everyone can write, but I can't. I've tried and I can't do it.'

The cigarette lies in the tin, already rolled. Ess lifts it to her lips, lights it and looks out of the window. Slowly, she is beginning to understand the depth of Dani's distress. She had thought that if only her daughter would try a little harder, then everything would be all right. For so long, she has thought that the problems with writing would disappear. In the past, things had not been too bad. There was always the frustration of getting her to write thank-you letters and stuff like that, of course, but when Dani was little, the writing problem had been manageable.

Last year things had started getting much worse. First, Esme thought that it must be adolescence. Teenagers often didn't want to study. Lately, she had thought that if only Dani were not stressed by Steve leaving, then her writing problems would start to disappear. But this was wrong. There was a problem here that was deep, a problem Esme had missed because it didn't seem credible. A problem that had lain hidden because her daughter had managed for so long to cover it up. Her daughter, so quick and clever, so competent at all things, could not write.

Ess grips the mug in her hand so tightly that it slips as she lifts it to her lips. Prays that Darius can help in some way, but it seems unlikely. She doesn't hold out much hope because she and Steve have tried for years to get Dani to write. Nothing has worked and the problem has become steadily worse. It was clear this morning that Dani had given up hope.

And then there is her bad dream. How does that fit in or isn't it connected? Dani has kept saying that the bad dream has come back. It's bothering her again. Esme knows about the dream. Dani has had it off and on since childhood, but it seemed to have gone away until recently. It's about her first father. A dreadful dream. Ess thought it had come back because of anxiety over Steve leaving.

The coffee is cold. Ess goes into the kitchen to make some more. Does it automatically. Sits down again. The words echo in her mind. *Everyone can write, but I can't. I've tried and I can't do it.* Esme starts to imagine what she would feel like if she were in Dani's position. To not be able to write well enough to cope in school.

Sitting still is no longer possible. Ess looks at her watch. It will be another hour at least before they get back. She pulls on her jacket and leaves the house. Feels the wind whip through her hair. Freezing. Makes her shiver. She sets off to the park. Needs to walk. To get things straight in her mind. She wants to understand so that she can start to help. Esme walks, strides, breaks into a run then slows down again. For years, she has tried to help Dani with the writing problem, but she has failed and has probably made things worse. She didn't understand that it was a problem over which Dani had no control. She has nagged and threatened with the best of intentions, but she was wrong. Esme walks as fast as she can then faster.

Half-running, striding on, she turns into the park and sets off on the path that leads straight ahead down the hill. Tall trees to her right. Squirrels. Smell of leaves and hedge. A man with a dog walks past. All this time, she has been preoccupied with Dani's distress over Steve. She had thought the writing problems were secondary.

Esme is walking so fast that she's out of breath, but she doesn't stop. Turns left where the paths fork at the bottom of the hill and heads up towards the play area. She's got to keep going. Faster. Faster. Is it the past that is distressing her daughter so much that she can't write? Or is it the present? Is it a physical condition that is hindering her? Or a mental one? Esme pounds on, slightly slower now. She is breathing heavily but steadily as she slows down and walks on. Past the swings. Past the rose garden and back across the top of the park towards the gate.

If only she could make life easier for Dani, Esme would do it. She would do almost anything for her daughter. Almost. There are some things that she cannot manage, even though she would like to do them. She has already tried and failed. Her separation from Steve is as undoable as was her separation from Andreas all those years ago. Even though Steve is still in the house, they are already separate. It is how things are. In the past, she couldn't stay with Dani's father, Andreas. Now she knows that she won't be able to stay with Steve. Ess will give up a lot for her daughter, but not quite her whole life. Is that wrong? She is running now. She ought to be a better mother. She loves Dani more than anything. She keeps trying.

Esme is out of the park, walking along the road towards home. She is still striding as fast as she can, still breathing hard. If only there was something that Esme could do to make Dani's life easier. Something other than staying with Steve. If only she could take Dani's problems away and bear them herself. If only she could. If only she could. If only she could.

If only she could, she surely would.

43

'Have you finished?' Steve asks as I go over to where he is sitting. 'Was it all right?

I'm sure he doesn't need to ask. He can see by my face and by the way that I bounce. I can't stop smiling.

'Yes,' I say. 'Come on, Steve. Let's go.'

I walk out of the room and out of the building feeling marvellous and warn myself to hold back. It can't be this easy. Can't be. Out into Roundhay Road. It's cold. I feel the wind on my face and want to run. But I hold myself back and walk with Steve to the car. With a spring in my step. Just a little spring in my step.

'What happened?' he asks and I start to tell him.

'It's dysgraphia,' I say and the words pour out of me. That's the reason that I can't write and I'm not the only one (although Darius said it wasn't particularly common). I tell Steve that there are ways to help so that I can write. Me, too. Just like everyone else. Maybe even better, I think, (but I don't say that, of course) as hope rises like a fountain, high in the air, unstoppable. No boundaries. 'Darius said I had a high IQ,' I can't stop myself saying.

'Well, we always knew that,' Steve replies and I'm amazed.

'You didn't mention it,' I tell him wondering if he's having me on, but no, I can see from his face that he means it. 'What does Mum think?'

'She thinks you border on genius,' Steve replies with a grin and although he's joking, I begin to believe that they really do think that I'm not a complete fool.

'Didn't you think I was stupid because I couldn't write?'

'Of course not,' Steve says. 'We thought you weren't trying hard enough.' He pauses. 'Because we didn't understand. But nobody ever thought you were stupid.'

'Mrs Richards did.' I can see that Steve is about to deny this but changes his mind.

'I don't know about that,' he says.

'Well, I do,' I reply but I'm smiling. Don't care about Mrs Richards because I'm going to be able to write. Darius says it will be hard work and it will take time, but he's sure that he can help me to write. And I believe him. I can't wait to tell Mum, my dear mother who thinks that I border on genius. It's a joke. But such a nice one.

***

It's Sunday afternoon and I'm still bouncing. Can't stop. And maybe I haven't got a high IQ. Darius might be wrong. But then again, he might be right. Perhaps it is true and perhaps I have. I'm on my way to the park to find Jaffa. To tell him all about my writing session. Not about the high IQ of course, I'll keep that to myself. But about all the rest. I'm on my way and pedalling as fast as I can.

THE END

Acknowledgements

Huge thanks to all my beta readers especially to Michael Kerrigan, Jill Tennison, Caroline Timus, Elaine Segura, Pat Eva Berger, Teija Haussalo, Anne Haussalo, Sandra Meredith, Chandra Masoliver, Norbert Berger and James Gallaugher.

For ongoing inspiration and discussion I thank Zoltan Patai-Szabo and Greg Savva.

For unfailing encouragement and technical help, I am grateful to Francis Booth.

For insightful feedback on multiple drafts and never-ending patience, I am grateful to Paul Way-Rider.

Want to read more?
Novels by angela j. phillip

The Daniela Hoffman series

Daniela Hoffman is Not Stupid (book 1)

The Third Father (book 2)

Please will you write a review? Feedback is the most precious thing and helpful for other readers. Even if it is only one or two lines, it would be very much appreciated.

For more information and to sign up for the newsletter and special offers, please go to:
https://angelajphillip.com.

Printed in Great Britain
by Amazon